When the going gets toffee . . .

A state police car crested the hill in front of me. I stopped, resisting the urge to run into the stand of trees on my right, knowing that trouble was about to ruin my day.

I waited on the side of the road, hands on my hips. Sweat pooled on my lower back, not all of it a result of my exercise.

Sure enough, Detective Roger Lockett slowed to a stop beside me, his arm on the open window. He looked at me through reflective sunglasses, smiling a little. Probably because I was a sweaty mess.

The last time I'd seen him was when he'd grudgingly told me the inside scoop on the deal to put two murderers behind bars for a long time. Two murderers that Erica and I had helped uncover. And then he'd demanded that I stay far away from police work in the future.

I'd readily agreed, convinced I'd never need to.

"Bad news?" I asked.

"That's the only kind I deliver," he said.

My chest constricted at his confirmation. "Leo?"

"No," he said emphatically. "Your brother's fine. At least as far as I know. It's about Dr. Moody."

I relaxed just a little. "Did he take off to Bora Bora with his ill-gotten gains?"

"Nope," he said, his eyes on me. "He's dead."

Berkley Prime Crime titles by Kathy Aarons

DEATH IS LIKE A BOX OF CHOCOLATES
TRUFFLED TO DEATH

TRUFFLED
TO
DEATH

KATHY AARONS

BERKLEY PRIME CRIME, NEW YORK

BERKLEY PRIME CRIME

An imprint of Penguin Random House LLC
375 Hudson Street, New York, New York 10014

TRUFFLED TO DEATH

A Berkley Prime Crime Book / published by arrangement with the author

ISBN: 978-0-425-26724-0
5651 9688 6/15
PUBLISHING HISTORY
Berkley Prime Crime mass-market edition / June 2015

PRINTED IN THE UNITED STATES OF AMERICA

10 9 8 7 6 5 4 3 2 1

Cover illustration by Mary Ann Lasher.
Cover design by George Long.
Interior text design by Laura K. Corless.

Penguin
Random
House

This book is dedicated to Shaina and Devyn Krevat—
you make me proud every single day!

ACKNOWLEDGMENTS

I'd like to thank Jessica Faust, my amazing agent, and Robin Barletta, my wonderful editor, for making my publishing dreams come true.

I cannot gush enough about the marvelous cover art of this book. Thank you to Mary Ann Lasher for perfectly capturing the theme!

Once again, this book (and my sanity) wouldn't exist without the help, and patience, of my critique group, the Denny's Chicks: Barrie Summy and Kelly Hayes.

A mountain of gratitude to Dr. Joe Ball, Professor-Emeritus, San Diego State University, and my expert on all things Maya. He graciously answered my endless questions and contributed plot suggestions that have made their way into this book. I could not have written this book without him!

It truly takes a village to launch a new book series, and I appreciate all of the family and friends who bought books across the country, attended my book signings, and spread the word, especially: Jim and Lee Hegarty, Pat Sultzbach, Manny and Sandra Krevat, Donna and Brian Lowenthal, Patty DiSandro, Jim Hegarty Jr., Michael Hegarty and Noelle DeMarco, Matthew and Madhavi Krevat, Jeremy and Joclyn Krevat, Lori and Murray Maloney, Lynne Bath, Amy Bellefeuille, Sue Britt, Cathie Wier, Joanna Westreich, Susan and Terry O'Neill and the rest of the YaYa's, my Moms' Night Out group, and my long-suffering and incredibly supportive book club. Thanks so much to publicist extraordinaire Danielle Dill.

A special shout-out to Terrie Moran, author of *Well Read, Then Dead*, for her friendship, encouragement and book promotion advice.

Special thanks to the following experts for unselfishly sharing their knowledge:

Isabella Knack, owner of Dallmann Fine Chocolates, the best chocolates in the world.

Elaine Payne for her expertise as a chocolatier and pâtissier.

Dr. Josh Feder for his expertise in treating PTSD and depression, and Caron Feder for her event planning knowledge, and both of them for being untiring cheerleaders for my writing.

Jill Limber for her cat knowledge that led to Coco's multiple identities.

Dr. Susan Levy for her medical knowledge.

Lori Morse for her special event planning expertise, theater knowledge and years of friendship.

Judy Twigg for her expertise in the world of academia and being a typo-finding guru.

Julie Gill for her enthusiastic help exploring Frederick, Maryland.

Kristen Koster for her Maryland knowledge.

Any mistakes are my own.

And most important, thank you to Lee Krevat, for twenty-four years of unending support, laughter and love.

"It's so beautiful," I practically cooed at the plain clay bowl sitting just inches from my face behind the glass. My fingers were itching to hold it.

"My niece could do better." My assistant manager Kona laughed at me as she scooted by with a silver, multitiered tray of appetizers to place on a small table.

My eyes moved to the detailed figurine of a Maya ball player wearing an ornate headdress and what looked like a sumo wrestling belt around his waist. Sports equipment sure had come a long way in the past few centuries. A large plate beside it showed a colorfully dressed member of royalty reading a book. Like from a thousand years ago. With the rest of the Central American antiquities artistically placed on dark red velvet, the display seemed to be made just for our store.

We were about to open our doors for Chocolates and Chapters' reception celebrating the recent donation of Maya art by the River family to the Baltimore Museum of Man. Since founding West Riverdale, Maryland, in 1860, the Rivers had been pillars of local society, and no one was surprised by their generous gift.

Our store looked fabulous. It was well over a year ago that Erica Russell and I had removed the wall between our businesses to create the best combination ever—my gourmet chocolate shop and her family bookstore.

Tonight, we'd rearranged a few bookshelves and pushed our comfy, mismatched couches and tables against the walls to open up our dining area for the guests who were soon to arrive. Colorful flower arrangements of varying sizes and strategically placed tea lights had transformed our normally homey shop into an elegant party area. We'd pulled up the blinds and our place glowed from every window. Erica had taken a lot of photos for the website, hoping that tonight's party would lead to more customers paying to hold their events here.

We'd closed early for a Saturday night, giving plenty of notice to our regulars, especially May Jensen, owner of next door's Enchanted Forest Flower Shop, and the supplier of tonight's arrangements. May and her best friend, Nara Prashad, stay-at-home mom turned bed-and-breakfast manager, had decided that my chocolate was their good luck charm in meeting men.

They looked as different as could be—May liked to say she was fifty pounds away from being a plus-sized model, and Nara was originally from India and as tiny as May was big. They'd become best friends while attending a perimenopausal support group and went out manhunting every Saturday night.

I suspected that they enjoyed the looking more than the having because they were in our store getting giggly over Champagne Milks and Spicy Passion Darks week after week.

I'd assumed this evening would be just another opportunity to spread the word about my fabulous chocolates and Erica's amazing books, but then I'd learned that the small brown bowl had trace elements of theo-something-or-other, which translated chemically into *chocolate*. This bowl held chocolate over eight hundred years ago.

Mine, my soul said. The security guard hired for the event eyed me a little suspiciously while he adjusted his belt and then crossed his arms over his potbelly. Drooling on the glass would be unacceptable.

I sighed and went back to arranging my chocolates. Besides my always-popular Mayan Warriors with their spicy cayenne pepper kick, I'd designed several new flavor combos that were sure to delight our guests: tangy Aztec Pineapple Milks, Rain Forest Bananas Foster with a hint of rum, and my favorite, the pyramid-shaped End of the World Caramels. Erica had told me how historically inaccurate my names were, but the great majority of our guests would care about that as much as I did. Which wasn't much at all.

She'd already given me the lecture about how the correct term was *Maya*; *Mayan* referred only to their language. It hadn't helped me to point out how *Mayan* was used all over the place and that changing my packaging to correct it to "Maya" would take time.

Erica was prepping her table display of *Secrets Revealed in Maya Art*, a beautiful coffee-table book of pottery much more colorful than "my" bowl. The book was causing some kind of uproar in the world of anthropology, but I'd tuned out as soon as Erica started talking about pre-Columbian, Mesoamerican something or other.

Erica's sister, Colleen, came running in from the back, tugging her black dress into place and smoothing her hair. "Sorry!" she said. "Mark was late picking up the kids."

She was in the middle of a divorce that was remarkably amicable given that Mark had cheated on her. I'd have strung him up. Or at least taken him for everything I could.

She hurried over to the bookstore cashier counter to handle sales of the Maya and other books. "This place looks amazing!"

"Thanks." I did a quick review of the whole store. "Do you need anything over here?"

"Nope," she said cheerfully. "Unless you can sneak over some of that yummy food I'm smelling from the kitchen."

I scowled. While I was glad the Rivers had hired a catering company to handle the appetizers, and *really* grateful I was being paid for the truffles we'd made for the event, it drove me crazy to have someone else using my kitchen.

Ever since I'd scraped together the money to open my chocolate shop, the only people who'd cooked there were me and my assistants. The thought of other people in there made my skin crawl.

Especially Juan Aviles, owner of El Diablo Restaurant. Not only had he sniffed at the size of my kitchen and said, "I guess this is sufficient for cooking your little chocolates," he was constantly berating his staff. I guess he'd decided to follow in the footsteps of Gordon Ramsay. Or he was just a jerk.

Vivian River had promised me they'd bring their own pots and utensils, but my assistant Kayla had caught them digging through a drawer for a melon baller and given them the evil eye.

"I'll work on the food," I told Colleen. "How are the kids?"

"Good." She shrugged. "They're hanging out with 'Dad's friend' tonight."

"Oh," I said. And then I realized who the "friend" was. "Oooh. Sorry."

She shook her head. "It's good that they like her. It's just . . ."

"I know," I said. "It's hard." I didn't really know. Who could?

Luckily, Erica saved me by calling from the dining area. "Ready, Michelle?" Her smile was totally stressed out.

"Are you sure you're okay?" I asked her.

"I'm fine," she said, her smile stretching so tight I thought her lips would crack.

"Because ever since you told me about this whole thing, you've been weird." After two years of working together and being housemates, I knew Erica better than almost anyone, and I'd never seen her this edgy.

Like every other time I'd asked her, she shrugged it off. "I'm fine."

At least the reception would be over soon and Erica would go back to her normal, happy self.

This was our first big event since Colleen had handed over management of the bookstore side of our space to Erica and gone back to school full-time. Maybe Erica's tension was due to the added responsibility of keeping the family business going all by herself.

Just as I was asking Kona to make sure some of the appetizers made it over to Colleen, Dr. Smug came in the back door, wearing a tux. Okay, his name was Dr. Addison Moody, which also said a lot about his personality and the reality of self-fulfilling prophecy. He was the hero of the evening, a university professor turned museum curator who had put together the arrangement between the River family and the museum. It was win-win-win for them all: The Rivers got to be the gracious, richer-than-anyone-else-in-town family who had so much money they could donate a bunch of centuries-old art without blinking. The museum got not only the art but also a chunk of money to create a permanent display for them. And Dr. Moody probably got a big bonus for bringing in such a huge deal. He was also planning to research all of the pieces and publish papers about his findings.

Something about this guy made me feel anxious and I wasn't sure why. He looked the part, like every professor on TV—tall, with thick, curly brown hair a little too long and graying at the temples in a dignified way. He had big brown eyes, and an enthusiasm for everything, which was contagious to everyone except me. It just made me nervous, like he was sucking his energy from everyone around him. One of those people who swept you along in his enthusiasm because it appeared so genuine. Childlike, which might seem somewhat gross for someone in his forties, but was more like Willy Wonka than Hugh Hefner.

At the moment, Dr. Moody looked very elegant in his tux as he gazed around the store, beaming.

Erica smiled even brighter, if possible, and asked him, "What do you think?"

"It looks wonderful," he said and walked over to the display case. "Look at my beauties." He stood staring as if he couldn't believe it.

I felt drawn to the art as well and joined him in silent admiration.

He leaned over to peer closely at a tall vase in the center of the display, a tiny spotlight emphasizing the rich colors of the detailed artwork depicting a seated man wearing a blue headdress. Erica had told me the man was a Maya lord gazing in a mirror being held by a servant. A few small pointed tubes were strategically placed around the base.

"Just think what wonders they've seen," he said reverently. "Used by the royal families for their religious ceremonies, and even their humble meals."

He pointed to a battered diary that looked like it had traveled in Indiana Jones's pocket. "It seems rather embarrassed, don't you think? Surrounded by so much glory."

The late Bertrand River had recorded his travels in that diary. He'd been the black sheep of the industrious River family, taking off for years at a time to explore ruins in Central America. There'd recently been whispers about the legality of bringing these pieces back. Maybe silencing the rumors was one of the reasons for the donation.

Our reverie was interrupted by Dr. Moody's assistant, who walked in from the back hallway with her perpetual frown.

There was no nice way to say it. Lavender Rawlings looked like a frog. And her oversized glasses and blunt pageboy haircut only enhanced the impression. She was the opposite of the professor's vitality. A true buzzkill. It probably had something to do with her peevish expression and her sniff of disapproval at everything.

Maybe her lack of energy somehow balanced the professor's exuberance. Like she grounded him or something.

Tonight she wore what would be a stylish cocktail dress

on anyone else. It had beautiful needlework and sequins on the bodice, showing off what wasn't a bad body if she would stand up straight and not walk like a mole in her black flats.

Erica would tell me I was mixing my animal metaphors.

Not that I'm a fashion plate. I was usually happy to find something to wear that didn't have chocolate stains, but tonight I could almost pass for chic. Erica had insisted on taking me shopping in Frederick and bullied me into trying on a dress that gathered in a high waist and then draped into a frothy blue and green skirt. It made me feel utterly feminine.

For some reason, Erica had chosen to go totally professional, with her most boxy black pantsuit. But even with her blond hair pulled back into a tight bun and her eyes hiding behind her librarian glasses, she managed to look sophisticated and sexy.

Lavender didn't bother with a greeting. "There's a cat out back trying to get in."

I groaned internally. Coco was a brown tabby who'd arrived in town a few months before and been quasi-adopted by almost every shop on Main Street. At first, she'd refused to go inside any of our stores, but lately it was hard to keep her out.

It didn't take long to figure out why: she was pregnant. We'd all stupidly trusted Reese Everhard, owner and editor of the town's newspaper, who had assured everyone that Coco was a neutered male.

I resisted the urge to check on the cat as Erica said, "It's time," and made a gesture for me to take off my apron.

I hurriedly threw it to Kayla, who stuffed it behind the counter. Kona opened the door with a flourish just as the River family's stretch limo pulled up.

Maryland's early September weather had cooperated

nicely with our party, the summer's brutal heat and humidity having grudgingly left the week before. A cool breeze brought in the smell of star lilies from the flower shop next door. May had decided to have her assistant work in order to show off her wares to the visiting Maryland royalty.

A camera flashed from across the street as Reese took photos, dodging a black SUV to get shots of the River family. I couldn't resist watching them arrive. The town gossips followed the Rivers as much as the latest Miley Cyrus debacles, and we all knew far too much about the whole family.

Vivian River, grandniece of explorer Bertrand River, was the first one out.

Vivian terrified me. She was one of those graciously wealthy, always totally put-together women who sported the latest designer clothing for the rich and not *too* fashionable. She was very unlike me: tall and thin with her hair ruthlessly under control.

I'd dared to ask Vivian if she was sure hiring Reese was a good idea, given her penchant for hysterical headlines like: *West Riverdale Stars Football Team Is Out of This World!*; *Keep Banned Books Off Your Kids' Kindle*; and *West Riverdale Council Abandons Town*, when the members took their annual vacation. Vivian had told me, rather frostily, that Reese's contract ensured that the Rivers maintained strict control over all of the photos. The warning in her voice made me believe Reese would stay in line.

Luckily, I hadn't been the target of Reese's sensationalist style of journalism for a while. Both Erica and I had done a good job of keeping a low profile over the summer after our amateur murder investigation had turned into a fiasco.

While we had outed two murderers, both Reese and I had almost been killed in the process.

Even though Reese had moved onto others after I'd practically saved her life, I suspected that getting the most hits on her "news" website wasn't the only thing she was interested in. For some crazy reason, her sense of high school rivalry went deep and it wouldn't take much for her to attack me again.

Exiting the limo behind Vivian was Adam River and his younger siblings, Gary and Jennie. At thirty years old, Adam had already taken over the real estate division and manufacturing plants of the River family businesses. Only a few years younger, Gary had none of Adam's drive. And young Jennie was facing her own demons.

Adam helped out his grandmother, Rose Hudson, and guided her into the wheelchair that had been unloaded by the driver. He waved away the driver's help and pushed her into the store, with everyone else trailing behind.

They were undoubtedly siblings, all three of them blue-eyed and blond with strands that lightened to white in the summer. The boys retained the distinctive nose, but every River female had the offending bump removed.

Adam had on a beautifully tailored suit with a red tie that flapped around his neck as he came in the store. Gary had thrown a sports jacket over a white button-down shirt and pair of khakis, and must have spent a lot of time on his hair to make it look so fashionably disheveled. Jennie wore a short skirt over colorful green and orange tights. If I tried those, people would think a Muppet had thrown up on me, but with her cropped leather jacket and dreadlocked hair, she looked more funky than I'd ever been in my life.

Our West Riverdale neighbors were the first to arrive.

The Rivers had spared no expense, and people who had zero interest in Maya history or hadn't even left their homes after dark for years had called the babysitter, dressed themselves up, and come down to enjoy the free wine and appetizers of the biggest party of the season.

Then the beautiful people from the neighboring cities and towns began to arrive, the men in designer suits and the women in little black dresses and glittering jewelry. Just one of those necklaces would pay for the industrial chocolate-tempering machine I constantly ogled in my chocolatier magazines.

Aviles came out to take one look at the crowd and rushed back to the kitchen. I didn't think we could fit this many people into our store. Normally I'd worry about the fire marshal complaining, but he'd just waylaid Kayla and was shoving crab taquitos into his mouth.

Reese was inside now, taking the regular high-society shots of glamorous donors, side by side, smiling perfectly into the camera.

My brother Leo was standing with a group of fellow veterans, his arm around the waist of his girlfriend Star. She was the first woman he'd dated in the years since he'd returned home from Afghanistan after losing his leg. He'd made so much progress in his fight against his depression, and his happiness with her was the icing on the cake. They'd been together all summer, and he'd even fixed up his apartment to make it more homey. I hoped it was in preparation for Star to move in.

"You look amazing," I told her.

"Thanks!" Star was wearing a shimmering navy dress that fell below her knees, accentuating her athletic build and highlighting her hazel eyes.

I pointed to the diamond necklace in the shape of a star. "Love the necklace." I'd helped Leo shop for it.

"Isn't it great?" She turned a blazing smile on Leo.

"Need any help?" he asked.

"No, but thanks," I said. "Enjoy the party."

Several people who I assumed were from the museum arrived, and the professor and Vivian greeted them. One man broke off from the group to talk to Erica. He was dressed almost like a toy soldier, with a short, buttoned jacket with brass buttons, and cigarette pants folded up to show an inch of white socks. His brown hair was manicured, and he'd obviously planned his appearance in detail.

I was about to bring out more Blackberry and Goat Cheese Darks when Gary decided to heave himself up and sit on my counter. My counter! Where I served food! Then his sister Jennie joined him and they sat there kicking their feet back and forth and watching the party as if they were little kids in a tree house.

I made a beeline for them. "Get down now."

Gary raised his eyebrows as if he didn't know what the problem was.

"Your butts do not belong where people put food," I insisted. "Off!"

They both reluctantly slid to the ground and then looked around for a new place to park themselves. When Gary eyed a small table without chairs that had been temporarily cleared of food, I told them, "Go sit on the stairs or something."

They turned for the big wooden staircase that we'd roped off for the party, but stopped as Vivian appeared at my elbow.

"Reginald." Vivian's voice was laced with disapproval.

Reginald? If that was my name, I'd use Gary too.

Everyone knew that Vivian was fierce in maintaining the

family reputation. "You have host duties." Her dour tone made it sound as much fun as Saturday morning chores.

Jennie slipped away silently and Vivian let her go with narrowed eyes.

"Sorry," Gary said with a shrug and joined a group of younger guests gathering around the glass drink dispensers filled with El Diablo's lethal punch of fruit juices and rum. I thought I saw him shoot a wistful glance at the stairs.

I'd heard all about Gary's dedication to doing as little work as possible while still holding on to his trust fund. Rumor had it that Adam had bought him the Big Drip Coffee Shop and made him manager as a last-ditch effort to instill some kind of work ethic in Gary.

"He takes after Bertrand in far too many ways," Vivian said bitterly. Then she changed back into her normal gracious self. "The event is going swimmingly, Michelle. Perhaps it's time for the professor to make his announcement."

I nodded, wondering how many people could get away with using the phrase "swimmingly" so easily, and tracked down the professor, who was plopping olives in his mouth while pretending to listen to an older woman. I couldn't hear her over the noise of the crowd, but the professor looked past her the whole time. As I approached him, he did a double take, obviously recognizing someone off to my right and not liking it. I couldn't resist following his glare to a gorgeous man strolling into the party. Whoa. This guy could be a model for Bad Boys R Us. He paused to pull on his shirt cuffs, as if he'd just put on his suit jacket, and I could see his diamond cufflinks flash from across the room.

Kona's hot-man radar was on full blast and she put herself in front of him in a split second, offering a tray of chocolate truffles, with her hip angled to imply another offer. He smiled at her, his teeth blinding against his resort-tanned skin.

Dr. Moody took an involuntary step toward the man, and I remembered my assignment. "Professor?" I said.

He stopped to focus on me.

"Vivian River would like you to make your announcement now?" His furious expression made me end the sentence on a question.

Lavender must have sensed a disturbance in her Professor Force since she was instantly beside him, glowering at me as if his anger was all my fault.

"Vivian said it's time to make the announcement," I told Lavender, sounding like a tattletale.

His face smoothed over and jovial Professor Moody was back. "Of course." He walked toward the display, pulling the microphone from its stand.

"Hello?" he said into the mic and it screeched, getting the attention of everyone in the room. "Thank you all for coming."

Kona scooted by me, and I whispered, "Who's the cutie?"

"Dibs!" she said. "He's got the most delicious accent." She sent a flirtatious look over her shoulder in his direction, but Gorgeous Man was watching the professor.

Jolene Roxbury, high school math and drama teacher, gave me an arch look. "If I was ten years younger and not happily married, I'd hit that."

"Jolene!" I said. She and her husband were the happiest married people I'd ever met.

"What?" she said. "I'm in love. Not dead." She took a champagne glass from her husband, Steve, who returned from the bar, and then she slipped her arm around his waist as the professor began his speech.

"Tonight we're here to honor the River family, the generous donors of this beautiful and important art to the very fortunate Baltimore Museum of Man." He gestured toward the display. "These pieces, along with many more antiquities in the collection, will help unravel the mysteries of the ancient Maya."

He went on. "We are all very lucky that Bertrand River's adventures took him to Central America at a time when he could discover so many different pieces from so many different eras."

I noticed that Adam was attempting to push his grandmother's wheelchair to the front, and I led the way, tapping shoulders to make room. Once she was in place, I moved around the side to the back of the room and saw a man standing by the kitchen door.

It was Bean. Erica's brother.

My crush.

My heart started beating faster. He hadn't seen me yet.

Mine, something inside me whispered again.

I shut down that errant thought. Bean was not mine. He belonged to the world.

What was he doing here? Last I heard, he was on the Canadian and West Coast segments of his worldwide book tour, riding a wave of rave reviews. He'd been in town for a few weeks in May and then taken off with barely a good-bye. Almost patting my head as if I were still the middle school kid he'd been forced to kiss in a spin the bottle game ages ago.

He was wearing a beautiful suit. His publisher probably

insisted on it. Then I realized that Erica must have known he was coming. Maybe this was what she'd been so stressed about. Wait. Had she taken me shopping so I could look halfway good for her brother?

It could be that she felt responsible for the sputtering end to what I thought was a pretty hot flirtation. I'd never told her about eavesdropping on their conversation. Soon after I'd been almost killed by West Riverdale's most notorious murderer in a century, I was sure Bean was about to seal the deal with our relationship. And then Erica had told him to think about what he wanted. That I had "abandonment issues"—like, who didn't?—and he should realize that he couldn't just fool around with me and then take off when the next story called to his journalist soul.

I'd almost screamed then and there that he could fool around with me all he wanted! No commitment needed. But after Bean left, I'd realized she was right. If it hurt that much when we weren't even involved, how much would it hurt if he left in the middle of something that I thought of as special and he thought of as a fling to fill the time between book signings?

Of course, Reese Everhard's blog highlighted every single photo she could dig up of Bean being hit on by some dazzling woman across the globe, along with some salacious headline. My least favorite was "Too Sexy for Sweden."

He saw me and all of that evaporated. He looked a little stunned and I realized he'd never seen me in a dress. And then he smiled as if he was really glad to see me. I walked toward him, feeling like I was in a fog. People magically moved out of my way, just like in a really cheesy romantic comedy.

I was almost close enough to say something when I heard

a noise. A low sound hidden by the professor's words. And then a wail rose and he stopped speaking.

The expression on Bean's face turned to concern and I fell out of my hypnotic state. Together we rushed toward the crying as the crowd pushed away from the source.

Rose Hudson was pointing at the display case, sobbing incoherently. The professor stood holding the microphone, openmouthed with surprise. Adam attempted to calm his grandmother down, but she moaned even louder, "Cursed! Cursed!"

2

Poor Rose covered her face with her hands, muffling her sobs. Adam got down on one Brooks Brothers–clad knee beside his grandmother. He pulled a handkerchief out of his pocket and wiped her tears. "It's okay," he repeated several times in a gentle voice as he rubbed her shoulder. "Do you want to leave now?"

When she bobbed her head behind her hands, he stood and wheeled her toward the main entrance, nodding at Professor Moody to continue. The limo driver appeared like magic to lift the chair to the sidewalk, ignoring our ramp.

Vivian made an imperious gesture for the professor to speak, her expression livid.

The professor stumbled back into his talk, and I followed Adam out. Rose seemed to have shrunk even smaller in her chair. "Is there anything I can do?" I asked.

Adam frowned as if he couldn't quite place me. Really? After all we'd done? Then his face cleared. "No, but thank you, Michelle." He turned to watch the driver lift Rose into the car, and I felt dismissed.

Which totally made me want to stay. "I could put together a little goodie bag for Ms. Hudson," I offered a little nonsensically, since the driver was already walking around to get into his seat.

He ignored me as he watched the limo go, a worried frown between his eyebrows.

"Does she really think the pottery is cursed?" I asked. No way could that little chocolate bowl hold anything except goodwill and grace.

"Of course not," he said, turning to go back to the party. "She's just confused."

Bean came to the entrance and this time I was more prepared.

"Benjamin Russell!" Adam said heartily. "How are you, you old dog?"

Old dog? Was he thirty or seventy? "He goes by Bean now," I said with what I hoped was a saucy smile. It may have quivered a little when Bean grinned at our inside joke.

"Benjamin is fine," he said to Adam and shook his hand.

Adam tried to put his arm around Bean's shoulder in the timeworn *let's you and I have a little chat* gesture, and said, "I'd love to hear about your book," but Bean executed a slick avoidance move that showed a lot of practice.

"Of course," Bean said. "I'll see you inside in a minute." He stared at me, and my heart started thudding in my chest.

Adam looked between us, clearly surprised, and then left us alone. Or as alone as we could be right outside a huge party.

"Erica didn't tell me you were coming back to town," I said.

"I wasn't sure I could make it." He took a few steps closer. "You look great." He winced.

Professional writers must feel like they should come up with better words than "great."

He tried again. "Like a fairy," he said. "Whimsical."

I tilted my head. "Whimsical?"

"Give me a break." He grabbed my hand. "I missed you."

"You did?" Pure delight danced through my veins.

"Michelle!" Kayla yelled and then saw who I was talking to. "Never mind!"

But she'd broken the spell. "I should . . ." I pulled my hand away and waved it aimlessly toward the door.

"Sure," he said. "You're busy. Would you like to go out to dinner sometime?" It sounded formal, which was totally weird. Was he nervous?

"Are you okay?" I asked. "Not, like, dying of cancer or anything, right?" It was my turn to wince.

He smiled. "Nope. So dinner? Steamed crabs? Tomorrow night?"

"Sure." Excitement fluttered in my stomach. And not because I loved steamed crabs as much as any Maryland native. Maybe it was the chicken tamales I'd pilfered from El Diablo. "Coming back in?"

He shook his head. "Just stopped by to see you and Erica. I've had to deal with too many . . . people lately."

That reminded me of all the "people" photographs I'd seen on Reese's blog, and my good mood deflated. "Okay. You staying with us, I mean, Erica?"

"Yep," he said cheerfully, as if he knew how that drove me crazy. "Right upstairs."

I made sure not to watch him walk away—okay, maybe a little bit out of the corner of my eye—as I went inside.

The professor had finished his words, and the crowd had seemed to swell even more in the few minutes I'd been outside. The Latin beat of the music had picked up and a few people were dancing in place, almost as if they didn't realize it.

El Diablo stepped out from the kitchen to see what was needed and frowned at me when he discovered holes in my arrangements. How could I help that my truffles were so popular?

I intercepted the tray Kona was carrying and filled in the open spaces. A breeze blew through the open door, a warning of the rain that would soon start. I had a moment of gratitude that it had held off so long, and then something prickled up the back of my neck.

A new gorgeous man, this one with long hair pulled back into a Johnny Depp ponytail, stood in the doorway. His eyes flickered around the room and I stopped to watch him, feeling like an animal about to cross the plains, knowing a predator waited somewhere. Or like turning left at the Jasmine Road stop sign right outside of town, where cars speed around Devil's Bend, ignoring the Stop Sign Ahead signs until it was too late.

He met my eyes, as if sensing my discomfort, and I swear his green eyes glowed for a second. In some ways, he was similar to the delicious man Kona had laid claim to, but just a little darker. Darker hair. Darker tan. The veneer of civilization wafer thin. Someone you wouldn't want to meet in a dark alley. Not that West Riverdale had many of those.

I brushed off the fanciful nonsense and looked away.

Kayla approached him with a tray, shaking her hair to

allow her cute blond curls to fall across her face. She must have won the coin toss with Kona.

I watched him take a bite of a Cherry Ambrosia truffle and close his eyes, as if he couldn't help himself. I could almost taste the kirsch and dried cherries along with him.

"Someone is having a sale on tall, dark and dangerous," May said, tugging at her Spanx through her sparkling green dress. "Maybe he likes 'em middle-aged and plump."

I laughed. "He should be so lucky."

Nara stared at him with wide eyes. "Maybe he likes 'em tiny and exotic."

I watched him lean closer to Kayla and say something that made her laugh. "Looks like he likes 'em young and adorable."

"Too bad." May sighed. "Have you seen Lentil, I mean Coco?"

"Lentil?"

She waved her hand. "Sorry. That's what Iris calls her. Says she's the exact color of the diner's lentil soup. Plus a few other choice names when Lentil, I mean Coco, threw up on her shoe."

Served her right for naming my cat after soup. "Someone said Coco was out back."

May was even more into Coco's kittens than I was. "I'll take a peek," she said, but then she didn't move.

We turned to look at Tall, Dark and Handsome 2.0 in time to see Kayla point to me. I felt rooted to the spot as he made his way over.

"Ms. Serrano," he said, his voice soft and low with a Central American accent. He wore some kind of woodsy cologne that made me think of the jungle. "I'm Santiago

Diaz. Your Miss Kayla told me that you made these delicious confections. I'm in awe."

My thank-you ended in a squeak as he took my hand and kissed it! Like in a movie. Right there in the middle of my store. In the middle of West Riverdale, which hadn't seen a hand kiss like that in probably ever. I think May and Nara squeaked along with me.

"These are my friends, May . . ." I couldn't remember her last name. "And Nara."

"Delighted." He kissed their hands as well, his ponytail low on his neck. "How lucky to have such a talented pâtissier as a friend."

They both nodded. They would have agreed if he'd said "such a talented serial killer."

"Oh no," I said. "I only make chocolates, not baked goods."

"Hmm," he said, as if reserving judgment. "Such a sophisticated palate you must have." His voice was mesmerizing, but then I sensed something underneath the smooth talk. My BS meter was going off big-time.

"Are you friends with the Rivers?" It came out a little more challenging than I intended.

His eyes widened just a tiny bit, as if he was surprised that his flattering words weren't working. "No. Just curious about the beautiful treasures from my heritage."

"That's wonderful," I said. Over his shoulder, I saw one of the catering staff gesturing wildly to me. "Excuse me. Duty calls."

"I'll show you the exhibit." May grabbed his arm and steered him toward the display.

"Eddie just quit!" The teen girl in the red shirt with the

El Diablo logo and black pants was practically wringing her hands.

"Eddie?" I asked.

"The sous chef!" Her voice rose with alarm. "Can you get someone to help me clear dishes so I can take his place?"

"Of course," I said. "I'll do it." It was a miracle Eddie had lasted as long as he had with the abuse Aviles piled on him.

I picked my way through the crowd, piling used plates on my tray to take back to the kitchen, but Vivian and Gary were blocking my way.

"Where's Jennifer?" Vivian held Gary's arm by the counter, their faces turned away from the crowd.

I loaded even more plates on my tray, and could almost hear his shrug. "I don't know. She was just here."

"You were in charge of watching her," she insisted.

I glanced over and saw him wince, but I wasn't sure if it was from Vivian's words or her tight hold.

"I'm sorry," he said, with the emphasis on the second word. "I was talking to the new mayor and she just disappeared." I wasn't sure if he was worried for his sister or mad for being called out about her leaving under his watch.

I'd finished cleaning up the plates at the edge of the counter and now couldn't avoid trying to scoot by them. "Excuse me."

Vivian let him go with a frown.

I could understand her worry. Everyone knew about poor Jennie River. She'd taken her father's death a few years before very hard. At twenty-one, she'd just been through her third attempt at rehab. From the concerned expression on Vivian's face, perhaps it hadn't been successful. But what did I know about young rich people and their drug habits?

I smelled it even before I opened the door to my kitchen.

The overflowing garbage can assaulted my nose, reminding me of why I was so careful with scents in my workspace. If any of my chocolates absorbed even a whiff of the cooked onions, charred garlic, or whatever else was part of that disgusting smell, they'd be ruined. Another reason to hate El Diablo, who was nowhere to be seen.

Cursing under my breath, I closed up the bag and took it out the back door, catching Gary River in the act of escaping.

"Just pick me up, man," he said into his phone. "I'm so done with this granny crowd."

I let the door shut and he turned around, mouthing an *I'm sorry* when he saw it was me. He'd pushed up the sleeves of his jacket to his elbows and untucked his shirt, looking way cooler than he had minutes before. I hadn't noticed his small cross dangling from his ear before.

"Okay," he said with his eyes on me. "Five minutes by the diner." He closed the phone. "Sorry 'bout that."

"No problem." I went down the steps to the Dumpster, the garbage scent trailing behind me.

Coco must have heard my voice and she came out from under the porch. She meowed piteously, like I was keeping her out in the cold, hard world.

"Hey, Coco," I said, but she took one look at Gary and dove back under.

"Is that your cat?" Gary asked.

"Not really," I said. "She's her own cat."

"She doesn't seem very friendly," he said.

I didn't know why I felt the need to apologize. "She's shy around new people."

"What's in there?" He waved his hand to try to move the smell away from his face. "Body parts?"

I laughed. "I hope not. Although I wouldn't put anything past El Diablo."

"Yeah," he said. "My mom loves his food but he's nuts." He checked his phone. "Gotta bail." He took off in a jog toward the diner.

I turned over and slammed off my alarm clock the next morning, still tired. The reception had gone way past what we'd planned, and it was eleven before we'd been able to convince Tonya Ashton, the last of the stragglers, that last call meant last call. Luckily, her patient and totally sober husband had eventually steered her out the door so we could clean up, but not before she'd told me several times rather emphatically that this was the best night out she'd had since her baby was born.

El Diablo had left my kitchen a mess, and it had taken us an hour to get it back in shape. We had to rethink the idea of using my kitchen for events. Although if every out-of-towner who'd told me they loved, loved, *loved* my chocolate and couldn't wait to order from my website actually did, it may have been worth it.

Once we got home, all I could think about was Bean. Right above me. Just lying there. Or laying there. Erica would know.

It probably would've been bad to do what I wanted during my restless night, which was to bang on the ceiling with a broom and demand that he come downstairs and help me get to sleep. Or not sleep.

Disgusted with myself for pining away for Bean, I jumped out of bed. Sunday was the one day of the week when running was optional for me, and the one day I didn't make chocolate. Instead I usually had a leisurely morning and opened the store with Erica at eleven.

After making coffee, I went out onto the porch. Maybe I let the screen door close a little too loudly, just in case a certain journalist was awake and wanted to join me. Left-over raindrops twinkled on our grass as the sun rose over the trees. A neighbor was baking, and the scent of cinnamon and sugar made my stomach growl.

After wiping water from the two wooden rocking chairs, I sat down and sure enough heard the creak of stairs and then the clink of the coffee mugs. I schooled my face into nonchalance as the screen door opened. It was Erica.

She must've seen my expression change. "Bean's not here." She took the wooden chair beside me and stretched out her legs. "He left a note that one of the sources for his new investigation was arrested and he had to go take care of it."

I tried not to let my disappointment show. "That's too bad. I know he wanted to visit with you." And me.

Erica got the hint. "I'm pretty sure he'll be back soon." She smiled at me. "Any reason you're asking?"

"No," I said, my hurried response showing I was totally lying. In defense, I changed the subject. "Where was Bobby last night? Working?"

Erica and one of our local police, Lieutenant Bobby Simkin, had restarted their high school romance over the summer, but from my point of view it was moving along very slowly.

"Bean's hoping to make it in time for your dinner," she said, letting me know I wasn't fooling her at all. She broke eye contact with me. "And I thought it was better if Bobby didn't attend."

"Oh." They were trying to keep their relationship quiet, but she had to know there were few secrets in a small town.

"I'm so glad the reception is over. Do you want to tell me why you were so stressed about it?"

She frowned, her eyes following a blue bird flitting among our oak trees. "Let's just say I have some unsavory history with Dr. Moody," she said in a dark tone I'd never heard her use before.

Erica had a complicated relationship with the world of academia. She was the town's girl genius who got a full ride to Stanford, then moved on to graduate school and a Fulbright scholarship overseas before returning home to West Riverdale. Some people thought she settled for being a bookstore manager, and was capable of so much more. But she loved to match the right books to her customers, and her outside research enabled her to use her vast brain to explore all kinds of topics. Which made her a know-it-all in the best way.

"Okay," I said, not sure I wanted to know. "Well, now we've done what we set out to do and he's out of our lives. No need to ever see that jerk again."

"Probably not. Although," she said, drawing out the word, "the museum asked us to do another event."

"Not another reception." My voice sounded a little whiny. I hadn't recovered from the last one.

"No." She paused dramatically. "A flash mob!"

"Really?" I asked. "That sounds so, I don't know, undignified, for a museum."

"No, it'll be great." Her enthusiasm was outweighing her dislike of the professor. "The museum is trying to appeal to a younger audience. I'll be working with Wink—"

"Wink?" I asked. "That guy who looked like a toy soldier?"

"Yes, my contact at the museum." She raised her eyebrows

when I smirked in amusement. "His name is William Kincaid but he's been called Wink since he was a kid."

"Do you always feel like winking when you talk to him?" I asked and gave her a slow wink.

"No, because I'm not a child," she said, and then relented. "Maybe a little at first. Anyway, when I heard the museum was attempting to improve their social media presence, I suggested that we work with the high school to do the flash mob. If we can get it to go viral, it'll help to advertise not just the Maya exhibit but the whole museum. And it'll be an excellent experience for the students as well. We're meeting at the store this afternoon."

"Because your life was so boring, you needed another challenge?" I asked.

She smiled. "I'm going to get the Super Geeks involved. I've already shown them how Maya art on ancient artifacts were very early comic books." Erica had regular meetings at her store with a group of comic-book-loving teens who called themselves the Super Hero Geek Team.

"Will it help Chocolates and Chapters?"

She made a face at my self-serving attitude but then smiled. "I'll get the store in there somewhere."

Last night's freebies hadn't hurt our Sunday business, as lots of people stopped in to gossip about the party and buy chocolate. Chocolates and Chapters looked back to normal, with the tall cocktail tables out and our comfy couches and side tables back in. I kind of missed the glass case full of treasures, especially my bowl, but I loved the hum of people talking and enjoying my truffles and picking through Erica's books.

The reception had been a ton of work, but this surge of business would keep us humming until Halloween, Thanksgiving and then the holidays.

I opened a new bag of coffee beans and fed them into the coffee grinder, appreciating the rich scent, my second favorite smell in the world.

"Can you watch the front for a minute?" I asked Beatrice Duncan after I hit the brew button. I'd told Kona and Kayla to come in late, but Beatrice had plenty of experience working as a cashier at the Duncan Hardware Store.

"Of course," she said. "I'll only steal a few of the Raspberry Specials as payment." She said their zesty infusion of real raspberries made her feel like she was being particularly decadent.

I went out the back door to see if Coco had eaten the Beef Feast cat food I'd left out for her when I arrived this morning, but she hadn't touched it. Most mornings, she ate breakfast on my porch. Even though I knew every store owner on Main Street fed her, I couldn't help but worry when she changed her routine. I called her name a few times.

Nothing.

Back inside, a gaggle of single women were speculating about all the available men at the party, particularly the identity of the two sexy strangers. Someone had heard that one of them was staying in Nara's bed-and-breakfast.

They shouldn't get so excited. This was West Riverdale. Even if one of the delectable duo was still in town, he wouldn't be here long.

"I bet ya they were drug dealers," one of them said. "They looked just like the bad guys on that *Person of Interest* rerun last week."

"Nah," another replied. "They didn't have those tear tattoos on their faces."

"That's for gangs," the first one retorted as if she were some criminal underground expert. "And he could have tattoos under his clothes."

Beatrice raised her hand. "I volunteer to find out!"

The bells on the front door joined the group's laughter as Chief Noonan came in with Lieutenant Bobby. One look at their solemn faces and we all went silent.

"What is it?" I asked. It took a lot not to ask if they were here because of my brother Leo, but after these last few months of stability, I managed to stop myself. I had no reason to doubt his progress in his fight against depression.

Of course, he was now riding a motorcycle. My heart started beating faster.

"Can we talk in the back?" the chief asked. His eyes didn't even go to his favorite Simply Delish Milks behind the glass. This must be serious.

Erica stood up from stocking Harry Potter bookmarks on a display rack. "What is it?"

"You come too," the chief said.

Beatrice made a shooing motion with her hands. "I'll handle them both. You girls go take care of whatever it is."

Erica and I exchanged *what the heck?* looks as she led the way back to my kitchen.

The chief and Lieutenant Bobby stood in the doorway, a contrast in so many ways. The chief, nearly seventy years old, tugged his belt up over his paunch. He'd earned every one of his gray hairs. And Bobby with his brown hair cut short, leaner than he'd been in high school, was totally at home in his uniform.

I braced myself on the metal utility table.

"The Mayan, I mean, Maya art display was stolen on its way to the museum," the chief said.

Relief flooded through me and I gave a nervous laugh. "Is that all?" I asked. "I thought someone had died or something."

Chief Noonan scowled. "It's no laughing matter. Those antiquities were worth over two hunert and fifty thousand dollars."

My mouth dropped open but Erica nodded as if she knew. Of course. She knew everything about everything. She might have told me that we had such valuable items right in our store. And we *definitely* should have charged the Rivers more for that party. That pottery was only part of what they were donating to the museum.

"What happened?" Erica asked. "Is the security guard okay?"

"Wasn't much of a guard," I muttered.

The chief's jaw tightened but I was surprised that Bobby still looked so grim. Usually he appreciated my sense of humor.

"Since you two are suspects perhaps you'd like to take this more seriously," Chief Noonan said.

"What?" I said. "That's crazy!"

He cleared his throat, clearly uncomfortable. "Someone has made accusations that we need to clear up."

"Who?" I demanded at the same time Erica straightened and asked, "What accusations?"

Before the chief could continue, we heard loud voices from the front of the store. "Where is she?" It was the professor.

We all moved quickly for the hallway, where we saw Dr. Moody attempting to get past Beatrice at the counter. She stood her ground with her solid arms sticking straight out to keep him back.

His face was red with rage as he pointed a shaking finger at Erica. "She did it!"

Lieutenant Bobby moved around Beatrice and pushed the professor back with one hand.

Dr. Moody snarled over Bobby's shoulder. "She's trying to ruin my life!"

3

"That's enough," Lieutenant Bobby said with enough menace that the professor stopped in his tracks.

Moody glared at Bobby. "So, now she's sleeping with *you*?" His contempt was unmistakable.

What? Did the professor just imply that Erica used to sleep with him?

I dodged past the chief's outstretched arm and almost made it close enough to smack that venomous look off the professor's face, when Bobby stopped me with an arm wrapped around my waist and lifted me off the ground. He'd seen me play enough softball not to underestimate me like the chief had.

The professor took another step back. "Did you see that? She was about to assault me! She obviously has anger issues. She probably helped that spiteful—"

"Watch it," Bobby growled and then visibly relaxed. I wasn't fooled. It was the way a kung fu expert prepared for a lightning-fast attack.

Chief Noonan must have been thinking the same thing because he inserted himself in front of Bobby as Lavender rushed into the store, huffing and puffing from exertion. She wound her way through the tables of fascinated customers to stand beside Dr. Moody.

Bobby stared down the professor over the chief's head. "Why would she want to ruin your life? What did you do to her?"

Lavender's face filled with vicious anger. "Nothing! He's done nothing! She's just jealous!"

The professor glared at her and she stopped, still seething.

"Dr. Moody and Ms. Rawlings," the chief said in his no-nonsense tone. "I already have your statements. You will both wait at your hotel until I require further information."

"And if I refuse?" the professor asked, blustering.

"Well," the chief said, scratching his head as if actually considering the question. "That would certainly move you up on my suspect list. You knew more about the security plans than anyone else. I could arrest you and hold you for twenty-four hours, and given that this is a Sunday and sometimes the judge is playing golf on Mondays, you'd most likely spend a few days in a cell."

"Bu—" the professor stopped in midword when Bobby shifted ever so slightly toward him. He turned his head toward Erica, trembling with rage. "You will not get away with this."

Lavender tugged at his arm to get him to leave, glaring at us the whole time. "You all think she's so smart but she's stupid if she thinks we'll let her do this." She slammed the door, causing the bells to jangle angrily.

"Lieutenant," the chief said. "Make sure they get where they're supposed to go."

Bobby nodded grimly and followed them out.

Our customers stared at us with rapt attention. Great. No matter how much they loved us, they had to be enjoying the firsthand view of the drama that would be making its way around the West Riverdale gossip train.

Erica stood still, shell-shocked. She'd attempted to keep her relationship with Lieutenant Bobby quiet, hard enough to do in West Riverdale. Would people believe the professor's accusations? And what had happened between Erica and Dr. Moody in the past?

"I'll start with you, Michelle," the chief said with a resigned air. He was still unhappy that we'd "interfered" with his murder investigation a few months before. I called it "helped."

"You know where to find me." Erica's voice was strained. She went quietly back to the cashier stand.

The chief gestured toward the back and I led him to Erica's office.

He sat down and the chair groaned. "Did you notice anything unusual at the reception last night?" he asked, bringing out his well-worn notebook.

Other than the chief hadn't been there for the free food? "Nope," I said. "Just a nice party for a nice cause." Then I realized something. "Wait," I said, outraged. "My bowl is gone?"

His bushy eyebrows went up.

"Not, like, *my* bowl." I stumbled over the words. "It had chocolate in it from centuries ago so I really liked it."

He made a note. Probably *Unusual attachment to inanimate object*. "What do you know about the security guard?"

I tried to remember. "I barely paid attention to him. I assumed he was hired by the museum or the Rivers." I thought about how he'd hovered when I was coveting my bowl. "Is he okay?"

The chief ignored that. "Anybody there that shouldn't have been?" He kept his eyes on me. "It was a fundraiser. You sold tickets, right?"

"Yes, but Vivian didn't want us checking for them, so I'm sure there were a lot who crashed. It was as much about publicity as raising money."

"Any strangers there?"

"Plenty of out-of-towners. You know, the upscale city types." And they'd loved my chocolates. I made a mental note to see if any of them had followed through on their pledges to place online orders.

Then I remembered the sexy strangers. "Did anyone tell you about those two guys who were kinda dangerous looking?"

He straightened in his chair. "In what way?"

I described them as best as I could without sounding like a fan-girl. "The second one's name was Santiago Diaz. Kona met the first one, but I never spoke to him."

He made a note. "I'll speak to her."

"The professor seemed to know the first guy," I said. "He looked angry to see him there."

The chief's eyes narrowed. Maybe the professor hadn't told him that detail. Of course, he'd been too busy heaping blame on Erica. "What do you mean? Did they speak to each other?"

"Not right then," I said. "I was about to ask the professor to start his speech, when the first guy came in. The professor saw him and looked mad for a minute, but then he had to thank everyone publicly. I was too busy to see if they talked later."

The chief made a note. "Where were you from ten last night to two in the morning?" he asked.

"Is that when it happened?"

He nodded.

"We cleaned up here until about eleven. And then Erica and I went home."

He wanted detailed answers about who left with whom at what time. And then he asked, "Who was here when the security guard left?"

"Other than us? Just Adam River. He watched him load up at about ten thirty, and then he thanked us and left. We were trying to get Tonya out the door so I'm not sure of the exact time."

"So Tonya provided a distraction?"

I rolled my eyes. Tonya as an art thief? "Are you kidding?"

The chief pointed to the security camera outside Erica's office in the back hall. "Do you have your security camera footage from last night?"

"Of course," I said. "I'll have Zane get it to you." Zane West was Erica's assistant for her rare and used book business, her website designer, and all-around tech guy.

"So, you know we didn't do it," I said, "no matter what Professor Bozo said. Can you tell us what happened?"

The chief squinted like he was deciding how much to reveal. "The security guard was drugged but doesn't remember how it could have happened. It appears that he was driven in his SUV to a side road near the highway where the items were unloaded into another vehicle."

I nodded, encouraging him to hand over more information.

"At five this morning, he woke up in his car, in the passenger seat." Noonan kept his eyes on me. That man would be suspicious of his grandma. "He was very confused and wandered around the area for a while, before he called 911."

"Wasn't someone from the museum looking for him?"

He shook his head. "There seemed to be a lack of communication with the museum."

"So he doesn't remember having someone else in his car?" I asked. "That's so weird."

"The last thing he remembers is getting a to-go bag from the caterer, Juan Aviles," the chief said.

"I knew it!" I sat up straight in my chair. "Anyone who could leave a kitchen as disgusting as he did has to be a bad guy."

He looked amused at my reasoning, or maybe at my certainty. "The bag was still in the vehicle, unopened."

"Shoot," I said. "Maybe Aviles gave him something to drink? He had these tropical juices that tasted like Hawaiian Punch."

His face tightened and I realized I might be asking questions he'd also asked, which could either sound like I was pretty smart, or that I was checking up on his work. "There was no evidence of that in the vehicle." He held up his hand as I sputtered in protest. "I know. It could've been removed. We're exploring every option."

"You know Erica didn't do this, right?" I asked. "How

would someone like her even know how to sell stuff like that?"

The chief frowned. "Money is not always the motive."

I walked the chief over to Erica. My side of the store was buzzing with news of the robbery. They couldn't resist sending speculative glances my way. The excitement of believing even for a second that Erica and I were art thieves was too much for them to pretend to be polite.

The only good news was that I had a few new customers ordering from my website. I was trying to figure out how to tell if they were from the reception when the chief left. No way could I ask Lavender to hand over the guest list to compare.

Erica sat by the cash register. Even from across the room, I could tell she was in her thinking zone, her mind miles away.

I waited impatiently for Kona to arrive so I could find out what Erica had learned, but Kayla walked in. She'd dropped her job as a yoga instructor and worked more hours for both Erica and me. She still made time for her other job—driving luxury sports cars from sellers to buyers all over the East Coast.

"Where's Kona?" I asked. "Are you covering for her?"

"Nope. Just came by for this." She went behind the counter and pulled out her cell phone. "You okay?"

I tried to appear calm and smiled. "However did you survive for twelve whole hours?"

"It was brutal," she said. "Want me to see where Kona is?"

"Uh, sure. But how?"

"We have this app." She tapped on her phone. "She's like a block away."

"Really?" I asked, appalled. "You keep track of each other?"

"Not, like, all the time," she said. "Just when we need to find each other. It's a safety thing."

"I guess," I said. "What's the app called?"

"Find My Friends," she said.

Then Kona walked in with a box of her specialty tortes. I'd recently promoted her to assistant manager and it was the best decision I ever made. During the summer, when I'd been deluged with orders for X-rated chocolates that I did not want to deal with, she'd taken over. She started a side business, Kona's Kreations, to make them. And she'd worked with Zane, technical advisor to practically all Main Street businesses, to build a website with everything anyone could want for a bachelorette party—boas of practically any color, *I'm the Bride* crowns, a seemingly endless variety of risqué party gifts, and much more. Luckily, she'd drawn the line at male strippers.

I followed Kona to the kitchen and filled her in while she unloaded the pastries into the refrigerator, out of earshot of our customers. "Do you remember the name of that guy with the accent you were talking to last night? He's one of the suspects."

"His name was Carlo Morales," she said. "But he couldn't have anything to do with taking those things."

"How do you know?"

She shrugged. "He was with me."

I tried not to look shocked. "Until when?"

She smirked and pretended to check a nonexistent watch. "Until an hour ago."

I thought of and discarded several disapproving statements. My assistant's love life was none of my business. "Are you sure that was a good idea?" I couldn't help myself.

"Yes, *Mom*," she said. "My roommate was home and I used protection."

I winced at the TMI. "Great. He coulda killed you both." And in five minutes, we were already down one potential bad guy.

Kona rolled her eyes at me, making me feel old.

"Go ahead and scoff," I told her. "Don't come crying to me when your next hookup cuts your head off." Which made no sense.

"How do you like those pants?" she asked, attempting to distract me. She was wearing the same kind, in khaki.

"I love them," I said. Kona had bought me a pair of clever cargo pants with tons of pockets and I'd ordered five more. Besides being comfortable and made out of some kind of magic material that even chocolate couldn't stain, they each had a cell phone pocket in the back waistband. We often wore long aprons, and it was so convenient to grab my phone out of the small of my back rather than trying to move the apron aside. The only thing I didn't like was when I had it set to vibrate and it rattled my whole spine.

With Kona in charge, I headed over to talk to Erica, who was still staring at nothing.

"He had to have been given an amnesiac," Erica said. She wasn't even offering to help the group of PTA moms debating the newest vampire novels in the Young Adult section.

I pulled a stool over to sit at her counter. "Who?"

"The security guard. From what the chief said, he doesn't

remember the time leading up to the robbery. Which means he was given a drug that caused retrograde amnesia."

"Retrograde?"

"It affects memory from the time right before the drug is administered."

Erica really did know everything about everything. "What can do that?"

"Probably Rohypnol," she said. "It's a common date rape drug."

"Where would someone get it?" I asked. Then I realized she believed this robbery was premeditated. "Wait. So this wasn't just some smash and grab deal. This was planned."

She nodded. "Someone knew what they were doing."

She went back into her own brain and suddenly I knew exactly what she was thinking.

"No," I said, pushing aside the flutter of excitement. "No. No. No. We are not looking into this robbery."

She went on as if I hadn't said anything. "There are actually very few possibilities of who it could be."

"What are you talking about?" I asked, feeling the impulse to investigate pulling at me like quicksand. Except for that part where I almost got killed, our last investigation had been an interesting time.

"I'm just agreeing with you. Someone planned this," she said. "Someone who knew the value of the items and at least some of the security details."

"Moody sent a press release to the whole art world," I protested. "Hundreds of people knew they were valuable."

She nodded. "But a lot less people were invited to the reception. And only a few people knew that the display items would be transported back to the museum last night." She raised her hand as I opened my mouth. "They could've assumed it. But the security guard trusted someone enough to take food or drink from him, or her. How many people would you trust in that situation?"

I frowned, knowing she was probably on the right track. "That doesn't mean we should stick our noses in."

Erica ignored me, moving along her own thought process. "Although, there's an outside chance that someone in the antiquities trafficking business stole them," she mused.

"What? Antiquities trafficking? In West Riverdale?" The flutter of excitement suddenly nosedived into batwing flappings of panic.

"Exactly," she said. "Very low odds. While these pieces are just the high-quality, high-profile art they'd love to get their hands on, they don't usually operate in the United States."

"That's nice to know," I scoffed.

"They certainly have clients here though," she said.

My eyes popped open.

"Of course," she said matter-of-factly. "Private collectors who are willing to pay top dollar for authenticated artifacts are what fuels the international antiquities trade."

"Like drug users?" I asked. "If there weren't so many customers, there wouldn't be Colombian drug lords?"

"That's more accurate than you'd imagine," she said.

Uh-oh. She was going into teaching mode. You could take the girl out of college, but you couldn't take the college out of the girl.

"It's the opinion of many experts that if the rest of the world wasn't willing to pay for Maya, Olmec and other pre-Columbian antiquities, the illegal looting of thousands of locations throughout Central and South America would stop. And then archaeologists could actually study them *in situ*, in place, to more accurately learn about how the Maya lived."

"Why doesn't someone do something about that?"

She shrugged. "Plenty of obstacles. Government officials are sometimes in league with the traffickers who are connected to drug cartels. Many of the sites are located in hard-to-reach places and are difficult to protect. Locals are often complicit with the traffickers in order to make enough money to survive. And the local police are simply outgunned."

My brain was stuck on "drug cartels" until she said "outgunned." Suddenly, this robbery didn't seem so simple. "In league with drug cartels? My bowl was stolen by a drug cartel?"

"No," Erica said patiently. "I think it was someone who knew the security guard. Someone who drugged him and stole a quarter of a million dollars in Maya antiquities."

A quarter of a million dollars. I couldn't wrap my head around that amount of money. That was like one hundred and twenty-five thousand truffles!

I was trying to come up with a way to bring up the nasty things the professor had yelled, when Erica said softly, "I'm sorry I never told you."

"It's okay."

She didn't meet my eyes. "I was embarrassed. And I thought I'd left it all behind." She paused, a hurt look on her face as if she was reliving something painful.

"You don't have to tell me."

She paused. "I told everyone that the politics of academia

were not for me. And that was true. Before I even met Dr. Moody, I was wondering what I was doing. It was all so much more . . . narrow than I'd expected."

She shrugged one shoulder. "And then Dr. Moody published my research on the Maya codices as his own. Without credit. When I confronted him, he threatened to say I'd made numerous passes at him and he had refused, and that falsely accusing him was my revenge."

I stood up, my hands closing into fists. "That scum—"

She waved that off. "He *was* scum, but it didn't matter. I actually could've proven that it was my work, but the whole thing was the proverbial straw that broke the camel's back."

"A straw," I said, fuming mad, "is something small. Not something this huge."

"But I have to thank him," she said. "Because I'm so very happy to be home."

That took the wind out of my sails.

"He did me a favor. Instead of trying to climb that slippery ivory tower, I'm in my hometown with my family, my store, and my best friend, who makes the best chocolate in the world." She smiled.

Her obvious contentment washed away some of my anger and I relaxed my hands.

"Thanks for telling me what happened," I said. "But now I really wish that Bobby hadn't stopped me from punching him."

4

Erica seemed fully recovered by the time Wink from the museum arrived. He gave her a big hug and Erica grinned. If he was one foot taller and she wasn't hooked on Bobby, I'd "'ship" those two, in the words of all the teens who frequented the store and used it to describe wanting a couple to be in a relation-"ship."

Erica called me over. "Wink, I'd like you to meet my partner, Michelle."

He surprised me by bypassing my outstretched hand and giving me an exuberant hug too. "So glad to meet you!" he said. "I *so* love your chocolates!"

"Uh, thanks," I said, smiling. "Are you always like this?"

He gave a delighted laugh. "Absolutely!"

Jolene Roxbury took me aside when she and her husband Steve arrived for the meeting. "You let us know if there's anything we can do for y'all, right?" She was dressed up for church in a fuchsia suit and matching shoes. Steve looked uncomfortable in his dress shirt and slacks. I knew he preferred his nerdy T-shirts and jeans.

"Of course," I told her.

"Because we don't appreciate nasty people stirring things up with our girls," she said.

They joined Erica and Wink at the large table in the back, which the whole town used as an informal meeting place. It looked like the flash mob was moving ahead despite the robbery.

Jolene taught math and drama, and Steve taught science at the high school. They both sponsored several clubs and knew how to get the best out of the kids. All four talked in excited tones about "expected production complications" and "authentic costumes" and a lot about a "Bottom Pack mural," with Erica busy typing away at one of her famous project plans, her absolute favorite thing to do.

By the end of the day, we'd had so many neighbors stopping by to gossip and look at us sideways, that we sold out of Mayan Warriors and End of the World Caramels. "It's like they were expecting us to pull an ancient Mayan vase from our back pockets and confess," I said to Erica as we shut down just a little earlier than our usual six p.m. on Sundays.

"Maya," she corrected absentmindedly while rearranging the books on the shelves in the dining area.

Someone knocked on the front door and I groaned. Who was having a chocolate emergency now?

I peeked through the blinds and groaned again. A more determined knock sounded.

"It's Reese." I went back to cleaning up.

"I know you're in there, Michelle." Reese's nasally voice was unfortunately clear.

"Just open it," Erica said.

When I looked at her like she was nuts, she added, "Maybe she knows something."

I slouched to the door like a reluctant teen being forced to do the dishes and opened the door. "What?"

Reese came in and started taking photographs of different angles of the couches now covering where the glass case had been. Twisting and turning her long limbs like that made her look like an ostrich trying to stick its head in the sand. "What do you know about the robbery?" she asked, practically upside down.

"It didn't happen here," I said in my *you're an idiot* tone reserved just for Reese.

"I know," she said. "But the crime scene is closed off. This is as close as I could get."

Erica looked amused at her contortions. "Actually, Highway 70 is as close as you can get."

"Don't you have about a million photos from last night?" I asked. I searched her carefully to make sure she wasn't using her pen camera.

"They belong to the Rivers," she said. "I'm not allowed to use them. Well, legally."

How could I get that kind of contract with this loony-tune?

"Do you have any suspects?" Reese asked. "You'll be investigating this, right?"

This time she set down her camera, focused her beady little eyes on me, and pulled out a notepad.

"Why would we do that?" I asked, not answering her question.

She made a note. "Because Erica is a suspect, so you need to clear her name."

"You know, you look like a normal person, and then you open your mouth and everyone starts to wonder," I said.

She ignored my insult. She'd probably heard them all. "I thought we could exchange some information. I've learned more about the security guard, who isn't a security guard at all."

Erica raised her eyebrows as if considering the offer. Had she forgotten how miserable Reese made our lives, not all that long ago?

"No," I said firmly. Working with Reese was a very bad idea.

Reese directed her question to Erica. "What do you know about the museum staff?" Reese said. "Maybe it was simply a publicity stunt."

I stepped in between them and didn't let Erica respond. "That's something only you would do. And it *has* been a slow news month. Did you . . . ?"

She gritted her teeth, and then moved to the side to try to get around me. "I heard what Dr. Moody told everyone this morning. I waited all day to get your side of the story before I write it up." She sounded like she was doing us a huge favor.

I scowled and raised my voice. "Then I guess you better get the same lawyer Dr. Moody will need when he's proven wrong."

She jutted out her chin. "The people of West Riverdale have the right to hear the truth."

I pointed to the door. "You wouldn't know the truth if it bit you on your tiny, bony ass."

S torm clouds were skidding across the sky when I went out to the car. By the time I made it home, the clouds were piling up behind each other as if the one in front had changed its mind on which way to go.

Erica had picked up Chinese food for dinner, and sometime after eating our chicken lo mein and before the fortune cookies, we'd progressed from thinking about possible robbery suspects to actually writing them down. And after a bowl of tiramisu ice cream, I'd even put them up on the whiteboard on the inside of the pantry we normally reserved for shopping lists.

Neither one of us said anything out loud about taking any steps forward in our investigation, until I said, "Maybe it was some kind of inside job. Do you think Bobby would tell you the name of the security guard, and you could ask Zane to look into him? Legally, I mean."

Zane was getting his computer science degree and had helped us with questionably legal information gathering in the past. The police had sternly cautioned him to never do it again.

"I know his name," Erica said, not acknowledging that she was making the leap with me to actually taking action on our investigation. "Farley Olsen. We talked for a little while about theater, now that I think about it. He does acting on the side. I'll ask Zane tomorrow."

Acting? He looked more like the bouncer type.

"Do you think anyone at the museum . . . ?"

"Not Wink," she said. "He's too decent."

"What does that mean?" I asked.

She paused to think. "Someone that dedicated to art education for youth just wouldn't be capable of planning a crime simply for the purpose of publicity."

Before I could question her logic, Erica excused herself to answer emails. She often took on research jobs for professors, which she handled at night. She needed less sleep than us mere mortals, and lately, I'd heard her pacing long into the night. Maybe she'd taken on more projects than usual.

My cell phone rang a little after nine. I was already in my pajamas, working on my laptop in bed. I debated answering it, but the Washington, DC, area code made me curious.

"Hi. It's Bean."

I sat up straight, shoving pillows behind my back. "Hi." My voice was a little breathless.

"Sorry I missed our dinner," he said. "Erica told you what happened, right?"

"Yeah," I said. "Your contact was arrested. Did she tell you about the robbery?"

"Yes," he said. "I talked to Bobby about it too. You're not going to look into that, are you?" The connection went fuzzy for a minute. He must be in a low-coverage area.

"I don't know," I admitted. "Dr. Moody is making some pretty serious allegations against Erica. Maybe"—I paused—"you should come back."

"Bobby said he'd handle the professor." Bean sounded grim. "But it's not the professor I'm worried about."

"Okay," I said, wishing he'd come back for another reason. "What are you worried about?"

"I'll fill you in—" Then I heard another man's voice. "Later." He hung up.

What did that mean?

By ten, I'd convinced myself to focus on my Monday plans to get my mind off Bean. "Later" obviously didn't mean today.

Monday was my favorite day of the week, when I experimented with new flavors and recipes and planned what delectable treats we'd make in the days following. I made a mental note to check on the supply of Bee Pollen and Fennel truffles, the current favorite of the group of PTA moms who rejoiced when school started again by meeting in our store every Monday morning. They'd heard something about the health benefits of pollen and they loved the hint of licorice flavor.

I decided to get a jump on fall selections, especially the ones that I'd need for Halloween and Thanksgiving. People instinctively wanted different flavors when the first hint of autumn hit. That need for more pumpkin-flavored everything probably started with the Pilgrims.

I'd already bought what I needed to play with pumpkin, sweet potatoes and butternut squash the next morning. Cinnamon and allspice. Apple cider. My mouth started watering at the possibilities.

The annoying beeping sound of Erica's electric car backing up woke me at midnight. That was weird, but not enough to keep me from falling back asleep.

At one in the morning, I woke with a start. It took me a few minutes to realize someone was banging on the front door so hard the sound was reverberating throughout the house.

"Who is that?" Erica called from the top of the stairs when she saw me heading toward the door.

"I don't know." I was still stupid with sleep.

More loud banging.

"Do you have your phone?" I asked.

She held up her cell as a reply.

"Who is it?" I called out without opening the door.

"It's Lavender Rawlings." It was definitely her voice and she sounded mad yet again. "Open this door immediately."

"Why should I?" I asked.

"I know Dr. Moody is in there," she said. "I need to speak to him urgently."

I gave Erica a questioning look and she shook her head. "He's not here," I called out.

"Please." Lavender's voice turned pitiful. "You have to help me."

"Just do it," Erica said, and I opened the door.

"What are you doing here at this time of night?" I said like it was the craziest thing I'd heard in a long time. "And how do you know where we live?" Although I could've answered that one myself: small town.

Lavender opened the screen door and brushed right by me. "Is he here?" She did a complete circle around the downstairs, slapping open the kitchen door as if we were hiding him from her.

"I already told you that he's not here," I repeated, trailing behind her and wondering how crazy she was. Hide-the-knives crazy? Too late, I realized the pantry door was open and our list of robbery suspects was totally out there. I closed it, hoping she was too upset to notice.

She saw Erica and took the stairs two at a time. I didn't think she could move that fast. "Addison?" she called out.

Erica put her hands up like she was under arrest and got out of her way. I ran and caught up just as Lavender thrust open the door to Erica's office and stomped in.

"Where is he?" Now that I got a close look at Lavender's face I could see that she was frantic, not just her usual angry-at-the-world self.

"I assure you I have no idea," Erica said behind her. "I think we both made it pretty clear we had no use for each other."

"Why don't you sit down," I suggested as Lavender eyed a closed door. "You're welcome to check out the closets if you like, but really, he's not here." I cleaned the pile of books off a ridiculously tiny embroidered antique chair and gestured toward it.

"He's missing!" Lavender flopped down into the chair, causing it to creak ominously, her distress apparent. "He hasn't been back to the hotel since noon. I just couldn't wait any longer to look for him."

It was only one in the morning. "Maybe he had a date and just didn't make it back yet?"

She shook her head. "Impossible."

"Does he always tell you his plans?" I asked.

"Always," she said emphatically.

"Well, things are a little topsy-turvy right now," Erica said. "Maybe he just forgot."

"He didn't forget," she said. "Something has happened. Something terrible."

"Let's back up," Erica said. "What did he have scheduled for today?"

"He had a meeting at the museum and then he was coming back to West Riverdale to meet with the Rivers," she said. "After that he called me to say he was catching up with a student and would see me back at the hotel for dinner."

"Did you call him?" I asked.

"Of course," she said. "It goes straight to voice mail."

I couldn't help but imagine that he'd left the country with the goods from the robbery. Erica avoided meeting my eyes. Perhaps she was thinking the same thing.

"Have you talked to Chief Noonan? Maybe they're, I don't know, working together on something to do with the robbery?" I suggested.

"I did!" Lavender practically wailed. "He hasn't spoken to Addison since this morning."

Now I was getting an uneasy feeling, which was reflected in Erica's expression for a moment before she hid it. "What did the chief recommend?" Erica asked.

"He told me to file a missing persons report tomorrow." Her voice quivered at the words.

A missing persons report? The thought made me feel a little quivery too.

We finally got rid of Lavender at two in the morning.

"Where do you think the professor is?" I asked Erica.

"I have no idea." Now that we were alone, she allowed her worry to show. "But none of the possibilities are good. He either had something to do with the robbery—"

I broke in. "And he's basking on some tropical island now while Lavender pines away for him."

Erica continued. "Which doesn't make much sense, because the Rivers' collection could make his new career."

She continued. "Or Lavender is right and something . . . bad has happened to him."

Then I remembered something. "Did you leave the house at like midnight?" I wasn't sure if I'd dreamed it.

Erica flushed a deep red.

"Oh my God!" I exclaimed. "I've never seen you blush like that! What did you do?"

"Nothing." She kept her voice calm, but her eyes slid away.

"Come on. Spill it."

Erica's face went solid red again. "This whole day was a little upsetting and I decided that maybe I should explain it all to Bobby."

"Explain?" I paused. "Wait. You went on a booty call?"

"Shush!" she said, instinctively looking around.

"Shush, what?" I said. "It's two in the morning. The only people awake in West Riverdale are you, me and kooky Lavender."

"Okay, okay," she said. "I drove to his house and it was dark. I changed my mind and came home."

"Likely story," I said. "You probably had a quickie and got home in time to entertain our unexpected guest."

"No." She shook her head, laughing at herself. "I chickened out."

That I could believe. "So what the heck's going on with you two?"

"We're doing fine," she said, as if reassuring herself. "I think he's waiting for me to make the, you know, first move."

"Like a midnight booty call," I teased.

She blushed again.

"That's going to be the name of my next dark chocolate truffle," I said. "The Midnight Booty Call."

. . . .

The sky was a deep blue and felt huge to me, as if the possibilities were endless. The late afternoon temperature was both warm in the sun and cool in the shade, perfect for exercise. A beautiful day in Maryland.

I was in mile three of my four-mile route, feeling strong. After being up so late with Lavender, I'd put off running so I could be rested for my morning frenzy of chocolate making and spent my favorite day of the week doing my favorite thing. I'd loved my new fall creations and got to see my customers loading up on them. Pumpkin Treats with a tinge of allspice. Sweet Temptations Truffles which were dark chocolate cups filled with sweet potato mousse. And the most risky, Butternut Squash Squares with cookie crumbles on top. I'd left early with Kona in charge until closing so I could sneak in a run before dinner.

Then a state police car crested the hill in front of me. I stopped, resisting the urge to run into the stand of trees on my right, knowing that trouble was about to ruin my day.

I waited on the side of the road, hands on my hips as I heaved a little. Sweat pooled on my lower back, not all of it a result of my exercise. I was sure my face was flushed deep red, which always highlighted my freckles. My hair was plastered to my skull, but most likely had some bizarre strawberry blond tufts sticking up.

Sure enough, Detective Roger Lockett slowed to a stop beside me, his arm on the open window and his bicep straining the sleeve of his uniform. He looked at me through reflective sunglasses, smiling a little. Probably because I was a sweaty mess.

The last time I'd seen him was when he'd grudgingly told me the inside scoop on the deal to put two murderers behind bars for a long time. Two murderers that Erica and I had helped uncover. And then he'd demanded that I stay far away from police work in the future.

I'd readily agreed, convinced I'd never need to.

"Bad news?" I asked.

"That's the only kind I deliver," he said. He had a strong Pittsburgh accent that came through even in that short statement.

My chest constricted at his confirmation. "Leo?"

"No," he said emphatically. "Your brother's fine. At least as far as I know. It's about Dr. Moody."

I relaxed just a little. "Did he take off to Bora Bora with his ill-gotten gains?"

"Nope," he said, his eyes on me. "He's dead."

5

gaped at him, probably looking like a fish, the kind with a big, wide mouth. "The professor is dead?" My face felt numb with shock.

The detective clicked open the locks. "Get in," he said. "I'll drive you back to your house."

"Really? I'm all gross," I said, not really waiting for his answer. It seemed easier to think about the mundane than the professor.

"I'll keep the windows open," he said.

I started around the front of the car and went to open the passenger door. "Nope," he said. "In the back."

"What?" I said, outraged. "Like a criminal?"

He shrugged, clearly amused. "State law."

I stomped over and got in, slamming the door.

I think I saw him wince in the rearview mirror, although the cage between us made it difficult to see him clearly. "Hey," he said. "That's government property."

The seat was hard plastic, and my sweaty legs stuck to it. "What happened to him?" I asked as he wheeled the car around and headed back to my house.

"Let's wait for the chief to fill you in," he said.

"So how bad is this?" I asked.

He shot me a look in the mirror. "That depends. Did you do it?"

I rolled my eyes at him. "Of course not. Well, at least you're not closing my shop this time."

"Not yet," he said.

I'd learned to take his tough attitude with a grain of salt but I still scowled at him.

"How ya doin'?" He pushed his Pittsburgh accent for me. I'd had a roommate from Pittsburgh for a while, and he knew I delighted in the unique expressions.

"Good," I said. "You bin back to the 'Burgh since I saw you in May?" I had a lot of practice copying that accent.

"Once," he said. "Fourth of July."

"Didja see the fireworks at the Point?"

Pittsburgh's Point State Park sat right where the Allegheny and Monongahela Rivers met to form the Ohio River. Since I had few relatives, my roommate had been kind enough to invite me on several of her family visits, and we'd had a lot picnics there.

"Yep," he said. "With the whole family."

"Nice," I said. "West Riverdale's fireworks were cancelled, so we went to Frederick." Our new mayor, Abby Brenton, was trying to get the town back on track after the previous mayor's debacle and had promised to have a celebration next year.

I focused on what he'd said. Family? "Do you have kids?" I asked. I'd never thought about his personal life.

"Nope." We pulled up to the house, and the chief's police car was parked in front for all the neighbors to see. Erica's car was plugged into its special charging station, so she must have come home early too.

"Lieutenant Bobby here?" I asked.

He gave me a sarcastic look. "Whatta ya think? I'm stupid?" He was well aware of the history between Erica and Bobby but maybe not the current state of their relationship.

I walked inside, the chief looking out of place at our kitchen table. Erica had given him coffee and a banana nut muffin, despite looking shocked at the news.

Luckily, the pantry room door where I'd written the beginnings of our robbery suspect list was still closed. Neither Chief Noonan nor Lockett appreciated our investigative efforts in the past.

I poured a cup of coffee for Lockett and handed him the cream and sugar bowls in the shape of monkeys with their arms as the handles. "Let's just get this out of the way," I said. "Where were we on the night of . . . ?"

The chief stopped in the middle of peeling the paper from his muffin. "How do you know it happened at night?"

"I don't," I said. "It was a joke. You know, '*Where were you on the night of June thirteenth?*' They say it on all the cop shows."

He sighed one of his sighs that showed how deeply disappointed he was in me that I wasn't taking this seriously.

He was right. Someone was dead. Even though I hated what the professor had done to Erica, it was still tragic that he was alive yesterday and dead today.

And it meant another murder that affected little West Riverdale, what we used to call "The Mayberry of Maryland." How was that even possible?

Erica's cell phone rang. She grabbed it and pushed the button to reject the call. It immediately rang again.

Then my phone rang. It was Leo. "I have to take this," I said and stood up to take the call in the hallway. "Hey, Leo."

"Worst day of your life?" he asked right away. It was our way of making sure the other one was okay. The absolute worst day of our lives was when our parents died, although Leo had too many days that were close to his worst when he was in Afghanistan.

"I'm okay," I said. "Talking to my best friend Lockett."

He laughed. "Call me later."

I went back into the kitchen. "I guess we better turn these off." If this news had already hit the town, then everyone would be calling us. After yesterday's scene, all of West Riverdale knew we hated the professor.

I decided to jump right in. "Lavender came here at one in the morning looking for her boss," I said. "I don't know why she thought he might be here."

The chief looked over his glasses at Erica. "Before he disappeared, he mentioned having a meeting with a former student. Was that you?"

"No," she said calmly. "I was at the store until closing and then here."

"He must have a lot of former students," I insisted.

"True," Detective Lockett said. "But not that many who wanted him dead."

My eyes popped open. "Why would you think we wanted . . . that?"

Too bad Lockett was such a smart guy and realized I hadn't disagreed with him. "Didn't you?"

"No! Just because we couldn't stand the guy and wanted him to leave West Riverdale and not come back doesn't mean we wanted him dead." And maybe lose his job, his hair, his teeth, and all of his friends.

Lockett stared at me.

"Let's keep this simple," I said. "Lavender said he left at noon yesterday. Both of us were at the store until closing. Then Reese stopped by. And then we came home and were here all night."

"Can you prove it?" Lockett waited with his pen poised for an answer.

"You mean, beyond vouching for each other? I don't know. We were both on our computers. Can't you track them or something? Our cell phones were here." I saw Erica's face flinch a little and remembered that she'd left the house at midnight. I rushed on. "What else do we need to do to prove it?"

The chief and Lockett exchanged glances and I sighed. "You're going to separate us, aren't you?"

Detective Lockett stood up. "You come with me," he said. "Outside."

"Why do I have to be the one who goes outside?"

"Cuz you smell," he said.

Oh yeah. I'd forgotten the whole sweaty mess thing.

We sat on the wooden rocking chairs and he looked out

over the field across from our house, rocking a little. "I have a bad feeling about this, Michelle."

I didn't answer. His getting personal thing was probably just a cop trick. "We didn't do anything." I turned to watch the kids who lived across the street playing a form of tag that involved calling out colors of the rainbow.

"I know," he said. "But you can't stick your nebby nose into this one. It could be a whole heck of a lot bigger than that last one."

"Really? You pulled out 'nebby nose' from your Pittsburgh grab bag?" I asked. Even my roommate had learned that no one outside of the 'Burgh knew that meant nosey.

"You didn't answer me," he said. It was hard to get anything past this guy. "You gonna stay out of my police business?"

"Of course," I said.

He didn't look like he believed me.

"Where did they find . . . him?" I asked, suppressing a shudder.

"In Bluebird Park," he said. His tone was casual but he couldn't help his cop instincts to stare at me and evaluate my reaction.

"Outside Frederick?" I asked. "What was he doing there?" Besides being murdered.

"Crime scene techs think he was killed at a picnic table and dragged into a creek," he said.

I shivered but managed a joke. "Don't you mean a 'crick'?" I was sure he was rolling his eyes internally. "How did . . . it happen?"

He gave me his *do you really think I'd tell you that?* look.

I tried to figure out a question the detective might answer. "What's near the park?"

He raised his eyebrows. "There's a self-storage business pretty close."

"What a waste of money," I said. "People need to learn to throw things away."

Lockett smiled, as if he knew I was trying to distract him with nonsense so I could ask more questions.

"Was the professor's car there?" I tried, knowing I was pushing it.

"Yes," he said with exaggerated patience. "Are we playing twenty questions?"

"I get twenty?" I asked. "Who found him?"

"Someone was playing Frisbee golf—"

I interrupted him. "Frisbee golf?"

"Yes."

"That's, like, a real thing?" I asked.

"Yes, it's a real thing." He shifted in his chair, annoyed that he'd used my words. "A sport."

"For old people?" I asked. "Like, bocce ball or something?"

He looked even more annoyed. "That's really one of your questions?"

"Wait." I pretended to be appalled. "You don't play Frisbee golf, do you?"

He shook his head, more at me than to answer. "No."

"Bocce ball?"

He smiled. "Maybe. I'm half Italian."

"So how did this Frisbee golf super-athlete find . . ." My voice trailed off.

"A Frisbee ended up in a 'crick' and our witness climbed down to retrieve it," Lockett said.

"Which is the most exercise he enjoyed during the whole game," I said. "Wait, is it even called a game?"

"Let it go." I'd pushed it too far. "When he slid down the small cliff, two vultures flew away and he saw the professor's body."

I felt sick to my stomach. "Vultures?"

"Unlucky for us, yes." He was probably enjoying the look on my face. "The damn things attacked the body and most likely destroyed evidence, but the professor was definitely murdered."

I sat in silence, but Lockett wasn't finished. "One thing was lucky."

"What's that?"

"If it had rained like it was supposed to last night, that crick woulda been a river and who knows where the body would've ended up."

I stared at him. "Do you think that was part of someone's plan? That it was premeditated?"

"We'll have to figure that out," he said.

I remembered my outstanding question. "What did the professor say about Carlo Morales?"

He raised his eyebrows at me, knowing what I was hinting at. "That he'd never met him and didn't know why anyone would think he cared if Mr. Morales was at the reception or not."

I frowned. "I saw him. He was mad."

He shrugged and changed the subject. "I hear Benjamin Russell was in town this weekend."

I felt a little frisson of alarm at the studied casualness of his question. "Yes. He left on Saturday."

"When's he back?"

"I don't know," I admitted.

He stared at me. "Okay." As if he sensed my disappointment and didn't want to dig further. "We need to talk to him."

"Question him, you mean," I said.

"I expect he wasn't too happy with the professor either," the detective said.

"Was anyone?"

They finally left. The only good thing was that they were on their way to question Reese, just because I happened to mention that she was actively investigating the robbery and might have learned something to help.

"They wanted Bean's new cell number," I said. "His old one is turned off."

"I don't have it," Erica said as if it didn't matter. "He uses burner phones when he's on assignment. But he wasn't in town during the time in question. If he was anywhere close, he'd have stopped to see us."

I wish I had her confidence in Bean's desire to see us. I was still somewhat dumbfounded. How could it be that someone we knew was murdered? And that once again, we were implicated?

I stared at the floor, sneaking glances to see if Erica was ready to talk. She looked out the window, legs outstretched and arms crossed, one of her favorite thinking poses. "The professor's murder must be tied to the robbery."

"Deciding to investigate a murder is a much bigger deal than a robbery," I reminded her, but the curious mixture of resignation, fear and excitement made me realize it was probably inevitable.

"We may need to," she admitted. "Lavender believes I did it. Or she wants to believe it. She's going to do her best to make sure the police focus on me."

I thought of the venom she'd directed at Erica in the shop on Sunday. "Okay. Let's talk suspects."

Erica smiled.

After returning way too many phone calls from concerned and gossiping citizens of West Riverdale, we
spent almost an hour discussing the "murder quotient" of
anyone involved with the professor. Erica had come up with
an equation to establish the percentage chance of each suspect actually being the professor's killer. Knowing Erica,
she'd write a paper and police departments across the
country would start using it.

I didn't care about her "MQ" and put vindictive Lavender
Rawlings first. According to every cop show I'd ever seen,
anyone who tried to cast blame onto other innocent people
was probably trying to deflect attention from their own guilt.
Given how much she disliked Erica, I doubted she would
talk to us directly, unless we came up with some serious
motivation.

We agreed that all of the Rivers except Rose were toward the top of our list, even though I couldn't imagine what they had to gain. They had a ton of money. They seemed very committed to making the donation, and surely, it was embarrassing to have it stolen right under their noses. What could make them risk their social standing for some ancient pottery? The "motive" column was empty for all of them.

We still wrote in what we knew about each one. Adam was ambitious and smart. He was quickly climbing the corporate ladder; maybe he made some enemies on the way up. There was also some lingering anger about a big layoff at one of the River manufacturing plants that had occurred as soon as he'd taken over. Maybe the theft was more about payback than the art.

Gary was a slacker who wanted to slide by in life. Jennie was a confused kid with a drug problem, but not so far gone that she was robbing people.

"I wouldn't put anything past Vivian," I said. "She'd knock off her mother to make sure the family reputation stayed intact."

"But killing the professor would have to outweigh the possible damage of something he could reveal," Erica said, taking me more seriously than I expected.

"I talked a little to Gary at the party and he definitely has issues with his mother," I said. "Maybe I can stop by the coffee shop and see if he'll tell me something that will help."

The security guard was moved ahead of the Rivers. "Even though he was drugged," she said, "he could've been part of an inside job."

"What about Carlo Morales and Santiago Diaz?" I asked.

Erica's face immediately grew concerned.

"What?" I asked when she didn't answer.

"I think we work on everyone else before we look into these two."

My stomach flipped a little. "Do you think they're dangerous?" I remembered the predatory feeling that Santiago gave me, even with that silly ponytail.

She shook her head like she didn't know. "They could be."

"Okay," I readily agreed. "Let's not get crazy. But write down that Dr. Moody seemed to know that Carlo guy, no matter what he told Lockett."

I moved the subject back to people who didn't scare the hell out of me. "We definitely have to put El Diablo there," I said. "Gary said his mother loved his food, but maybe Aviles was into something she didn't know. If his store wasn't doing well, he may have needed the money."

Erica wrote in her computer. "We should ask Zane to see what he can find on him, and everyone on the list. As long as he does it all on the up-and-up."

"And maybe we need to take a road trip to Frederick and check out the El Diablo Restaurant," I said.

Thinking about Juan Aviles's crab tamales made me realize how hungry I was. "What do you think about eating dinner at the Ear?"

Erica perked up. "Really?" She knew what that meant. The Ear was the best place to hear the town gossip. Too much of it would be about us, but maybe we'd learn something helpful. We didn't even bother to change before we left.

"I'm sure Jake would love to tell us what he knows," I said.

The Ear got its nickname back in the sixties when the neon stopped working in the curves of the *Bar* sign of

O'Shaughnessey's. It was a West Riverdale landmark, welcoming anyone who wanted to have a drink, shoot some pool, or eat the best double-stuffed potato skins in Maryland.

Jake Hale was the owner and regular bartender who could be in a commercial for any product that wanted the image of an easygoing handsome guy going about his business in a flannel shirt and worn jeans.

We walked in, the scent of stale beer and peanuts washing over us. "Walk Like a Man" played on the old-fashioned jukebox. Conversation in the whole place dribbled to a halt before it exploded, as two of Jake's cousins rushed toward us, both with high ponytails normally seen on toddlers.

"Are you guys going to investigate this murder too?" one of the cousins asked, holding on to my arm, at the same time the other said, "Did you do it?" earning a fierce scowl from the first.

Jake was plagued with about a million female cousins who all looked alike, and he always had a few working for him.

The second cousin stood in front of Erica. "I'm totally kidding. I'm sure you'll do a better job than that state police guy, but can you introduce me to him? He's just my type. Rugged and doesn't talk much. I bet he's a tiger in bed."

Erica recovered faster than I did. "We can't possibly do a better job than the state police with all of their resources. And I'm sorry, but I don't know anything about the detective's private life."

Neither of them realized she hadn't answered their question about whether or not we were investigating. Or if we'd done it.

"I think that pottery really is cursed, like their grandma Rose said." The first one moved her shoulders in an exaggerated shudder as if enjoying the thought. "I bet beetles ate him, like in *The Mummy,* for disturbing the grave."

"Those were scarabs," Erica said. "They don't attack people. And the professor didn't—" She stopped, maybe realizing there were way too many things wrong with what the cousin had said and she couldn't fix them all.

The other cousin tossed her hand towel over her shoulder. "I think it was one of them Mayan gods or something. It came back from the dead to protest all that 2012 end of the world stuff."

"Maya," Erica corrected.

I sent her an exasperated look, even though I should've been used to it by now.

"Which god?" Erica asked politely, as if the girl really knew what she was talking about.

"I don't know," she said. "That chicken guy maybe?"

"Chichen Itza?" Erica tried.

The cousin got distracted by a rumpled man coming into the bar from the poolroom and dropped my arm. "Ah, sweetie, you out already?" She completed an elaborate hair flip and went over to console him.

Jake met us at the end of the bar with a Pearl Necklace beer for me and a glass of chardonnay for Erica. "Leave 'em be," he told cousin number two, who went back to cleaning tables. Jake shook his head. "Don't mind them. They spend too much time watching reality TV." He tapped the beer bottle and asked me. "You tried this yet?" Jake knew I was a fan of the local breweries.

"Isn't it made out of oysters or something?" I asked.

"Just give it a shot," he said. "Money-back guarantee."

I took a sip. "This is awesome." I pointed the glass at

Jake's T-shirt, which read *Nobody trains to ride the pine*. Of course, he had his trademark open plaid flannel shirt over it. "What does that mean?"

"You know," he said. "The bench is made of pine. Nobody trains to sit on the bench." He put some used glasses in a small tub behind the bar. "Trouble seems to be following you girls around lately."

"Hey!" I said, offended. "It's been months since we had any trouble. And this has nothing to do with us."

"I don't know," he said. "You guys are up there in the betting pool."

"These people are already gambling on who killed the professor?" I asked.

"These people would gamble on who had to go to the bathroom first if I let them," Jake said.

Erica smiled. "Who's ahead of us in the pool?"

"That Lavender woman, Vivian River, and tied for third are those two strangers who made such an impression on the ladies."

"Why Lavender or Vivian?" Erica asked.

"Well, according to our amateur bookies, Lavender killed him in a fit of jealous rage when she finally confessed her love for him and he laughed at her. And Vivian because she decided she didn't want to donate all that stuff after all."

"Really? That's all they got?" I asked.

"What are our odds?" Erica asked.

He pulled his cell phone out. "Michelle's odds are three to one that she killed the professor."

"This sounds like a game of Clue. Miss Scarlet killed Professor Plum in the billiard room with a candlestick," Erica said lightly.

"More like *Gilligan's Island*," I muttered.

"What're my odds?" Erica asked.

"Four to one." He looked apologetic. About her odds being worse than mine or mine being better than hers, I wasn't sure.

"What are our fictional motives?" I asked.

He pulled a rubber plug out of the bottle of wine resting in ice. "Some people are saying that you guys killed him when he discovered you stole the Mayan stuff."

I frowned at Erica and she held back from correcting him. "And why did we steal it? In their bizarre view of reality?"

"For the money." He said it in his *isn't it obvious?* tone as he topped off Erica's glass of chardonnay.

"And how would we know how to get rid of stolen Maya antiquities?"

He shrugged. "They didn't get that far." At my outraged look, he laughed. "It's harmless, Michelle. Let the idiots have their fun."

"Who else is on the list?" Erica asked.

"Well, under the premise that it's always the ones you least suspect, there's Iris, Nara and Abby."

"A waitress, hotel manager and mayor?" I asked. "None of them make sense."

"What can I say?" he said. "They watch too much *CSI*."

Erica frowned. "Actually, approximately seventy-seven percent of the time, the murder victim had a personal relationship with their assailant." She took a sip of her wine. "Who else has better odds than we do?"

"Adam River. Everyone else is a long shot."

"Why the Rivers? They don't need the money," I said.

"Eh, there's never enough money for folks, especially

rich folks," he said. "Again, this is not my list or my odds."
He smiled as if to say they were all crazy and he loved them
for it. "So, are you guys putting on your Sherlock Holmes
hats for this one?"

"Oh no," I said.

He shook his head, bartender instinct at work. "I knew
you couldn't keep your noses out."

"That got us in a lot of trouble before," Erica reminded him.

"Right," he said. "Heard the police questioned you both."

"And we have solid alibis," I insisted.

"Ouch," he said, pulling out his phone and changing
some numbers.

"Did our odds just drop?" Erica asked.

"You bet. Ignore the pun." He put it away. "Since you're
not investigating, you'll have no interest in hearing the latest
news."

"What latest news?" I asked.

He frowned as if pretending to be totally serious. "I know
you're not interested. So I won't bother you with it."

"Jake," I said in a serious tone.

He took his time, pouring nuts into small bowls before
answering. "The River family fired Deirdre."

"Their housekeeper?" Erica asked.

He nodded. "Interesting timing, don't ya think?"

"But hasn't she been with them, like, forever?" I asked.

"Yep," he said. "Her whole life. And her mother worked
for them her whole life too. It's their family tradition to work
for the Rivers. Did you know that Deirdre was actually born
in the house when her mother refused to leave until the silver
was polished? And that by then, it was too late."

Erica sent me a look. "Wow. It would take something

very big to fire someone after that long. I wonder what she did."

"I don't know," Jake said. "But Iris at the diner said Deirdre is spitting mad and ready to dish some dirt on the whole River family."

"Why hasn't she already?" I asked.

"Maybe waiting for someone to pay her for what she knows. People like the Rivers must have some enemies who'd be willing to cough up a lot of money for secrets to use against them."

One of his cousins yelled, "Jake! We need ice."

He sighed. "What can I say? Murder is good for business."

"Where are you in the pool?" I called after him.

He smiled over his shoulder and didn't answer.

"Sounds like we gotta find ourselves a housekeeper," I said to Erica.

She tapped a fingernail on her wineglass, not really listening. She was already putting this into her mental vision of her project plan and analyzing what it could possibly mean. But I bet that at least some of the Rivers' murder quotients just went up.

One of Jake's cousins came to the waiter station. "Two Buds," she told him, and then stopped by our booth. "I know who it is. Wasn't there some Mayan god named El Chocolate something? And they made chocolate offerings to him?"

A chocolate god? My heart started pounding.

"Ek Chuah?" Erica asked. "Actually, that's an Internet myth. He was a minor deity, most likely a patron of long-distance merchants. And the Maya drank considerable amounts of chocolate, for every meal actually, but didn't make chocolate offerings. They performed bloodletting cere-monies and offered their blood to their ancestors, not to gods."

I got stuck on "chocolate for every meal." That sounded awesome.

"So maybe one of their gods demanded a human sacri-fice," the cousin said, wide-eyed. "And someone gave them the professor."

He'd be my first choice.

7

Bean was in my kitchen when I woke up the next morning. Delighted surprise broke through my sleepiness. "Hey," I said, curiosity in my voice.

He'd made coffee and was waiting at the table. I peeked outside and didn't see a car.

Bean launched right in. "Look, I'm sorry. I know I started something that I can't . . . finish. And now I'm in the middle of a story and it just wouldn't be safe for you to be seen with me. Or for me to be anywhere around here."

"Why?"

"I may have . . . crossed a line." He paused. "I made the call to insert myself in this group. Into the story." He stopped as if not sure what he could tell me. "They don't trust me yet and I know they're following me off and on. So I have to stay away from here."

"Who is 'they'?" I asked. My thoughts were tumbling

around. Relief that he wasn't totally blowing me off. Worry because he appeared truly troubled about his undercover role. And dismay that I hadn't brushed my teeth and couldn't kiss him hello. Or good-bye. Or whatever this was.

"I can't tell you," he said. "Sorry."

"Be careful, okay?" I tried to put all of my troubled emotions in my voice.

His face softened into a smile. "Yeah, I will."

I ducked my head and took a sip of coffee, wondering how uncool it would be to scoot out and at least swish around some mouthwash.

"So when this is over," he started to say.

"Your 'this' or my 'this'?" I joked.

"You're not supposed to have a 'this.'"

"How will I know you're okay?" I cringed at the plaintive tone in my voice.

He didn't meet my eyes. "You won't. Unless . . ."

I finished the sentence. "Something terrible happens."

"Well, that's one murder you won't have to investigate."

When I looked horrified, he grabbed my hand. "Nothing is going to happen."

I blinked, worried I was going to lose Bean before I even had him. "Okay." But then I got a little breathless thinking about the "having."

"I came back for another reason," he said. "I talked to Bobby and I want you and Erica to stay far away from Dr. Moody's murder. Given the robbery, Bobby thinks there's a chance, a small chance, he was involved with some criminals who work with international art traffickers."

"Erica said that was highly unlikely," I said, even as his words made me feel shaky.

"This isn't like those TV shows where rich people with European accents steal from each other. Traffickers are vicious, nasty people who don't let anyone stand in the way of their profits." He actually seemed worried. Last time he was encouraging us to investigate the murder.

"Okay," I said. "We'll be careful. But isn't what you're doing dangerous?"

"It's my job."

"I know," I said. "But you could be doing a lot of other jobs in the world where you don't have to sneak around because you're in danger." My breath caught in my throat a little. It would totally suck if something happened to him. He was in actual danger and we were maybe, possibly in hypothetical danger. Wait. Were we having our first fight?

Then I heard Erica at the top of the stairs and rushed out the words. "Um, so Kayla and Kona have this app. I think it's called Find My Friends or something. Maybe you and Erica can kinda, I don't know, keep track of each other." The "or me" was implied. I could almost see it hanging out there in cartoony words hanging between us.

He thought for a moment. "Would it make you feel better?"

"Yes," I said, probably a little too emphatically. So uncool.

"I'll check it out," he said. "If I can hide it so my new buddies can't find it on my phone."

Erica appeared in the doorway and her face brightened. "Bean!" She gave him a hug. "Can you stay for breakfast?"

I let them have a moment alone and hurriedly brushed my teeth, but Bean didn't seem interested in kissing me good-bye when I came back.

He was telling her about a story one of his reporter buddies was working on. "He's becoming somewhat mythical
in Central America."

"Who is?" I asked.

"He goes by El Gato Blanco," Bean said. "No one knows
who he is. But if even half the stories are true, he's responsible for returning hundreds, if not thousands, of looted
artifacts back to their country of origin."

"A modern-day Robin Hood," Erica said.

"Yes," Bean said. "And just about as violent. He's willing
to do whatever it takes to obtain the art. Sometimes he buys
it—so he has considerable resources—and sometimes he
simply takes it, even if it means shooting his way out."

"Where did the name come from?" Erica asked. "The
White Cat. It's not very intimidating."

"No one knows for sure, but a small town in Belize is
alleged to have a white jaguar that they protect from poach-
ers and other outsiders," he said. "And perhaps the idea of
someone in a white hat being the good guy. Supposedly, he's
pissed off enough traffickers that there's a considerable
bounty on his head."

"But no one knows what he looks like?" I said. "Probably
nothing like the fluffy white kitten I was imagining."

Bean smiled. "How's the kitten watch going?"

"She's going to pop any day now," I said, not liking the
image as soon as I said it. "Wait. Do you think El Gato
Blanco stole the museum's display?"

Bean shook his head. "West Riverdale is too far off of
his stomping grounds. It sounds like the kind of job he'd do,
but he's never acted on the East Coast. The only time he's

been rumored to operate in the U.S. is a rash of burglaries in several small museums in California. He certainly has enough work to do in his own part of the world." He checked his watch. "I gotta go."

I felt a little lurch in my heart as Erica and I took turns hugging him good-bye. "Take care of yourself."

He went out the back door with a *don't worry* smile, but Erica looked concerned. "He parked behind the barn on Whispering Pines, and walked across the fields to make sure he wasn't followed."

We stared at each other for a moment. "Life is sure complicated," I said. "Don't you think?"

"It'll calm down," she said, but I wasn't sure even she believed that.

I downloaded Find My Friends and got ready for work.

On the way, my phone pinged with a Find My Friends invitation from a "John." I accepted, only slightly appeased.

I stopped at the shop and was happy to see Coco waiting for me outside the back door. She wound around my legs and demanded that I feed her *now*. With so many kitties inside that fat tummy, it was no wonder that she was starving. She let me sit and pet her while she ate some special canned salmon food that May insisted was for pregnant cats, and then wiped her furry little face on my pants. Nice. I had to clean that up before my early morning mission: trying to catch Gary River at his Big Drip Coffee Shop after he opened but before his early morning coffee rush started.

Again, Coco tried to sneak inside when I opened the door, and I had to scoot her out with my foot. May had made a perfect bed for Coco in the back of the flower shop, but she would never stay there long.

Trying to air-dry the spot on my pants, I locked up the shop again and headed off to check out Gary on the slim hope that he'd spill on his family members.

Somewhere I'd heard that Adam had given Gary an ultimatum to make the coffee shop a success or lose his trust fund. The Rivers were the only "trust fund babies" in West Riverdale. I couldn't imagine what it would be like to not *have* to work. I hoped that even with all the money in the world, I'd still want to make my delicious chocolate creations that made so many people happy. Although it would be nice not to worry about meeting payroll during those tough months.

Coco must be psychic, because she met me halfway there, coming out from the tiny alley by the Knit Wits Yarn Store. It was oddly comforting to have her company on my early morning walk through the quiet downtown streets.

The Big Drip was open with lights blazing and I could see Gary behind the counter, placing pastries in the glass case. He'd propped the front door open, probably trying to gather the cool morning air before it warmed up, and Coco followed me right in.

"Hey, Gary," I said.

"That cat can't come in here."

"I'm sorry," I said, trying to pick her up. She wriggled right out of my hands and went out the door as if she knew she wasn't wanted. "She just started doing that. Should I close the door?"

He watched her walk away, her tail in the air as if totally offended. "Nah. She's gone."

"This place is great!" The shop was decorated in an

upscale retro diner style. Metal chairs with burgundy leather seat cushions surrounded a few chrome tables plastered with postcards of old cars and famous diners from the past and then coated in thick plastic. Shiny red seventies-style bar-stools cozied up to a shiny counter, while a small couch and love seat made a perfect little corner to chat. Small menus with red frames were placed artistically on the walls.

Photos had been taped in between, and sometimes on the art itself, with little regard for the decorator's hard work.

"Thanks," he said.

"I can't believe I haven't been here before." I'd seen advertisements when they first opened "under new management" but never made it over. I should've at least checked out the coffee competition. The pastries looked like they were from the grocery store. Kona's tortes would kick their butt. "How's it going?"

"Good," he said with a quizzical look.

"Our coffee machine is broken and I'll never make it through opening without some caffeine," I told him. "I can't wait for Kona to fix it when she comes in."

"She can fix those things?" He seemed impressed. "Cool."

I better make sure to tell her she had a new skill. I looked up at the menu in chalk on the wall and then reached out to touch it. "Wow. You painted the wall to be a chalkboard?"

"Yeah," he said. "Duncan Hardware carries the paint. My sister makes the letters look all cool like that."

"I'd love a large cappuccino." I wanted something that would take a few minutes to make. I drifted around the store and checked out the photographs. They all contained skate-boarders doing impossible jumps and surfers riding waves higher than my building. Then I recognized one of the close-ups. "Is that you?"

"Some of them," he said. "I surf." He ground some coffee beans and tamped coffee into the portafilter.

"That's hard to fit in as a business owner," I probed, keeping my eyes on the photo.

"Tell me about it. Especially with my brother—" He cut himself off.

I gave him a sympathetic look over my shoulder. "I have an older brother too. Man, they can guilt you into anything, right?" I said, while sending silent apologies to Leo who was the lowest-key big brother I knew.

Then Coco strolled in from the back of the restaurant. "Do you have a back door?" I asked.

"Yeah," he said in a *why are you asking me that?* tone. Then he saw the cat. "But it's closed." He hit some buttons and the coffee dripped in the small metal pitcher.

"I'll get her," I said as I herded her out the back door like a sheepdog. The screen door had a gap at the bottom that she must have squeezed through, so I shut the heavy wooden door. "Sorry about that."

Gary was working the steamer like a pro, when a group of four skateboarders came in with a bunch of "Yo's!"

"What're you slugs doing up this time of day?" Gary smiled, working the steamer with one hand and high-fiving them with the other.

"House of Vans in NYC, man!" the one with the red headband tied around his leg said. "We need the brew."

He heaved himself up onto the counter to reach over to the to-go cups Gary hadn't put out yet, tossing them over his head to another skater in a move that looked well practiced. The four of them filled their cups from the carafes at the end of the counter and began piling in sugar and cream.

"That's five bucks, guys," Gary said.

"What?" The red handkerchief guy sounded outraged, and then looked at me. "Sure, dude."

He dug in his pocket and slapped a few singles on the counter, dropped a quarter in the tip jar, and slammed open the door.

"Friends of yours?" I asked to dispel the awkwardness.

"Yeah. My friends are cheapskates," he yelled after them. One of them made a vulgar gesture and grinned to show he didn't mean it. "They pay me back eventually, whenever they have money." He poured the perfect foam on top of my cappuccino and handed me my cup. Looking at it made my mouth water.

"I have a few friends like that." I tried to establish some kind of connection. "The ones who come in for free chocolate."

"I know, right?" he said. "They don't understand what it takes to run this place."

"Your shop is really great." I blew on the coffee. "I'm impressed."

"Thanks," he said.

Then Coco came in from the back of the shop again. "What the heck?" I asked. "Is there another way in?"

"No." He stared at the cat as if she was supernatural.

"These old buildings have lots of nooks and crannies." I shooed Coco out the front. This time she seemed to get the message and headed off toward where lights were coming on closer to Main Street.

"That's too bad about the robbery," I said. "All your beautiful things." *My beautiful bowl.*

He shrugged. "They already belonged to the museum, but it sucks anyway."

I took a sip. "Yum," I said. "I don't think your mom likes all that publicity. Especially with the professor's death."

"Yeah." He shook his head. "Adam and his ideas."

I filed that one away. "He wanted to make the donation? That's nice."

He scoffed. "My mom doesn't think so now."

"It sucks that such a nice idea got ruined," I tried. "Did you hear that the police questioned us? We had nothing to do with it."

"Yeah, they're nuts," he said. "Our lawyer is keeping them off our backs, which is good because I do *not* want my mom finding out where I was."

I nodded. "Would she be mad?"

He snorted. "She'd have a fit."

"Sounds like you were doing something interesting."

"Nah," he said. "I was just babysitting Jennie at a party. That's the part that would crank off my mom."

"How long did the party last?"

But I'd pushed it too far.

His eyes turned suspicious. "Our lawyer says we're not allowed to talk about it."

"I'm sure the police will let us all know when they figure it out." I grabbed a plastic lid and carefully put it on. "Are you still going ahead with the other donations?"

"Yeah," he said. "That's a done deal. There's a lot of stuff they didn't get." He slouched toward the cash register. "You want anything else?"

My cue to leave. "No," I said, pulling out a five-dollar bill. "Thanks so much for the caffeine. I can't get enough today."

He gave me change and I put it in the tiki jar with a hand-made *Tips are for kids!* sign. "Thanks," he said. "Have a good day."

I cleared the table after the elementary school's coffee klatch moms left, their normal stop on Tuesday mornings after dropping their older kids off at school and then playing in the park with their younger children. One of their toddlers had insisted on playing peekaboo with me every time I came close, yelling, "I see you," and then squealing with laughter while hiding behind the totally see-through slats of the chair.

One of the moms, Samantha, had taken one bite of a Mocha Supreme and not finished it. I grinned and took the evidence to show Kona. "Samantha's pregnant."

Kona laughed as she wiped down the counter. "Diagnosis by truffle?"

"You'll see," I said. "Sometimes pregnant women can't handle the coffee flavor." No coffee? I couldn't imagine. "Can you check website orders?"

"Sure." She clicked a few keys on my laptop behind the counter. "Oh my God. There are a ton!"

"Really?"

She turned it around so I could see.

"Wow!" Then I got a sick feeling in my stomach. "Do you think it's because the professor . . . ?"

"Don't go there," she said. "It's just because the news reminded all those people at the reception how amazing your chocolates are."

I took a few deep breaths, staring at the screen. Then I met her eyes.

"It's still pretty creepy," she admitted.

At noon, I got a call from our next-door neighbor, Henna Bradbury. "I'm sorry to be the bearer of bad news, but your house is filled with crime scene investigators."

"What?" I yelled. "I'm gonna kill Chief Noonan." Did I say that out loud? I looked at the customers staring at me. "I mean, what a funny guy."

"Oh my goodness," Henna said. "There's a police officer coming this way. Bye!"

Erica was back in her office, holding an ancient, leather-bound book in her hand and talking to a customer for her rare book business on the phone. "I know. It's terribly disappointing. But I'm confident that it's not a first edition."

"I need to talk to you now," I whispered loudly.

She held up one finger. "Of course," she said to whoever was on the other end. "I'll do that right away. And again, I'm sorry I don't have better news." After a few "uh-huhs" and "that's fines," she finally hung up.

Before she could ask, I told her, "The crime scene techs are at our house!" I felt frantic at the thought of strangers going through my stuff. My clothes. My dirty underwear. And oh no, my high school diaries.

Her eyes widened, but her voice was calm. "That's okay," she said. "We have nothing to worry about."

"Should we go home?" I asked.

Erica thought for a minute and then said, "No. Let them come to us. I have a date with a flash mob."

8

I was on pins and needles, waiting for Detective Lockett to arrive. Erica looked relaxed during her production meeting with Wink from the museum, teachers Jolene and Steve Roxbury, who had snuck away during their lunch break, and Janice the Costume Lady. Janice worked with all the local high school drama classes and junior theaters to transform kids into characters on a shoestring budget. They all seemed very excited about the video they were planning, but not too busy to ignore my new fall assortment of truffles.

I'd asked Erica if the flash mob was a good idea given the professor's death, but they'd all decided that positive press was more important than ever.

Wink wore a bright yellow sweater vest with tiny blue stripes, his starched white sleeves folded up neatly to right above his elbows. His pants were rolled into a little cuff, showing off his contrasting psychedelic socks. Rolled up was big with this guy. "Is that allspice in those pumpkin truffles?" he asked.

I smiled. "Good taste buds."

"Genius!" he said. "I've never tasted anything like it."

"What's with the getup?" I asked Jolene, who wore an African-print turban around her hair and matching dress.

"It was 'Diversity Day' at school." She used finger quotation marks. "The new principal has a bunch of ideas for eliminating bullying on campus." She sounded dubious. "We're all supposed to wear something that shows our heritage."

The colors were gorgeous against her dark skin. "You look beautiful," I said and turned to her husband, Steve, who wore a neon green golf shirt and outrageously loud, orange plaid Bermuda shorts. "Where's your outfit?"

He flashed a grin. "Can't get any more WASP-y than this."

Jolene drew him away to discuss backdrops with Wink, and I cleaned up their dishes.

Detective Lockett held the door for Colleen and her three children and then strolled in behind them. Even though her divorce was not what she'd planned, she seemed happier than she'd been in a long time.

Her two-year-old twins made a beeline for me. "Aunty Schmell!" they yelled and grabbed onto my legs. I wasn't much of a kid person, but made an exception for Colleen's. Nine-year-old Prudence waved and headed over to the bookstore, which she loved almost as much as Erica did. The twins let go of me and raced for the play area on Erica's side. I was sure Erica was about to pull out her recording device. Ever since she realized they were losing their twin talk the more they learned how to really talk, she'd been trying to save what was left. If Colleen wasn't careful, she'd write a paper on the whole thing.

Lockett raised his eyebrows. "*Aunty Schmell*? Can I call you that?"

"Not if you want to live," I joked, and then realized that was probably not something to say to a cop investigating a murder. "I thought you needed probable cause to search someone's home." Being involved in a prior homicide investigation had its advantages.

"You want to talk about this out here?" he asked. "Erica should join us."

I rolled my eyes and collected Erica, who was sitting on the floor in the play area reading a book about a snoring bear to a toddler on her lap while the twins ran cars up and down her back.

I pointed out Lockett. "You're needed in the back," I told her, not bothering to keep the resentment out of my voice.

"No problem," she said and then spoke to Colleen, who put down the box of books she'd begun to stock on the shelves.

Erica's assistant Zane was working at her desk, looking like the preppiest kid in Maryland with his khaki pants, blue button-down shirt and argyle vest. I think he had vests in every known shade of pastel. Maybe he and Wink shopped at the same vest store.

He turned around in his desk chair and Lockett nodded to him. "Hey, West, you keeping your nose clean, kid?"

Zane looked deadpan. "As far as you know, yes."

"Great," I said. "Now he'll get a search warrant for you."

Zane seem unfazed and spun back to focus on his screen.

"You want him to stay for this?" Lockett asked Erica.

When she nodded, he pulled out a few sheets of paper and handed over a very official-looking warrant. "I'd like to know why you left the house at midnight the night of the murder."

"What?" I asked. "How do you know that?"

Erica looked over the papers. "I'm sorry, Zane. Can you check the post office box?"

"No problem." His wide-eyed *let me out of here* expression made it clear he was happy to escape.

We waited for him to be out of earshot and Erica explained to me, "My car tracks my usage, including pretty detailed GPS monitoring." She turned to Lockett. "Right?"

When he nodded, she continued in a calm voice. "It's easily explained. I couldn't sleep and wanted to tell Bobby what had happened with Dr. Moody. He didn't know anything about my . . . history with the professor."

"And did you?" Lockett leaned casually against the doorjamb but he couldn't hide his intense expression.

"I'm sure the data tells you that I stopped outside Bobby's house and then left after five minutes."

"Why?"

Her voice faltered. "I was embarrassed. That was a difficult time in my life when I made several bad judgment calls and I didn't want anyone, especially Bobby, to know."

"And that's the only reason?" he asked.

I moved to stand beside her. "That's the only reason," I insisted.

Erica put a hand on my shoulder. "I would prefer this not get back to Bobby."

Lockett nodded, which seemed pretty noncommittal to me.

"As I'm sure you know, Bobby and I have a complicated

relationship and we recently began dating again." She held her chin up. "I was considering taking our relationship to another level. Unfortunately, it was terrible timing. In more ways than one."

"So you didn't tell him anything," he clarified.

"No," she said. "I didn't even get out of the car."

He nodded, as if her statement matched what he already assumed. "We checked your store's security footage, and it corresponds with what you told us."

"Of course it did," I said. "Did you see anything useful on it?"

"Erica," Colleen rounded the corner.

"Are you done with me?" Erica asked.

"For now," he said.

"Why does that always sound vaguely threatening?" I asked him as Erica and Colleen headed over to the bookstore side.

He shrugged. "Probably because you're always *vaguely* guilty of something."

As long as he was here being a pain, we should get something out of it. I stopped halfway down the back hall and turned to face him. "So nothing on the video?" I asked. We'd looked at it too, but he was the expert.

"No."

"What were you looking for in our house?" I asked.

He stared at me for a long moment and then answered, "We have the autopsy results. The coroner determined that Dr. Moody was killed by a small, sharp tube, which was not found near the body."

"Like a straw?" I asked.

"Exactly," he said. "And Lavender Rawlings insisted she saw items that could've made such a wound in Erica's office."

"For the love of—" I broke off and took a deep breath. "Lavender is a vengeful idiot who doesn't know what the hell she's talking about."

"We know," Lockett said. "But she made quite a stink so we followed through."

"Did you find the so-called murder weapon at our house?" I asked.

"If I had, we wouldn't be having this conversation," he said. "A piece of the murder weapon broke off and lodged in a rib."

I had a sudden vision of a scene from the *CSI* show demonstrating the internal workings of how victims died in horrific, bloody detail, and felt a little faint.

"Are you okay?" Lockett asked.

I nodded. "I'm fine."

"The tube was made of jadeite," he said. "Have you ever heard of it?"

"Jade, yes. Jadeite, no," I said. "What is it?"

"I'm told that it's a stone used a very long time ago to make Maya bloodletting tools."

It took me a while to find my voice. I definitely paled this time. "Like for human sacrifice or something?"

"Exactly." He grimaced. "You don't want to know what they did with them."

If it freaked out an experienced homicide detective, I definitely didn't want to know.

"So I should let you know if I see any jade tubes lying around?"

"Jadeite," he corrected me. "Sure."

"I'm assuming you can't find them at the Duncan Hardware Store," I said. "You know, aisle fourteen for gardening, ceiling fans, and bloodletting tools?"

He smiled. "Not unless they sell items worth about one hundred thousand dollars."

"What?" My voice was shocked. "He was killed by something that was worth one hundred thousand dollars? How big was it?"

"Not big," he said. "Say seven or eight inches long."

"That's like twelve thousand dollars an inch."

He sighed.

I stated the obvious. "So you're going with the assumption that this had something to do with the disappearance of the display." Then I remembered that it had contained some tubes. "Wait. Weren't some of those things used in the display?"

"Yes," he said.

I felt a little sick to my stomach. "So one of them was used to . . . ?"

"We won't know for sure until we recover the murder weapon," he said.

Lockett seemed in no hurry to leave, and I got an uneasy feeling. "Can you tell me again why you're here?"

He stared at me. "Gary River said you were in his coffee shop asking weird questions."

"I was just getting coffee," I insisted, but at the last second my glance slid away. I knew I'd blown it. I had to get better at that interrogation stuff. "But you have to suspect someone in that family."

"They all have alibis," he said. "Stop asking them questions." He pushed off from the wall and left.

Erica joined me back in her office, and I told her about the murder weapon and Lavender's accusations. "She's definitely out to get you," I said.

Erica didn't seem concerned. "She's grieving. All those emotions have to go somewhere." She opened her laptop and clicked a few times. "A bloodletting tool. That's fascinating."

"Really?" I asked. "I'd have gone with incredibly gross."

"You're not far off," she said. "Much of Maya art documents their many rituals, including perforating their, let's just say their most sensitive places, to collect blood on paper. Then they'd burn the paper as an offering."

I so didn't want to hear about that. "Did I really need those images in my head today?" No wonder Lockett had seemed squeamish about it. "There were some in the display case."

"As we suspected, his murder could easily be connected to the robbery." She turned to Zane, who came back with a bunch of mail. "Did you have time to research Farley Olsen?"

He dumped the stack of envelopes and packages and dug through his desk for a few sheets of paper. "He's not really a security guard. He's an actor."

"Has he at least played a security guard on TV?" I asked, but neither of them responded to my joke.

Erica read from his research. "He works part-time at Eastern University of Baltimore."

"The professor's college?" I walked over to read over her shoulder. "That's pretty suspicious. Maybe it really was an inside job."

"The police have to know this," she said. "They must've cleared him." But her voice was thoughtful.

"Can you ask Bobby?" I asked.

She gave me a *you gotta be kidding* look.

Zane was looking at us with interest.

"Any chance you can get a, like, *totally legal* peek at the professor's past students and see if there's anyone with some correlation to West Riverdale, or the museum, or something?" I asked him.

He shrugged. "I can do that."

"But it won't get you into trouble, right?" I asked.

"Nah," he said. "A lot of this stuff is posted on public sites. Easy pickin's."

"Not that we're investigating or anything," I said.

He snorted and turned back to his computer. "Let me know if there's anything else I can be *not investigating* for you."

We left him alone with his sarcasm and went back to work. My chocolates weren't going to sell themselves.

Reese the crazy reporter banged on the front door again right after we closed. "Michelle. Erica. I need to speak to you."

"I'm not opening it," I told Erica. "It's been a long, long day." The delightful scent of almost-burnt sugar wafted through the store as Kayla expertly stirred the caramel in the kitchen. It would cool overnight and I could finish my half-sized Fleur de Sel Caramels in the morning. We all called them my "gateway drug" for good reason. I gave them away on the street to lure potential customers into my store, and no one could resist their gooey sweetness mixed with a tang of sea salt.

Erica did the honors. "What can I help you with, Reese?"

Anyone with half a brain would know from Erica's tone

that she was simply being polite. But not Reese. "The whole town is horrified by the gruesome murder of Dr. Addison Moody. Can you tell me your relationship and why you're considered a suspect?"

"Out!" I rushed over to get in her face. "We're closed." Too late I noticed Reese had an overly large pen in her pocket that everyone knew was a camera. "Really, Reese? You're back to illegally taping your neighbors? So you're bouncing back down to rock bottom in the tabloid journalism food chain?"

"Michelle," Erica chided as Reese drew in a quick breath.

"We are in a public place and you have no expectation of privacy," Reese said.

"We're in a place that is *closed*, where I have all the privacy I want," I shot back at her. Then I pulled the "pen" out of her pocket and looked for the power switch.

"How do you turn this thing off?" I asked.

"Give that back," Reese said.

I tossed it toward the door where it fell onto the welcome mat. "We are not answering any of your questions. We are not working with you. We are not sharing information on our invest—" I cut myself off but it was too late. I couldn't believe I did that!

"Ah-ha!" Reese pointed her finger at me. "You *are* investigating his murder."

"Reese, please." Erica tried to fix the situation. "Surely a journalist of your caliber is aware of the chance that very dangerous people may have killed Dr. Moody."

Reese stared at her.

Erica continued. "If they murdered an eminent man like the professor in such a horrific manner, then they are willing to kill anyone who gets in their way. You need to be very, very careful." Erica sounded even snottier when she was lying.

Reese didn't seem to fall for it. "The items were that valuable?"

Erica nodded. "They were worth over two hundred and fifty thousand dollars."

Reese was not the type to give up. "Is that what they'd sell for on the black market? That doesn't seem like enough money for someone to kill over."

And what would be enough money? I wanted to say, but Erica seemed to be considering the question.

"No one will know the true motive until the police find out who did it and why," Erica said.

Reese pounced on that. "Would art thieves really come to western Maryland for that much money? Or does it make more sense that someone connected to the whole thing, who had a motive other than money, did it?"

Maybe she wasn't as stupid as she looked.

Erica turned her hands up in an *it's not up to us* gesture. "I know from my brother that journalists are more courageous than others, in a way I don't understand. But Michelle and I are not the type to risk our lives when the police are much better equipped to handle this." She continued while Reese gave her a sour look, trying to figure out if she was telling the truth. "I wouldn't be surprised to hear that the FBI gets involved."

Whoa. Erica was getting good at lying. I almost believed her myself.

"Fine," Reese said flatly. Then she took something out

of her pocket and slammed it down on the counter. "Maybe that will pique your interest."

It was a flash drive.

T he flash drive contained about a gazillion photos from the reception. Erica sat at our kitchen table scanning them while I cleaned up dinner dishes. We'd picked up a half-pepperoni (for me) half-black-olive (for Erica) pizza from Zelini's on the way home, and I was pleasantly stuffed.

"You really believe Reese gave this to us because contractually she can't use them?" I asked. "Or is she going to say we stole them or something?" Reese would never voluntarily share her leads with anyone, especially us.

"No one needs to know we have them." Erica frowned. "She probably views this as a goodwill gesture so we'll help her." She clicked through the photos, stopping occasionally to enlarge one and look at it closely. "Look. Here's one of you."

I looked over her shoulder. Reese had taken a shot of me staring at the bowl. The look of blatant longing surprised me. But my hair was totally under control for once that night.

"Did you ever wonder why the professor wanted the reception at our store?" I asked when she'd moved on to a photo of him in his tux. "Did he want to taunt you or something?"

She paused, considering. "Vivian said that she chose Chocolates and Chapters."

"But?" I prompted.

"I guess we'll never know."

"Why did you say yes?" I asked.

"It was supposed to be good for the store." She squinted at an image and then enlarged it to fill the screen.

"What?" I asked. "Do you see something?" It was a photo of a short, wide vase, its color much more faded than the others in the display case. But it was still gorgeous.

"Hold on." She enlarged the photo even further and focused on some designs along the bottom.

I waited impatiently.

"This could be it." Erica turned the laptop for me to see a photo of Santiago Diaz staring intently at the display case, and then another of him frowning into Reese's camera.

"What's he looking at?"

She ignored me, reading the press release the professor had sent out that detailed some of the pieces. She clicked on the vase photo again, this time enlarging the little card beside it that provided basic information. "I have to look up this glyph. Hold on." She pushed back from the table and ran upstairs.

"What's a glyph?" I called after her and stared at the computer screen.

"It's a symbol, of sorts," she yelled. She rushed back downstairs. "In this case, it might be a very important one."

She showed me the book—*Chronicle of the Maya Kings and Queens*—and then opened it on the kitchen table. "So there's an extra glyph on this vase." She compared it to a page in the book several times, before sitting straight up and staring at me, looking stunned.

"What?" I couldn't remember seeing her so shocked.

"If what I think is true," she said, "this vase is worth far, far more than the amount the professor valued it."

"How much more?" I asked.

"Instead of about forty thousand, it could be worth . . ." Her voice trailed off.

"How much?" I insisted.

She shrugged. "A million?"

"A million dollars!" I shrieked.

9

sat down on a kitchen chair, hard. "We had a million-dollar vase in our store?"

Erica shushed me. "If I'm right, this vase is something the archaeologists have been trying to find for decades."

"Could the professor have made a mistake?" I asked.

She shook her head. "It's unlikely. He's an expert. He must have misidentified it on purpose." She stared at the photo, obviously trying to analyze what this new information meant.

"Why would he do that?" If I'd just landed a million-dollar vase, I'd be shouting it to the stars. I pulled my chair closer so I could see the photo better.

"Hold on." She pulled up other photos and I saw one of my bowl flash by. "These photos went out with the press release announcing the deal with the Rivers. Here's one of the vase. It's positioned so that it doesn't show the extra glyph."

"What could he possibly gain from hiding that?" I asked.

"I'm not sure," she said. "Maybe he was worried that the Rivers would sell it rather than donate it." She pulled her eyes away from the photo with effort. "Maybe he planned to reveal its true worth when it was firmly in the museum's collection."

"Can you show the photo to someone else to be sure?" I asked. "Someone who won't blab."

"Yes." She returned to the photo of Santiago staring at the vase and bit her lip. Even in a photo, his expression seemed dangerous. "But I'm not sure I want to . . . involve anyone else."

"Maybe someone who lives far away?" I asked. Far enough away to avoid international art traffickers.

She took a deep breath. "I have a friend in Africa who might be able to help." She opened an email and sent him the photo along with a message.

"What would we do if it is worth that much more?" I asked.

"We'd do the right thing and tell Detective Lockett." She shut down the photo application and opened a spreadsheet outlining our suspects. "If anyone else knew about this . . . it opens up even more reasons for the robbery. And the professor's murder."

"You don't really believe the BS you told Reese, right?" I asked. While I probably should be afraid of anyone who killed the professor, ruthless international art traffickers terrified me much more. "Wait. Do you think Reese knew about that vase? And that's why she gave us the flash drive?" I couldn't imagine she'd be that smart.

Erica tapped her pen on the table. "I don't know how she

could. She'd have to pinpoint the one photo that showed the glyph and meant something. And she'd have to know more about Maya art than most people."

Reese was definitely not an expert on anything except for ridiculous conspiracy theories. "So she just randomly wanted us to look for possible clues?"

"It was probably just a fishing expedition." Erica looked over our suspect list. "I still can't help but believe that someone who knew the professor stole the items and then killed him."

"Even if that vase is worth as much as you think?" I pointed out. "Maybe the professor was involved in the robbery and then had a problem with whoever he was working with."

"Then we still have to figure out who that was," she said, but I could practically see her brain working overtime.

"Or maybe his death is completely unrelated to the Maya stuff," I said. "He was a jerk. Maybe he pissed someone off we don't know about."

She narrowed her eyes. "Let's find out why he changed from being a professor to a museum curator. Hold on." She clicked away on her computer. "I heard of a new website. It's like Rate My Professors but without the moderator controls."

"That exists?" I asked. "A professor gossip site? You have to take that with a grain of salt. Anyone who didn't get the grade they wanted could put whatever they want there."

"I'm not sure how seriously anyone takes it, but maybe . . ." She took her time reading while I picked up the book on Maya kings and queens.

Before I could turn a page, Erica looked up at me, dismayed. "Oh no. Someone accused him of sexual harassment."

She clicked the mouse a few times. "And some other women said he did the same thing to them."

"Are you sure?"

"This is terrible. Eight students?" She got agitated and stood up to pace. "And there could be more who never came forward. I could have prevented this. If I had just stood up to him, and reported him, a few years ago."

I turned the laptop around to scan what they said, my stomach dropping at every entry. It was textbook harassment, starting with sexual innuendo and graduating to grade manipulation and outright groping.

"How could he get away with that in this day and age?" I asked, outraged.

Erica stood at the window, rubbing her temple with her fingers. "Something was probably done, but quietly, so as not to hurt the school's reputation."

"But he didn't do . . . that to you. How could you know what he was capable of?" I said.

"I could've had him fired two years ago," she said flatly. "I had all the proof I needed."

"He is responsible for all that. Not you," I said. "But if it's true, then it explains why he was at the museum and not at Eastern University anymore."

"I should've done something," she murmured.

I had to get her attention off of her guilt. "One of these women, LibrarySophie, is really angry. Do you think we should talk to her?"

She straightened her shoulders. "Not yet."

"But there's a lot of rage in there," I said. Talk about motive. "Maybe we should tell Detective Lockett?"

"Absolutely not," Erica said in her determined voice.

"Those women have been victimized enough. It's too late to make sure Professor Moody never does this again. Now, let's change gears and get to work on our suspects."

It wasn't like Erica to leave a rock unturned. Or even a shiny little pebble, if it could reveal something important. And this was practically a boulder, potentially hiding a bunch of slimy, worm-like information.

"Okay, but maybe you should at least ask Lavender if she knows anything about this website." I held my hand up to keep her from arguing. "Don't tell her anything that's on it. Just that some students made some crazy accusations and you want to find out what she knows about them."

She frowned at me.

"If we're going to investigate, we have to examine every aspect." I kept my voice quiet and reasonable. "You know that."

Her shoulders lowered. "Okay. I'll call Lavender. But that's all we're doing right now."

I reread LibrarySophie's comment. *I say we all meet up with him and KICK HIS ASS!!! so he never does this again. He deserves that and more.*

Maybe one of them really did make sure Dr. Moody never did it again. I kept that thought to myself.

"Jake said our favorite waitress Iris knows something about Deirdre," I said. "Do you have time to eat lunch at the diner tomorrow?"

"I think we have to," Erica said, still worrying.

I'd have to work harder to get her mind off what those girls wrote. "What about Lavender's murder quotient? Do you think she finally became jealous enough to knock him off?" If I were her, I'd claim insanity due to Stockholm syndrome. I kept that to myself.

Erica considered it for a moment and then shook her head. "If she hadn't come here looking for him, maybe. But I doubt that she's that great of an actor."

"The odds are incredibly low that Reese is right about anything, but what if it was someone at the museum?" I asked. "What would they have to gain?"

"Not Wink," Erica protested. "But I'll try to get him to answer a few questions about the other museum employees." She typed a note into her computer. "By the way, I volunteered our living room Thursday night for some costume planning. Jolene's going to start making the props for the flash mob at the school."

"No problem," I said, looking at the list of suspects on the door.

We both heard a car screech to a halt in front of our house. I stood up and saw Bobby get out of his police car and come up the porch stairs, his steps deliberate and his face determined. Too bad we hadn't locked the front door, because I barely had time to slam the pantry doors closed and move away, when he walked directly to the same spot and opened the doors. Our list of suspects was right there in black and white. Well, whiteboard.

He turned to face Erica. "You need to trust me to do my job."

"I do," she said.

"No, you don't," he said in a voice that would piss me off if I were Erica. I just hoped she could hear the hurt underneath.

"Um, I'll just . . ." They didn't hear me. I escaped upstairs to Erica's room, wanting to both listen to what they were saying and bury my head under pillows in case it ended badly. It felt like parents arguing.

Too soon, I could hear the front door open and angry stomps down the porch stairs. That couldn't be good.

I walked down slowly and peeked into the kitchen. "What happened?"

She sat in the same place with a troubled expression. "We agreed to disagree."

"Did he threaten to throw you in the pokey to keep you safe?" I joked.

"No," she said. "But he wants to . . . take a break."

I sat down, stunned. Anyone could see he was hooked on her. "What? Why?"

She frowned. "I'm not exactly sure. Something about me not trusting him to be smart enough to solve this case on his own."

"Oh," I said. "That again." I could totally imagine being intimidated by her. I paused. "How did he even know about our list on the pantry door?"

"Lavender saw it when she was here looking for the professor," she said.

"He seemed way more mad at this investigation than the last one."

"I think because we're dating," she said, as if figuring it out as she spoke. "*Were* dating. And maybe he heard about my . . ."

"Booty call?"

She winced. "Yes. So learning that we've been asking questions bothered him even more."

I sat silently for a moment. "Does that mean we should stop?"

"Absolutely not," she said. "We can find out things the police can't." And then she said her most favorite words. "Let's make a plan."

. . . .

The reassuring smell of sweet pancakes and hamburgers frying on the griddle greeted us as soon as we walked into the West Riverdale Diner for lunch the next day. The owner believed in offering breakfast all day, and keeping the food cheap, fast and greasy.

Iris stood by the host stand. "It's about ta-ime you come 'n seen me," she said, her bright blue eyes snapping. Iris had been a waitress at the diner since I was a kid. Outside of the diner, she smoked like a fiend and tanned herself until she was bronze year-round.

"Sorry, Iris," Erica and I said in unison.

She grunted as she grabbed two menus, their cracked plastic coating yellowing with age, and led us to our usual booth. Where the Big Drip had retro diner décor, this place was authentic diner through and through. "Yourn spose to be here within twenty-four hours of breakin' news," Iris admonished.

"Sorry," we both said again.

"And that a-hole gittin' hisself kilt sure is breakin' news, ain't it?" she asked.

"Sure is," I said. I found all accents totally contagious, especially Iris's strong southern Virginia one.

She took a minute to get us our diet sodas. "Not that he din't deserve sumpin' pretty awful, just not them vultures." She paused as if considering that. "Well, maybe even them."

I did not want to talk about vultures before my lunch. "What have you heard about him?"

"Well, he ain't been here so long so's I know anything.

Jus' 'at he came in here 'n' yelled about a dirty glass, so I done tole him to leave."

"Who was he with?" Erica asked.

"That purple woman, poor thing," Iris said. "She tried to talk some sense into him but he din't listen." She left to take an order from a group of construction workers who sat at the counter.

Erica waited patiently until she came back. "Do you know Deirdre?"

Iris raised her painted-on eyebrows. "Not nobody knows Deirdre. She hardly goes anywhere. Fixin' to be one of those agoraphobics, I believe."

"Is she afraid to go outside?" Erica asked.

"Nah." Iris slid her tiny butt into the booth beside Erica, facing out so she could keep an eye on the diner. "She git herself into some trouble when she was young 'n' her mom put her on a tight leash. Just kept it up, I guess. Too much if you ask me. She needs a life."

"Did you hear she was fired by the Rivers?" I asked, hoping Jake had been right about Iris knowing something.

"Iris," a man in a Baltimore Orioles cap yelled. "My waffles are up."

"Hold your horses, you old coot," she shot back and didn't move.

He sighed and went behind the counter to get them himself. Everyone knew that Iris was not above slapping an established customer upside the head if he gave her a hard time.

She turned to face us and talked quietly. "I'm gonna tell you sumpin' I ain't tole nobody, especially that chief. I heard Deirdre tell her mom she ain't stole nothin' and Vivian knows it."

Erica kept her voice low as well. "Why didn't she go to the police?"

Iris shrugged. "Those Rivers kept everything private and maybe it rubbed off on her."

"Did the chief talk to her yet?" I asked.

"Nope," Iris said. "And not for lack of trying. She's up and disappeared."

"Oh no," I said. "We were hoping to talk to her. Is there any way to get her a message?"

Iris grimaced. "I kin sure try. The Rivers' gardener comes here every other day just about. They're good friends." She stood up. "Jasper! You git your feet off that chair!"

Zane was working on updating the page of available used books on the website when we got back to the store. While Erica was busy with a customer, I stopped in to talk to him. "Is there any chance you could find out all you can about someone and not tell Erica?"

He blinked at me for a moment. "Is this person Erica?"

"No!" I said, offended that he'd think I'd do that to my best friend.

"Then no problem."

"Oh good," I said. "Can I show you something on your computer?"

I was still uncertain about going behind Erica's back, but if it helped to get the suspect label off of her, I'd do it. I brought up the page that highlighted the professor's alleged sexual harassment. "There's the website."

Maybe Erica wasn't thinking clearly about the possibilities because she identified with those girls too much. She couldn't really believe that we shouldn't investigate them; just because they were harassed by the scummy professor didn't mean they could get away with murder.

"I know that site," Zane said.

I brought up the info on Dr. Moody and pointed to LibrarySophie's comments. "Can you find out anything you can on this person?"

He took a moment to read what she'd written and then pushed my hands away from his keyboard. "No prob."

Erica stopped by my counter when I was dipping fresh long-stemmed strawberries into chocolate. We often did some of the showy finishing touches out front to entice customers into ordering more. Who could resist a juicy, ripe strawberry dripping with the finest Felchlin milk chocolate? Especially when I decorated it with a glistening sprinkle of raw sugar.

I put a newly dipped strawberry on a plate and gave it to her. "If you wait a minute, it'll harden."

"I like it this way." She took a small bite of the end and then licked the smudge of chocolate off her lips. "Yum. I left a message for Lavender."

"Did you tell her why you're calling?" I asked.

"Not specifically," she said. "I said I found something online and needed to speak to her."

"Okay." But it made me feel uneasy. Then I saw Zane come down the hall with papers in his hand. As soon as he saw Erica, he did a quick U-turn and went back to his office.

I waited until Erica finished her chocolate treat and went back to her side of the store, before running back to see what Zane had found.

"That website is pretty tight," he said. "I can probably get more with my comp sci professor's help, but all I could get right away was that she signed in from one of Eastern University's library computers."

"So she's trying to stay anonymous?"

"A couple of them were posted after hours," he said. "She may work there."

"Oh," I said. That explained her online name.

"And then I did some digging on Facebook and found this." He handed me a sheet of paper with the photo of a young Sophie Anderson, smiling into the camera with huge brown eyes and light brown hair. "And this." The next photo was the same girl, but with angry eyes made up with heavy black eyeliner, her hair dyed goth black, and a leather spike collar around her neck.

I looked up at Zane. "That's a pretty major before and after."

He frowned. "Remember when you guys asked me to find any connection the professor had to West Riverdale?" he asked.

I nodded.

He pulled up a website of student research projects for Ancient Maya Civilizations. Twenty-three students had submitted papers on the assignment titled, "The Significance of Trade on the Art of the Maya People."

Jennie River was one of the students.

10

I was wondering when I could fit in a trip to Baltimore to track down LibrarySophie without Erica knowing, when Carlo Morales walked into the store wearing a suit that probably cost more than my entire wardrobe. Plus a month's rent for the store. I sucked in a breath. What was he doing here?

"Hi," I said, as if he was like any other customer. "Sit anywhere and I'll get you a menu."

"Thank you," he said in a low voice that would've been sexy if I didn't think he might be a murderous art trafficker. "But I'm here to see Kona."

I was sure my surprise showed on my face. "Um," I stumbled. "I'll get her."

He nodded as if used to people doing his bidding. I sedately walked back to the kitchen when I felt like running and asking her what the hell she was doing with a man like that. Again. If there was any time I'd prefer she have a one-night stand to a relationship, it was now. I closed the kitchen door behind me. "Kona. That Carlo guy is here to see you!"

She stopped filling the Hazelnut Darks with a pastry-piping bag and looked up at the clock. "Damn it! I lost track of time." She squished the ganache toward the bottom of the bag and started filling faster. "Can you talk to him while I finish these and change?"

"I guess," I said. "But are you sure you know what you're doing?"

She gave me an *are you kidding* look and leaned down to finish the tray. "Really? You're going to go all mom on me?"

"It's just—" I stopped. "You don't know anything about him. He feels . . . unsafe." Maybe I shouldn't tell her my real fears about him unless I had even a scrap of proof.

She laughed. "And that's a bad thing?" She waved one hand. "Go. Keep him entertained for a minute. But not too entertained."

I walked back to the front where Carlo stood by the counter. How the heck should I handle this? "She'll be right out," I said. "Would you like something while you wait?"

"No, but thank you. Your chocolates are delicious." That word sounded even better with his exotic accent in that low rumbly voice. No wonder Kona couldn't resist him.

I felt an overwhelming wish to protect my friend. "So how long are you going to be in town?"

"Not long," he said. "Until I complete my business."

"And what business is that?" I tried hard to sound

interested and not investigatory but there was a definite edge in my voice.

"I'm a fine art dealer." His voice was calm.

"Oh," I said. "Is that why you were at the Rivers' reception?" I asked.

He nodded once. "Indirectly."

I raised my eyebrows, expecting more information.

"When a museum obtains such pieces, and obviously sets such store by them," he explained, "it encourages my buyers to purchase similar items at significantly higher prices."

"You have clients here?"

He looked amused at my questions. "I have clients all over the world." He paused. "You feel motherly towards our Kona, no?"

Our Kona? "No. I mean, yes." I decided to put it all on the table. "She's very young. And you're very . . ."

His eyes widened. "Old?" he said in a challenging tone, as if daring me to be rude.

"Sophisticated." I held my chin up high, looking straight at him. "Why would someone as worldly as you be interested in a young girl like Kona?"

His jaw tightened, but before he could answer, Kona walked down the hall in a colorful sundress, looking as lovely and fresh as a dandelion in the spring. I kept my eyes on his face and saw his expression become almost uncertain as if he was realizing the difference I'd just noted. And then he went back to the suave guy he was so good at pulling off.

Kona seemed to sense that something was going on and she gave me a *back off* look.

Carlo took Kona's hand and kissed it, and she grinned and gave him a sloppy kiss on the cheek, which seemed to surprise and delight him. "See you tomorrow, Michelle," she said.

Carlo gave me little bow. "I will take good care of her."

I gave him a hesitant nod. That's what I was afraid of.

Zane joined me in staring at the door long after Kona and Carlo had gone. "I don't like him," he said.

Zane and Kona had dated a few times over the summer, but both had agreed right away that there was no chemistry between them. From what I'd overheard Kona telling Kayla, they'd tried. A lot.

I probably couldn't trust Zane's instincts in this, except that they meshed so well with mine. "Maybe you can check him out? I know he has . . . a solid alibi for the robbery."

Zane winced.

"But that doesn't mean he didn't mastermind it."

He nodded. "Absolutely."

Erica and I were usually both on shutdown duty Wednesday nights. She'd tried to reassure me that Carlo wouldn't hurt Kona when we knew he was with her, but the worry weighed on me. Was that what it was like to be a parent?

I called Kayla to see if I could find out more, but she was reluctant to tattle on her friend. "I'm just worried about this guy," I told her. "Have I ever cared who she was dating before?"

"No," Kayla said, still sounding a little dubious.

"Well, what do you think about him?" I asked.

"I don't know anything," she said. "Don't worry. It's not like she's marrying him or anything."

By the time I got home, I was exhausted but wired. "You

have to calm down," Erica said as I paced the kitchen. "Make some chocolate or something."

Her cell phone dinged with a text. "Or, maybe we can take a road trip."

"Where?"

"Farley Olsen, the security guard, is willing to meet us tonight after his rehearsal," she said. She pulled up her map app. "We can be there in less than half an hour."

"That's great," I said. "I need to do something." Action might help me get rid of this anxiety.

She texted him back. "He can do it. Let's go."

Her car was low on charge, so I drove my Chocolates and Chapters minivan. We waited outside the locked lobby doors of the local theater where Farley was starring in a production of *Noises Off*. The theater was gaining an excellent national reputation, known for its actors graduating to theater in DC and even New York.

"This script is quite funny," Erica said, looking closely at the play posters advertising upcoming events. "It's a great example of a play within a play."

Farley came out from the theater area, and my mouth dropped. He looked totally different, like he'd dropped at least thirty pounds. He let us in. "Sorry," he said. "I should've told you to come around to the stage entrance." He wore stage makeup that made him look older and an elaborate ascot around his neck.

"Not a problem," Erica said. "Thanks for meeting with us."

We sat on the benches lining the lobby that the lucky few who arrived early to a play got to use.

"We're not done yet so I have only a few minutes," he said.

"Wow," I said. "You guys work long hours."

He shrugged. "Tech rehearsals go until we're done." The stage makeup emphasized his weariness.

Erica got right down to business. "So how did you know Dr. Moody?"

"I work security at E.U.," he said.

E.U.? Did he know what that sounded like? "What does 'working security' mean?" I asked.

"I sit at the security desk and make sure students have ID to get into the dorm." Farley had the precise enunciation of most actors I'd met.

"What did you need to do to get that job?" Erica asked.

"Basically, just pass a background check," he said. "I got the gig when I was a student there and just kept doing it when it fit into my schedule."

"Why do you think the professor hired you?" I asked.

"I'm not sure," he said. "Except one time I caught someone stealing a load of construction wood that would've cost his department hundreds of dollars to replace."

"Do you know why he didn't use a more . . . official security company?" Erica asked.

Farley didn't seem offended. "He said there was no budget for security and he was paying me himself. And that it was just a show for the donors. It's not like the stuff was paintings or fine art. So I got the uniform, the stomach pouch and the muscle pads from the costume shop and acted like a security guard."

"What do you think happened that night?" Erica asked.

He shook his head. "I really don't know. Everyone keeps

saying there's never been a robbery like that, of Maya art, in the United States. The last thing I remember, I'd finished packing up and said good night to Mr. River."

"Adam?" I interrupted.

"Yes. And then it was the next morning and I was stumbling around on some hill by the highway. It was like a freaky rave party weekend when I was a kid." He paused.

Erica cocked her head. "Did you just remember something new?"

"Yeah," he said thoughtfully. "Someone called my name."

"Can you close your eyes and remember the sound of that voice? Like, play it over in your head? Think of it as waiting offstage, listening for a cue."

He did as he was told, but gave up, shaking his head. "It's so bizarre not being able to remember."

"Female or male?" Erica asked.

He closed his eyes again. "Male. I'm pretty sure."

"That's great," she said. "Any chance it was Dr. Moody?"

He squinted with his eyes closed, as if trying to see the memory in his own mind. "I don't think so. Sorry."

Erica changed gears. "What do the police think happened?"

He shrugged. "If they know, they haven't told me."

"Did you know any of the Rivers before the party?" I asked.

"No. I met them earlier the day of the party."

I persisted. "What about their housekeeper, Deirdre Cash?"

"No." Farley laughed, and I realized we were tag-teaming him pretty hard.

Erica didn't let up. "Did you recognize anyone at the party?"

He shook his head. "Just Dr. Moody. The Rivers were nice to me."

Erica got that look on her face when she had an inspiration. "What did you think of the Rivers?"

"Like I said, I barely spoke to them." He was beginning to sound impatient.

"But you must have got an impression," Erica said. "If you were casting them in a play or a movie, what role would they play?"

His eyes lit up. We were finally speaking his language.

"What about Adam?" Erica asked. "Just say the first thing that comes to mind."

"Gordon Gekko, *Wall Street.*"

"That's perfect," she said in an encouraging tone. "What about Vivian?"

"Lady M—" He stopped. "I can't say her last name inside a theater."

I didn't know what he was talking about but Erica did.

"Shakespeare, right?" she said with assurance.

"Macbeth?" I filled in.

Farley reacted with horror, his mouth a big O. "Sh!" He pretended to throw something over his shoulder.

"It's considered bad luck," Erica explained to me, exasperated that I hadn't followed her lead. "What about Gary?"

I could tell she was trying to distract him from my faux pas.

He considered Gary for a minute. "Bodhi in *Point Break.*"

"That surfing movie?" I asked.

"Yeah," he said. "I never saw it, but you know, the surfer-dude type."

"Wasn't he a criminal?" I asked Erica.

She didn't look at me but I could sense her wanting to tell me to shut up.

"No, not a criminal," he said. "Maybe like the surfer guy in *Fast Times at Ridgemont High*."

"What about Jennie?" she asked. I'd told her about Jennie's connection to the professor.

He shook his head. "I don't think she ever spoke to me. But if I had to guess, I'd say Amber from *Parenthood*."

The lost teenager, I thought.

"Interesting," Erica said. "You've helped a lot."

We thanked him and watched him walk away.

"What did that teach us?" I asked.

"I'm not sure," Erica said. "Let's see if we can watch him a little bit."

We slipped through the door and sat in the back seats of the small theater. Someone called out for the actors milling about on the stage, "Let's start at the beginning of act two."

We watched as Farley squared his shoulders, lifted his chin and totally became a world-weary director.

"He's an excellent actor," Erica said.

"I was thinking the same thing," I said. "So how do we know if he told us the truth?"

My phone woke me up the next morning. "Your cat had kittens in my storage room!" an outraged voice yelled in my ear, or at least as close as I could get the cell in my comatose state.

"What? Who is this?" I asked, sitting up and trying to figure out what planet I was on. I looked at my clock. It was five thirty in the morning.

"This is Gary," he said with exaggerated patience. "I came into my coffee shop this morning and went to get something out of the storage closet and your cat hissed at me. She had kittens in my storage room! And she made a disgusting mess in there."

"Coco had kittens?" I felt a weird rush of joy and pride. My little Coco was a mom? "I'll be right there." I jumped out of bed. It took me a minute to figure out what to do first. Clothes would help.

I ran to the bottom of the stairs and yelled up to Erica. "Wake up! Coco had kittens!" Then I dashed back to get dressed and brush my teeth.

"Erica!" I went out to the hall to yell through my tooth-brush. "Are you there?"

She came to the top of the stairs, in jeans and a T-shirt, pulling her hair back into a barrette. "One minute."

"What should we bring?" I asked. "Towels? Boiling water? Food?"

She laughed. "Well, I think Coco took care of all of the hard stuff. You grab two bowls and some cat food, and I'll bring a couple of boxes and clean sheets. We'll evaluate what else we need when we get there."

I drove too fast, while she calmly cut the sheets with scissors and then ripped them into small pieces. I parked in front of the Big Drip and dashed in through the open door. Gary stood at the counter, scowling. "You need to get them out of there." His blond hair was heading in different direc-tions, like he hadn't brushed it yet.

I rushed right by him and went to look. He'd opened the top half of the door, so I could see over.

It was the cutest thing ever. Coco had made a nest of torn-up paper napkins, a lot of them, in the corner under a shelf filled with boxes of sugar packets and coffee stirrers.

She looked up briefly and then went back to licking what appeared to be six little brown rats either mewing, nursing or squirming. Their tiny paws seemed not to be doing what they wanted, skewing off in different directions as they tried to scooch closer to their mommy.

Tears came to my eyes as I saw the new lives right there. Coco had done such a great job, all on her own.

Erica came up beside me. "Would you look at that?" she murmured. She squeezed my hand. "Congratulations, Grandma."

"Thanks." I sniffed and wiped my eyes.

We stood there for a few minutes until Gary came up behind us. "Are you getting them out or what?"

Erica turned to face him. "I'm very sorry, but they must stay right here a few days."

"What?" Gary and I said at the same time.

"She chose this place because she feels comfortable here. And it could be bad for the kittens to move them unless it's for their safety," Erica explained.

"I can't have these animals in my shop," he said, alarmed. "It's a health code violation."

"It's only four days at most," she said. "And then we'll move them."

I chimed in. "We'll totally take care of them. I'll bring food and water over and she won't leave the closet. You won't have to do a thing."

"Are you kidding me?" he asked. "This is crazy. All my supplies are in there."

"What do you need?" I asked. "Erica and I will get them all out and you can store it somewhere else. It's just four days."

His face turned surly. "Fine. Get out all the cleaning

supplies and the cups and other stuff. I'll deal with it." He stomped behind the counter and started making coffee.

I sure wouldn't like being pushed around by a litter of kittens and some women I didn't know in my own store.

"We'll take care of everything," I tried to reassure him.

Coco hissed once when I opened the bottom door of the storage room, and then went back to her important work of roughly licking her squeaking kittens. "It's okay, Coco," I said quietly. "It's okay, Mama." I reached in and started handing the supplies to Erica, who piled them in the hallway. Coco swatted at the mop and broom as they went by.

Then Erica slid in the box filled with clean strips of cotton sheets while I got the dishes from the car and filled them with food and water. Coco was already moving the kittens into the clean box when I came back.

"What a good mom," Erica murmured.

We waited for her to move all six and settle them in for a feeding before cleaning up the mess of paper napkins.

It was hard to leave the kittens. "We'll be back soon," I told Gary, who at least looked resigned to having the kittens in his shop.

I called May as soon as I got back to Chocolates and Chapters. She was even more delighted than I was and hung up so she could rush right over and see the kitties. She also agreed to bring a litter box with her.

Kona came in on time, looking well rested, and I followed her to the kitchen.

"How was the date?" I tried to sound casual but my voice gave me away.

She stopped in the middle of grabbing a tray of truffles from the refrigerator. "What is your problem with Carlo?"

"It's. I'm—"

"Look, it's just fun," she said. "He's an interesting guy and he likes teaching me things."

"I'll bet," I said.

"Not those kind of things. Although he is great in bed." She laughed at the face I made. "Like wine. And he loves theater. He's going to take me to a show at the Woolly Mammoth Theatre in DC to see a drama about women's rights in Africa."

"I just think you should be careful with someone like him," I said. "And not get too . . . attached."

"I'm too busy for anything serious," she said. "Which reminds me. Kona's Kreations has been cranking lately. You don't really care about the pastries anyway and Gwen's over in Walkersville are almost as good as mine. What do you think about her supplying us with tortes? Maybe she'd give us a really good discount if we put up a sign saying they were from her."

I hid my surprise. "That's fine with me if it's okay with you. I thought you liked making them though."

"I do," she rushed to reassure me. "It's just fun to throw myself into something new."

"Go for it," I said out loud, while I thought, *I'm going to lose her.* Maybe not soon, but eventually. Everything that made her a great employee would make her a great employer.

Then I realized something. "Wait. Did you bring that up to get me off the topic of Carlo?"

She sighed. "Just stop worrying. He's in town for a couple

of weeks and then I probably won't see him again. Why shouldn't I learn about another whole country, another culture?"

"Are you going to be sad when he leaves?"

"Sure," she said. "But not laying around, eating bonbons and watching *Beaches* kinda sad. I'll be fine."

11

I snuck away during a lull in customer traffic to see the kittens, and my phone beeped with a text. Assuming it was Kona wanting me to come back, I checked the screen.

It was from "John," aka Bean.

Heard that the white cat might be headed to eastern US. My friend is trying to get more accurate info. Sent you an email. Be careful. B.

What? That was it? No *Love, B.* Or at least *Best, B.* Just *B*?

I opened the attachment and read it. It contained notes about El Gato Blanco. Bean's reporter friend was careful to note that none of the information could be confirmed. But what was established was that hundreds, if not thousands, of pre-Columbian artifacts had been returned to only a few museums in Central America over the past few years. Those museums were known to be run by management not under the control of traffickers, and a government that supported the museum management's desire to have their looted treasures back where they belonged.

That's where the known facts ended. The reporter had interviewed several eyewitnesses who claimed to have seen El Gato Blanco in action. And their descriptions were extravagant tales of a man dressed in black who seemed to have the weapon and spy skills of James Bond. He participated in auctions through intermediaries and paid fortunes for antiquities that soon appeared in one of his pet museums. He beat up local looters on their way to their traffickers. He stole looted artifacts from heavily secured private collections and indiscriminate museums. He regularly bombed heavy construction equipment to prevent them from destroying entire archaeological sites for a few valuable bowls. And he was blamed for the assassination of a known drug cartel leader who had purchased some of that equipment.

No one could say what he looked like. No one knew who he was. Not even law enforcement.

And now there was a huge bounty on his head.

Bean said the guy was thought to be heading east. I couldn't imagine that someone who operated at the level he was rumored to work would be interested in anything happening in West Riverdale. And besides, how could anyone know where a ghost like El Gato Blanco was heading? It was impossible.

May was still at the Big Drip, keeping a watchful eye on the crowd that had gathered outside the storage room, all vying for the best angle. May wore pale pink from head to toe, and I tried to figure out what she had on sale.

Gary was staring at the crowd with his arms crossed.

I wanted to elbow my way in to see the kitties, but decided I better buy some coffee first. There were a lot of empty hands in front of the storage room.

"I'd love another one of your cappuccinos," I said to Gary and he turned to make it. "You know, it's really cool that Coco trusted you enough to have her kittens here."

He gave me a *you've gotta be kidding* look over his shoulder.

"You holding up okay?" I asked.

"Yeah," he said. "The whole town's been in here."

"Are they at least buying coffee?"

He shrugged. "Some. That's the only good part." He glared at a bunch of squealing moms in yoga pants. The others shushed them.

"You should charge them," I joked. "Buy a coffee or pay the kitten viewing fee."

"Or offer a kitten special," he said. "Instead of a bear claw, call them kitten claws." His heart didn't seem into it.

If I were him, I'd be offering free samples. "I don't know," I said. "You've got a good thing going. Now all the shops in town are going to have litters of kittens to draw a crowd."

"If they can figure out how to make some money off them, they're welcome to have them," he said, with a rueful smile.

He was coming around.

Reese arrived with camera in hand, pushing her way to the front. She was about to take a photo when May moved faster than I'd ever seen her. "No flash photography!" she hissed. "It'll hurt the kittens' eyes."

Reese frowned but changed the setting on her camera.

She started clicking away and I could hear Coco hiss at her deep in her throat.

"That's all you get." May stepped in front of her. "Mama Coco's the boss."

Reese joined me at the counter with Gary. For once she didn't harass me with questions. She barely even looked at me. "I have an idea that will help keep the crowds down and promote your store at the same time," she said to Gary. "I can install a webcam—we'll call it the Big Drip Cat Cam—so people can keep up with them online instead of trooping through here all the time."

Gary shook his head. "No way."

"Why not?" She gestured toward the crowd at the storage room door. "It's great advertising. It'll make people feel good about your shop."

I backed away from that conversation and went to look at the kitties.

May gushed, "Michelle! Aren't they darling?"

She pushed someone aside so I could join her in front. The kittens had either fluffed up a little or had grown in a couple of hours. I felt a little melty inside.

"I already talked to Gary about moving them to my shop in a few days," she said. "I hope that's okay with you." Before they were even born, May had nominated herself honorary grandma to the kittens. If anyone would do a good job mothering the mother, it was her.

"Absolutely," I said, happy they'd be so close. "We'll just have to make sure they don't get into the back hallway. Hey, who won the kitten pool?"

She gave me a pleased smile. "I got the delivery date on the nose."

"That will help pay for cat food," I said.

Reese pushed her way to the front of the line, a laptop and a separate webcam in her hand. She must have won her argument with Gary, and brought the equipment with her. She opened the bottom half of the door, pushing back the crowd, and Coco snarled deep like she was a leopard about to attack.

"That girl has good taste," I said.

Reese ignored that, handing me a webcam with a clip. "Here, you set it up." She pointed to the bottom shelf. "Attach it there."

I sat down slowly, not sure Coco wouldn't object to even me getting close to her kittens, but she didn't seem to mind. I moved aside a big box of napkins and clipped the webcam to the edge of the shelf while Reese folded her long legs and sat down beside me with the grace of a drunken giraffe. She fiddled around with her laptop until a video of the storage room showed up on the screen.

"Cool," I couldn't help but say, even if it was Reese making the cool stuff happen.

"Push it down. Now up a little." Reese directed me to move the webcam until it was perfectly centered on the kittens.

"Done." Reese set down the laptop and stood up. "Check my website in twenty minutes and it'll be working," she called out to Gary as she left.

I had to give it to her. She knew what she was doing.

With one last peek at the kittens, I went back to my store. I took my laptop out to the counter and brought up Reese's blog. The webcam was working perfectly, right beside a dozen ads for local businesses. That was why Reese had pushed Gary into the Cat Cam. The more clicks she got, the more money she made. I hoped she shared some of that with Gary, who had to put up with the whole thing.

Then I got an email from Reese with the subject line "Hero Cat Gives Birth to Six Kittens." It advertised the link to her website, and it looked like she'd sent it to everyone in West Riverdale. Maybe all of Maryland.

I could practically hear Gary groaning from his shop and hoped the health department wasn't on Reese's distribution list. The click counter on the bottom of the page was already at 540 hits. Coco was sleeping all curled up around her kittens, and I could imagine the collective "aw's" in homes across town. Then the counter went crazy.

Erica peeked over my shoulder. "Look. People are sharing it. That's what we want to have happen with the flash mob video."

"Then you should add some kittens," I said with a smile. "So, what's the game plan for today?"

"I'm going to call Lavender again," she said. "I couldn't sleep, so I put in the info we learned at the theater." She became deliberately vague as new customers came in.

I wasn't sure how anything Farley had said would help. "What's next for me to work on?"

She waited until the customers were sitting at a table out of earshot. "I'm on the fence about something." She looked pensive. "Zane can't find out much information on the River family, other than the superficial. They don't frequent social media. Their companies are privately owned and don't have to publicly file financial information."

"What did you want to do?"

"I'm wondering how ethical it would be to ask Rose why she thought the art was cursed," she said, sounding unsure.

I understood her dilemma. Rose was obviously suffering from some form of dementia. But she knew *something* about the artifacts. "We could bring her some flowers or something and see what she has to say. Not interrogate her or anything."

Erica didn't look convinced. "Let's table that for now."

"Who else is on our list?" My cell rang. It was Leo. "Hold on," I told Erica.

"Are you with Erica?" he asked.

"Yes," I said "We're working."

"I'm coming over," he said.

The urgency in his voice scared me. "What's wrong?"

"Have you guys seen it?" he asked.

"Seen what?"

"Reese's blog."

My heart dropped. "What did she do now?"

"She has an article on Erica that . . ." He stopped as if not able to explain. "I'll be right there."

"What is it?" Erica said.

I clicked my mouse to bring up Reese's page again.

A photo of Erica photoshopped with the professor filled half the screen with the title *Love Triangle Murder?* slashed across it.

I led a stunned Erica to her office in the back hallway, where we both finished reading. The article was devastating, filled with innuendo and salacious lies about Erica's past relationship with Dr. Moody. It claimed that Erica had a stalker-like passion for him, and when he'd threatened to have her brought before the disciplinary council at her university, she'd falsely accused him of plagiarism.

It went on to say that "someone close to the professor" noted that students fell in love with their professors all the time, especially someone as charming and handsome as Dr. Moody. But this time, perhaps it led to murder.

The blog post ended with a question that shook me even more than the rest. "Why aren't the police cracking down on these amateurs with an ulterior motive investigating the tragic murder of a respected academic?"

"Lavender," Erica said in a flat tone.

"Yep." I was sure my face was red with anger. "But mostly Reese. This time, we'll sue. Both of them."

Leo stalked in, looking as furious as I felt. "This time she's gone too far," he said. "We're shutting her down." He limped over to give Erica a gentle hug, the opposite of the expression on his face. I gave him a nod over her head. We would make it happen.

He pulled back to look her in the eyes. "Worst day ever?"

I felt tears come to my eyes at his thoughtfulness. He was on her side, even though he didn't know her history with the idiot professor.

Erica closed her eyes and took a deep breath. When she opened them, her face was determined. "Okay. Let's go see Lavender."

Lavender had made the unfortunate decision to stay at the Williams Suites in the nearby town of Normal. Unfortunate for her because the owner was such a huge fan of my Electric Currant Milks with their mix of black currants and strawberry-flavored Pop Rocks candy that she ordered a box every week. She loved the way the black currant tingled her taste buds at the same time the Pop Rocks set off tiny explosions in her mouth almost as much as I did.

With one phone call I found out Lavender's room number and soon Erica and I were knocking on her door. The hotel had an Asian décor with elaborately flowered blue carpeting in the hall and several large Chinese pottery pieces by the windows. She opened the door, her frog face puffy and red with recent crying, and I stuck my foot in it before she could close it again. I pushed once and she was backing up, looking around as if for an escape.

"I didn't mean it!" she said. "Reese took it all the wrong way!"

"Really?" I asked. "You didn't mean to tell crazy Reese those lies? You didn't mean to shove Erica under a bus and make the whole world believe she has a motive for murder?"

"No!" she wailed. "That Reese . . . witch bought me drinks next door and then asked me a bunch of questions like she cared . . ." She stopped and her voice hitched. "Like she cared about me." She crawled into her bed and threw the rose-covered comforter over herself as if trying to hide.

It was hard to maintain my anger at such a pitiful person, but I managed. "You need to send in a retraction. Today." When she didn't respond, I added, "And then we might not sue your ass."

She nodded with her face in the pillow. I was beginning to feel a little bad for her.

Erica's eyes narrowed. "I'd like to talk to you about the professor's special projects."

Oh good. She was going to take advantage of Lavender's guilt.

"Is there anything he was working on that was making people angry?" she asked.

"No," she said, sitting up. "He was focused on this exhibit. It's all he cared about." A tear leaked from her eye and she wiped it away.

"I'm sure he cared about you too." Erica changed tactics and spoke in a reassuring voice. "It's why he trusted you so completely, isn't it?"

Erica turned the desk chair around to face Lavender and sat down. "Can we start at the beginning of this mess?" When Lavender nodded uncertainly, Erica asked, "How did your Addison learn about the Rivers' collection?"

I slowly sat down in the rust-colored chair in the corner so I wouldn't distract her, resisting the urge to pop my feet up on the matching ottoman.

Lavender took a huge, shuddering breath as if preparing to unburden herself. Now maybe we'd learn something. "He met Adam Rivers at a museum fundraiser, and Adam told him about the pieces his great-uncle brought back," Lavender said. "Dr. Moody volunteered to verify that they were authentic." She paused. "When he saw them, he knew they were special. He was so excited that Adam was willing to make such a generous donation."

"So Dr. Moody convinced Adam?"

"Yes," she said. "He told Adam that the pieces were historically important and should be in a museum. Addison wanted to 'get back in the game.'" She used finger quotes. "He'd just quit the university and started working at the museum. He thought the Rivers' collection would establish his credentials."

"Why did the professor change careers?" Erica asked.

Lavender's face reddened. "The museum lured him away," she said. "It made him a very generous offer that he couldn't refuse. He's a brilliant scholar and in high demand."

Right, I thought. She sounded like she was trying to convince herself.

"Oh," Erica said, and then carefully added, "We saw some ridiculous claims online—"

"That was nonsense." Lavender sat up. "A bunch of hussies with bad grades getting together to try to ruin his reputation. It was shameful!"

"I agree," Erica said. "As you know, we had our differences but I never heard anything like that before this."

"He was a good man," Lavender said, shaking in her anger.

Did she really believe that? Usually when anyone said such a thing with such vehemence, the opposite was true. Deep down, she had to know the truth.

"He was." Erica nodded. "Some people will say anything to get attention."

How did Erica do that? She had to be burying her feelings deep to get the information we needed.

"So Adam talked his family into making the donations?" Erica asked. "Do you know if any of them objected?"

"I don't know what happened before, but by the time I met the Rivers, the deal was set," she said. "They all seemed happy with it."

"What was Dr. Moody most excited about in the display?" Erica asked. If Lavender knew her better, she'd realize Erica's casual tone meant she was the most interested in this one answer.

"That short vase," she said, which certainly gave points

to Erica's theory that it was worth far more than the professor said. "And the diary."

"Why the diary?"

"It provided the documentation needed to authenticate the art," she said. "And the amount of historical detail fascinated him."

"It's too bad it's gone," I said. "It might provide a clue."

"I have a copy," she said.

Erica couldn't help a little jump of surprise, and probably anticipation. "Could I see it?"

"Sure." Lavender reached over to yank her oversized purse onto the bed, and pulled out a large envelope. She tossed it toward Erica.

I had to give Erica credit. She just picked it up from the bottom of the bed and tucked it into her own huge bag as if it was no big deal. She must be dying to read it.

"Is it the whole diary?" Erica asked. "Dr. Moody had mentioned that pages in the back were damaged."

"Those were analyzed by some lab," she said. "I don't have the results yet."

"I'd love to see them when they arrive," Erica said.

I stood up, wanting to get out of there before Lavender changed her mind. "You'll send that retraction?" I reminded her.

She nodded, an earnest expression on her face. "I really am sorry."

12

Erica had the envelope open and was reading the diary before I drove out of the hotel parking lot.

"What does it say?" I asked, trying not to look at it and focus on the road.

"Right now, just writing about his preparations for travel," she said. "It looks like he was planning to visit sites I've never heard of."

"Wow," I said. "One thing in the world you don't know about."

She smiled. "It could be that those spots were destroyed, or simply swallowed up by the jungle." She flipped through to the middle and showed me a page. "Look. He was an artist too."

I glanced over to see a detailed sketch of a monkey holding a shirt up as if examining it for defects. Bertrand had even captured the mischievous look in the monkey's eyes. Erica turned it back to read more. "Can you drop me off at home? I need to get ready for the flash mob meeting."

"Sure." We were cresting the hill near our house when a police car zoomed up behind us, sirens blaring and lights flashing. I pulled over to get out of the way and the car stopped behind us.

"Damn," I said. "I wasn't speeding." I so did not need a freakin' ticket on top of everything else today. I sighed and started pulling my wallet out of my purse.

Erica turned around. "It's Bobby." She pushed the diary into her large bag and we both tried to look innocent.

Bobby strode over to Erica's side of the car, looking mad as hell. "Hand it over," he demanded in a voice that threatened bodily harm if we didn't comply.

"Hand what over?" I asked.

His face turned red. "The diary. Now."

"Don't you need a warrant?" Erica asked.

"I can see the papers sticking out of your bag," he said. "It looks like evidence for a murder investigation."

When she still resisted, he said, "You can't win. Give it to me."

Erica grumbled as she dug into her bag and gave him the papers. "We were on our way to take this to the chief," Erica said, "since you're not speaking to me." She kept her tone light, but we couldn't miss the undercurrent of hurt.

His expression faltered a little and then he looked down at the papers as if proof of why they were no longer dating.

I jumped in. "So you also figured out that Reese's lies came from Lavender? Did she tattle, or are you following us?"

He left without another word.

We watched him drive away, and I pulled back onto the road. "Now what?" I asked.

"Screw it," Erica said. She made a call. "Lavender?"

There was a torrent of excited conversation from the other end.

"I know," Erica said. "It's not your fault."

She let Lavender spew a little longer as I continued driving. "I understand. But you can't let that stop your efforts to find your friend's killer."

What efforts? That was Erica all over—giving other people missions they didn't even know they had and making them happy about it.

All I could hear was silence from Lavender's end. I raised my eyebrows and Erica gave me a little smile. Maybe Lavender was wavering.

"If you could request another copy of the diary be sent to you by email," Erica said slowly, "and then forward it to me, it might break this case wide open."

Case? Erica was starting to talk like a TV PI.

Still nothing from Lavender.

Erica continued. "And we can both get off the suspect list."

That gave Lavender something to say, in what sounded like a very shrill voice from my side of the car.

"I totally understand. And you must definitely follow your conscience," she said. "But if you could find the courage to forward the document to me, along with the analysis done of the destroyed pages, it might be just what we need."

I pulled up in front of our house and put it in park, listening to Erica say good-bye to Lavender. "Did Bobby tell her not to give us another copy?"

"Yep," Erica said. "But she'll come around."

I thought about how most people viewed orders from the police. Lavender probably wouldn't help us anytime soon. "I wonder if Rose Hudson knows something about the diary."

Erica's face lost its determined look. "Let's hope we don't have to go there."

She opened the door to get out, but we both received a text at the same time, which couldn't be good. It was from Leo. *Check out the Examiner's office.* We drove the short distance into town, cutting through an alley and pulling to a stop across the street from the small storefront that served as Reese's office. The afternoon had started to turn cool, the first hints of a crisp fall breeze blowing through our open windows.

A crowd of uniformed veterans, Leo's buddies, stood in front with signs that said *Shame on Reese Everhard* and *Shut down the Examiner.* They stood silently at attention, which was somehow more powerful than if they'd been shouting and chanting.

"Wow," Erica said, with a mixture of awe and worry.

"Reese deserves it," I said. "Every bit of it."

"But why is Leo doing this?" Erica asked, surprising me.

"What do you mean?" I asked defensively. "You're like a sister to him."

She bit her lip. "Maybe you should ask his therapist if this behavior is okay. It's not like Leo to go . . . this far."

I looked at the soldiers lined up. Maybe he was going a little overboard, but I knew his therapist wouldn't reveal anything to me. "What do you think Reese will do?" I asked.

"She'll probably try to ignore it all and wait for the anger to wear off."

We could only hope that she at least changed her ways first. We parked and got out so that Erica could hug all of the protestors.

"This is cool, Leo," I said to my brother. "Do you think it will work?"

"Well, she already took down that article," he said proudly. He pointed to an older man at the end of the line. "Jennings is organizing a boycott of all of her advertisers, and his brother is meeting with the mayor to see what the town council can do."

Reese's office was dark and empty. A tattered *West Riverdale Examiner* banner flapped over our heads, no longer attached to the wall on one corner. "Has she seen you guys yet?"

"Oh yeah," he said. "She just kept driving." Some of the vets close to us chuckled.

"What's the goal?" I felt a little overwhelmed, wondering what new problem this could cause. Sometimes the devil we knew was better than someone new taking over.

Leo's eyes narrowed. "Make sure she finds a different line of work."

"Did Bean send you that info about El Gato Blanco?" I asked Erica. She looked more concerned than happy that Leo and his friends had her back, but maybe the fictional story of White Cat Man would take her mind off of our real troubles.

"No," she said. "Does he have news?"

"Not really." I told her what the reporter had written, but at the last minute decided not to burden her with Bean's suggestion that he might be headed east. She didn't need to be worrying about a homicidal white rabbit, regardless of his charitable goals.

I dropped Erica at home and drove back to the store.

Kona was happy to see me. "Is it okay if I leave early? I have Kona's Kreations orders backed up." Of course I agreed.

Colleen was studying at the cashier's counter in the bookstore. She had only one customer who was perusing the Travel section, trying to decide between *Rick Steves' Ireland* and *Lonely Planet Ireland* travel guides.

I brought Colleen a cappuccino and a few of her latest favorite, Ginger Grant Darks, which only my most adventurous customers loved. Their chocolate ganache exploded with ginger and wasabi, and were sprinkled with sesame seeds. "I'm about to order dinner from Zelini's. Want anything?"

Colleen closed her calculus book with a sigh. "No, thanks. I brought something."

"That looks complicated," I said.

She stretched her arms above her head and wriggled her shoulders. "Yeah, but it's fun too. Being in just a few classes makes me feel like, I don't know, the whole world is bigger."

"Erica said you're busting the curve all the time," I said.

She smiled, delighted that her sister was bragging about her.

"What else are you taking?" I asked.

"I'm trying to figure out what I want to major in," she said. "So I'm kind of all over the place." She ticked off the classes on her fingers. "Bio, U.S. History, and English Literature."

"You have to be killing the lit class, working here all these years."

"Yeah," she admitted, a little shyly.

"How are the kids handling all of this?" From what I'd

seen, they seemed fine. But as I knew, home could be a different story.

"Actually," she said, "better than I'd hoped." A look I didn't recognize crossed her face. "Mark's being a little . . . weird."

"What do you mean?" I was ready to jump to her defense.

"He . . . drunk-dialed me a few times," she said with a look that could only be described as sweet satisfaction.

"What?"

"Yeah," she said. "You know what men do. The whole 'I was an idiot to give you up' kinda nonsense. My divorced friends said it was more common than you'd think."

"Does he want you back?" I asked.

"So far, only when he's drunk," she said lightly, as if not taking him too seriously. "He wanted to come over one night, but I told him absolutely not."

"If he's bothering you, I know more than a few people who'd be happy to set him straight," I said. Including me. And a whole bunch of customers who now officially hated him. He'd caused Colleen a whole lot of hurt just a few months ago.

She smirked. "Nah. I kinda like it." She rushed to add, "Not that I would ever let him come back, but it's nice knowing, even if it's too late, that he has some regret. That he realizes what he gave up was, I don't know, pretty special."

"You certainly are." I noticed someone standing at my counter. "Oops. I'll be back in a minute."

"It's okay," she said. "I'm going to get back to taking derivatives."

I took care of a few customers, and then my neighbor Henna rushed into the store. Henna's coming-of-age happened rather later than most. Straitlaced her whole life, she'd decided to let her hippie flag fly when she'd become a widow in her sixties. Now an artist, she wore brightly colored outfits every day, and recently had taken to dying her hair unusual colors. Today, the bottom was tinged with purple like it had been dipped in an ink pot.

"I have a clue for you," she said in a conspiratorial voice, leaning over the counter to get close to me.

"What are you talking about?" I asked.

"Oh stop it," she said. "Everyone knows what you and Erica are up to, and we're all rooting for you to win."

"Win?"

"Win," she insisted. "Find the bad guy before the police do."

"Why in the world would we want to do that?" I told her.

"Who knows why anyone does anything?" she said. "It's just what you two girls do."

When I just stared at her, she grew impatient. "Do you want to hear it or not?"

"Fine. What is your 'clue'?" I asked, resigned to the fact that she would tell everyone she knew that we were investigating and that she'd "helped."

"I was out at the River estate meeting with Vivian about their annual grant for the Arts Guild," she said. "For some reason, she's having everyone jump through extra hoops for River Foundation money this year. When I finally got her to agree to give us the money and went out to my car, I heard raised voices in the barn." She stooped over and mimicked tiptoeing over to the barn with her fingers pinched together. "Gary was yelling at his sister, Jennie. He said that boot camp was next for her if she doesn't do what she was supposed to. The military kind." She stood up straight. "I feel so bad for that boy."

"Is that all you heard?"

"Yes," she said a little defensively, and then she got an eager look on her face. "What do you think it means?"

"Right now, I have no idea," I said.

When she looked disappointed, I reassured her. "But thanks for telling me. Maybe it'll be the puzzle piece we need."

I couldn't help but wonder if his warning wasn't something else entirely. Maybe someone in the family was telling her to keep her mouth shut and Gary was warning Jennie what would happen to her if she didn't listen.

I texted the information to Erica, sure that she'd add it to her notes on the investigation.

I usually loved being in the store when it was empty, but tonight it made me feel a little unsettled. Kona had already cleaned the counter and the tables, but I wiped them all down again. I turned on my Find My Friends app and saw that Bean was on his way to West Riverdale! My bad mood vanished.

Closing time seemed way too far away, so I called Kayla to see if she was available to work. She was happy with the extra hours and I checked to see Bean's progress. Shoot! He had turned around and was heading back northwest.

There went my good mood.

Then he actually texted me as if he could read my mind. *How's your this?*

I texted back. *Making progress. How's your this?*

No answer. Maybe he'd accepted that Erica and I were investigating.

Erica was busy at home with her flash mob meeting. I

could sneak away to check out LibrarySophie and she'd never know. If I figured out something having to do with the murder, she'd totally forgive me. As soon as Kayla arrived, I hopped in my minivan and headed east. Our extracurricular activities were certainly taking us out of the store a lot.

Since Eastern University was west of Baltimore, at least I didn't have to drive into city craziness. I still hit a bunch of traffic heading toward the nightlife, which gave me a lot of time to worry if I'd made the right decision. What if Erica meant it that she didn't want us victimizing those girls again?

Eastern University of Baltimore looked like a smaller, younger sibling of its superior educational neighbors, especially the world-renowned Johns Hopkins University. I drove around the college, getting stuck in a total dead end by some delivery bay. With all the hysterical warning signs, it must service some mad scientist's lab.

I pulled over to type "visitor parking" into my map app and followed its annoying directions, paid for two hours and pulled into a slot. Luckily I had my backpack in the car, and took it along as cover. I walked across what felt like the whole school, until I found a campus map and followed a meandering walkway to the library, which was a massive building. How was I supposed to find someone working in there?

I should've thought this through. How did I know LibrarySophie was even working tonight? And maybe Zane got the Facebook connection wrong and LibrarySophie wasn't even Sophie Anderson.

An information desk right by the front door was manned by a bored girl with two uneven braids and eye makeup that resembled a cat. I panicked for a minute when I saw the turnstiles guarding the entrance, and then decided to bluff my way in. I pulled out a random card and waved it in front of the card key machine and looked dumbfounded that it didn't work. Cat-eyes girl barely glanced over and hit a button that let me in. I waved my thanks, and called over to her, "Sophie working tonight?"

She gave me an elaborate philosophical shrug as if to say, *Who knows if anyone is working?* and turned her attention back to her book.

I started on the ground floor and walked through every aisle, paying close attention to anyone who acted like an employee. It was hard to tell them apart from the students. Fortunately, employees wore purple lanyards with IDs on them. Unfortunately, not all of them were turned around so that I could read their names.

I took the stairs and went from floor to floor, each one with an assortment of young adults with all the trappings of being studious—laptops open, books strewn about and notebooks at the ready—but a lot of them were playing video games, texting, or flirting with the students at the next table. Anything but studying.

After the tenth dark-haired female employee in an Eastern University hoodie, I looked at the photo again to refresh my memory. Other than being totally goth, Sophie Anderson had the pointiest ears I'd ever seen outside of a *Lord of the Rings* movie.

I was about to give up when I noticed 1B, 2B and 3B in the elevator, indicating underground floors. And then I found her right away on the first basement floor. Even the ears matched the photo. She was putting books away from a cart.

Too late, I wondered how to approach such a delicate topic. I was sure asking her, "Are you LibrarySophie and did Professor Moody sexually harass you?" would not get her to open up.

She'd added a large nose ring with a chain attached to her earring since the photo. Her parents must be horrified. Or maybe they were the kind to encourage their kids to be creative and express their individuality. Even if it was stupid and hurt like hell.

I gathered my courage. "Sophie?"

She looked at me like she was trying to place me.

"My name is Michelle. I'm looking for someone with the online name LibrarySophie, and another student told me she worked here."

Her black-ringed eyes narrowed suspiciously. "Who?"

Shoot. "Excuse me?"

"Who told you?"

"Um." I stuttered for a second. "It doesn't matter. I just want you to know that I hate him as much as you do."

"Him?" she asked, but seemed to know what I was talking about.

I leaned closer and talked quietly. "Addison Moody."

"I don't know what you're talking about," she said in a flat voice. "I'm busy."

"I'm really sorry that . . . happened to you." I tried.

She scowled.

"He's dead, you know," I said.

"I know," she said. "Good riddance. He was a waste of skin anyway."

13

Whoa. Sophie was that open about wanting the professor dead? I took a step back.

"So he can't hurt you," I told her.

She scoffed. "He couldn't hurt me before," she said. "I kicked him in the nuts and he fell over like a baby."

I couldn't help it. I laughed. And then I felt bad. Laughing at the dead would not earn me good karma points. "Did you hear what happened to him?"

"Yep. He got what he deserved." Her eyes narrowed in satisfaction. "Especially the vultures."

Whoa. This girl was bloodthirsty.

"So what were you doing Sunday night?"

She looked me up and down. "Are you a cop?"

"No!" I said, flustered. Did I look like I could possibly

be with the police? "I'm just kind of . . . trying to figure out what happened."

"What happened?" she repeated. "I didn't do it, if that's what you're getting at."

"Where were you?"

"I was in Chicago," she said. "Which I guess is good for me, because for sure, if I could've done that and got away with it, I would have."

I was wondering how I could find out if Sophie was telling the truth as I pulled out of the visitor parking lot right when a police car drove by. Too late, I realized it was a West Riverdale Police car and that Bobby was staring at me from the passenger seat. Uh-oh. Even if he didn't see me, he couldn't miss my truffle-photo-covered Chocolates and Chapters minivan.

At least I didn't have to worry about confirming Sophie's alibi. Bobby would certainly take care of that. I drove a little too fast out of there, my pulse not calming down until I reached the highway heading home. The whole way back, I kept looking at my rearview mirror, sure that a police car would be pulling me over soon and Bobby would yell.

I walked into our house filled with teenagers. Steve Roxbury waved at me from the living room. "Welcome to chaos!" he said cheerfully. The furniture had been pushed back against the walls, and two small card tables now held sewing machines. A long worktable straddled the couch with piles of material strewn around. Students were pinning patterns to various swatches while others cut and sewed.

The dining room floor was covered with drop cloths, and Jolene was monitoring papier-mâché projects that were beginning to resemble heads. Or helmets. Or Dolly Parton's wigs. An almost life-sized copy of a section of the Maya mural Erica had shown me after an earlier meeting was cut in pieces and haphazardly stuck with blue tape on the walls.

Erica came out from the kitchen, holding a large bowl filled with white goop. "Hi!" she said.

"This is all for the flash mob?" They were going big-time.

"Yes." She looked around as if realizing it wasn't what she'd told me. "Sorry. They were kicked out of the theater workroom and we got a little carried away in here."

"No problem," I said. "What's the plan?"

She set the goop down in the middle of the covered dining room table, and the students dipped their newspaper scraps into it with glee. "Not too much glue, guys. It has to dry fast or it'll rot." She turned to me. "I found great patterns for the costumes. The students will take the machines home for a few days until they finish sewing. And the helmets will take until Monday for them to dry sufficiently to paint."

"Why does it smell like cinnamon?" I asked.

"I knew you'd catch that," Erica said. "One of the girls was complaining about the glue smell and I'd seen online that cinnamon helps."

I followed her to kitchen.

"I have some students working on the script in my office upstairs," Erica said.

"What kind of script? Isn't it about a mural?"

"It's much more than that," she said. "We're trying to re-create a part of this famous Maya mural from Bonampak, an archaeological site in Mexico." She grabbed a book that seemed to be a cross between a coffee-table art book and a textbook. "There's so much to choose from! Nobles and rituals and battle and conquest and defeat. It's going to be amazing."

"Your Super Geeks will love the battle scenes," I said. Those guys loved the gore. I'd once kicked them out of the dining area of the store for loudly discussing the artistic detail of the "entrails and rib bones" from the *Walking Dead* comic books.

Her enthusiasm was infectious. "Can I do anything to help?"

She looked around. "Sure! Pick a spot and go at it."

On my way to drop off my backpack in my room, my cell phone rang. It was from a blocked number but I answered it anyway.

Even with the door closed, the sounds of laughter and general teen fun came through the walls.

"Is this Michelle Serrano?" I didn't recognize the gravelly voice that could have been male or female.

"Yes."

"I hear you're looking for me," the voice said.

"George Clooney?" I asked.

"No." The voice answered with a smile in her voice. Unmistakably female.

"Deirdre?"

"Bingo," she said. "What do you want?"

"Well." I scrambled for something less straightforward but settled on the truth. "We're trying to find out everything we can about Professor Moody's death and hope you can help us."

She didn't respond.

"We'd just like to understand . . . how things worked out there on the River estate."

"Why would I want to do that?"

"I don't know," I said. "Because you want to help the investigation? How about for your own justice? From what I understand, you were let go for no reason. Why not tell us what you know?"

She was silent, and I began to feel a little desperate. "People suspect Erica, which is totally unfair. If there's anything you can do to clear this up, we'd be grateful. Very grateful."

"Okay," she said. "I'll meet you. At the store?"

Her fast response left me speechless for a moment. "Um. Sure?" I assumed she'd want to be more discreet than that.

"I'll be there at noon on Saturday." She hung up.

I tracked down Erica. "Well, that was weird."

"What was?" She was showing a student how to wrap the papier-mâché around a stick to get it to stay in place, while pointing to a picture of an elaborately decorated spear.

"Deirdre called me," I said. "She wants to come in and talk to us."

"That's great!" Erica said. "What's weird about it?"

"She's coming to the store at noon on Saturday," I said. "We're pretty busy then."

Erica shrugged. "Maybe she doesn't know that."

"Why would she want people to see her at all?"

"You won't know until you hear what she has to say," she said. "So don't worry about it until then."

Like that was possible. I walked back to my room, trying to take Erica's advice, but all I could think about was what Deirdre would be willing to tell us. Would whatever she said be a huge breakthrough and clear Erica completely?

. . . .

Friday morning, I was ringing up a pound of Cappuccino Darks, their mocha bite enhanced with a coffee bean on top, when my phone rang in my spine pocket, as Kona now called it. I reached behind my back to pull it out.

"Jennie River is hanging out in the park by the church," Zane said.

He hadn't been able to dig up much info on her, which was very odd for someone barely out of her teen years. She'd never even had a Facebook account that Zane could find. Talking to her was an opportunity I shouldn't pass up.

"What is she doing?"

"Swinging."

"Really?" I asked.

"Yep."

"Is she alone?"

"Yep."

"Okay, thanks."

I told Kona I was heading over to the grocery store for heavy whipping cream and would be back soon.

The church was the most beautiful building in West Riverdale, built in the mid-1700s of stone that had lasted centuries. Even though I didn't belong to the church, I thought of it as the anchor of our little town. Its stained glass windows let in gorgeous light. Ancient oak trees covered the tiny cemetery with weathered gravestones on one side, and the other side held a small playground.

I walked along the street that lined the playground and pretended to do a double take. "Jennie?"

Jennie sat in one of the swings, pushing off with one foot

to sway back and forth. She looked up at me with a blank stare.

"It's Michelle," I said. "From the chocolate shop?"

"Oh, hi," she said, continuing to swing.

"Are you okay?"

She put one foot down to stop as if seriously considering my question. "Yes." She started swinging again. She wore a bright yellow flowing shirt that billowed just a little when she moved, with cutoff jean shorts and green flip-flops.

I felt like I was talking to someone much younger than twenty-one.

"I'm going over to the grocery store and then back to Chocolates and Chapters. Want anything?"

She touched her toe to the ground and paused again to consider. "No." She started to swing again. "But thanks."

"Okay."

I rushed to the store, instinctively grabbing two spoons from the deli counter and two pints of ice cream, Ben & Jerry's Chocolate Fudge Brownie and Chunky Monkey, along with my cream. I stayed away from their Hazed and Confused, Cherry Garcia, and Chocolate Therapy, although I really wanted that last one.

Jennie was still there when I got back. I walked across the grass and joined her on the other swing. "Ice cream?" I held out both flavors and she chose Chunky Monkey. Yes! I preferred all chocolate all the time.

"How's it going?"

"Fine." She wrapped her arms around the chains of the swing so she could hold on by her elbows, and took the lid off of the ice cream. I handed her a spoon and opened my own pint.

We swung back and forth a little and I looked at her out of the corner of my eye. She looked fragile. And lost. No way could I ask her questions about our investigation.

I'd spent some years lost, not knowing what I wanted to do with my life. I didn't have the added burden of drug addiction, but figuring it out without parents had not been easy. I struggled to come up with something to say that might help her. "So what's next for you?" I asked.

She took a small bite of the ice cream and let it melt in her mouth before answering. "I don't know."

"What do you like to do?"

She paused her swing to focus on a butterfly meandering across the lawn. "At the moment, swing."

I tried to remember anything about her. "What about art?" I asked. "You won that special state art contest a few years ago, right?"

"That was before." Her voice was sad.

Before her dad died or before rehab?

"Did you know that both of my parents died when I was fourteen?" I asked.

She looked at me as if trying to figure out how old I was.

"My brother took care of me. He was only a kid himself."

She dug into a vein of chocolate and put it into her mouth.

"Who's taking care of you?"

"Adam." She paused for a second. "And Gary, I guess."

"Your mom?"

She kept her eyes on her ice cream, jabbing around a chunk of fudge before lifting it up. "She's not the nurturing type," she said without a trace of bitterness before eating the fudge. "She thinks I should be over it by now, but my therapist told her to stop telling me that. She's thinking it though."

"I was sad for a long time after my folks died," I told her. "And then I was mad for a longer time. It wasn't until I started making chocolate that I figured out what I wanted to do with my life, and I started to feel way better."

She stared at me, and I thought I saw a little hope creep into her eyes.

"Maybe you should get back in the studio and see if that's your thing," I suggested gently. I looked down at my ice cream, and it was more than halfway gone. "I'm going to have to run extra miles to get rid of this."

She kept eating. She probably didn't need to exercise to stay thin.

I stood up. "Have you heard that the high school is putting on a flash mob for the museum exhibit?"

She nodded.

"If you want to practice some really basic art, you could paint the backdrops. I know Jolene Roxbury would love any help she can get, especially a real artist. You know how much those high school boys like to slap it on."

She squinted up at me. "I had her for math. She's really nice."

"I have to get back to the shop," I said. "That group is meeting on Sunday afternoon at the school if you want to help them."

I started to walk away, when a large luxury sedan screeched to a halt right in front of us. Adam River got out, his face tight with anger. "Jennie! In the car. Now."

A blank look settled back over her face and she got to her feet, handing me the ice cream.

Adam waited until she got in the car and then slammed the door after her. Didn't he have a company or two to run?

He turned, blocking my view of Jennie. "Stay away from my family." His words were low, but anger leached out of them in an unmistakable warning.

Erica was smiling when I got back to the store. "Look," she said.

Reese had posted the letter from Lavender taking back everything she'd said about Erica. It wasn't a full retraction—morally deficient Reese didn't apologize at all for her role in the debacle—but at least people would know the truth.

I told Erica the little I'd learned from Jennie, including my run-in with Adam.

"Did he threaten you?" she asked. "Do you think it's something about the professor?"

"Not really," I said. "I think he's just protecting his little sister. Leo would do the same thing."

"I'll add it to our notes," she said. "Dinner tonight at El Diablo?"

Our next target was Juan Aviles, owner of El Diablo Restaurant. After leaving a message for Jolene suggesting she invite Jennie to help with the flash mob, I made the mistake of looking up his menu and lusting after his pork pupusas and fried yucca root on and off all day.

Once again, we left the store in our capable assistants' hands to handle closing. They had to know what we were up to, but neither one of them said a word.

We found the El Diablo Restaurant on State Street in Frederick, which looked like a younger, hipper version of our Main Street. But this one had sculpted trees, neat flower window boxes and charming flowerpots hanging from the street posts, and not enough parking spaces. Frederick had its share of colonial buildings, but seemed to have pushed all of its centuries-old bricks back into ruthless uniformity more fitting for this century. I wondered how they did it.

"Erica?" I heard a man's voice call out. Mark Harris, Colleen's soon-to-be ex-husband, stood outside a restaurant just two doors down. We met in between and stood awkwardly for a minute. "So you're going to El Diablo's, eh?"

"Yes," she said in a cool tone. "They catered our big reception and the food was great."

She looked at the sign for the restaurant he'd almost gone in. "New Orleans jazz? I didn't know you liked live music."

Mark seemed distinctly uncomfortable and then we saw why. A young woman swinging a guitar case walked down the street in what looked like ballet shoes. She called out to him. "Mark!" and then ran up to kiss him exuberantly on the lips before turning to us. "Hi! I'm Gretchen."

Oh my God. The other woman!

"Hi," Erica said with way more grace than I'd be able to muster up in the same situation. "I'm Erica, and this is Michelle."

Gretchen's eyes widened and her mouth made a perfect little O. She obviously knew who we were. And knew that we knew who she was. Erica looked her up and down, something I'd never seen her do before. It wasn't a mean girl move, just a seriously curious look-see at the woman who had broken up her little sister's marriage.

I pulled on Erica's arm. "We won't keep you," I said to them. I should've said, "Have a nice night," but it got stuck in my throat.

Erica seemed a little dazed as we walked back to the restaurant. I doubt that she noticed how the outside of El Diablo matched the charm of the rest of the street, and inside it had glossy wood booths, with red touches of color in large pottery and tablecloths. We stopped at the podium, where a discreet sign ordered us to wait to be seated. "Two?" the host asked in a bored tone.

"Yes, thank you." Erica pointed to a booth off to the side. "Could we have that table?"

"Sure." She picked up two leather-bound menus and led us to the corner where we were partially hidden by a huge fern.

"Do you want me to go kick her ass?" I asked when the waitress left, only half kidding.

Erica shook her head, still out of it.

We'd arrived for an early dinner and only a few tables were filled with mostly young businesspeople in their twenties sharing huge pitchers of the restaurant's colorful specialty drinks.

I opened the menu and found even a more extensive menu than what was online. Suddenly I was ravenous.

A woman with a dramatically asymmetrical haircut in a red business suit stood at the end of the bar, efficiently clicking away on her smartphone. A waiter brought her a to-go bag and she thanked him, placing what looked like a five-dollar bill into the tip jar. He thanked her and she went on her way.

Then Juan Aviles, El Diablo himself, came out of the kitchen. "There he is," I whispered. I slid further back into the booth, and then realized the fern offered better cover, and slid back to the front.

The waiter grabbed two steaming plates and walked them

to a table, while Aviles scanned the restaurant, as if checking to make sure everything was in place. His eyes stopped on the tip jar and quicker than I thought he could move, he'd grabbed the cash and shoved it into his pocket.

"Did you see that?" I asked.

"Yes," Erica said. "That just may be the leverage we need."

14

The same waiter who'd just lost his tip welcomed us to the restaurant and asked for our drink order. "Vince," according to his name tag, had a waxed mustache with small curls at the ends.

"Just water for now," Erica said. "I hate to mention this, but that manager took money out of your tip jar."

He looked back at Aviles and shrugged, but his voice held a trace of bitterness. "Happens all the time. Would you like an appetizer to share? I recommend the beef empanadas. They're our specialty."

"We'd love to try that," Erica gushed.

"And the pork pupusas," I added. "We'll need a few minutes for the rest."

When he smiled and went to the kitchen, I asked Erica, "We're ordering full meals, right?"

"Oh yes," she said. "And then we can insist on talking to the chef."

I was all for eating. "But what if he sees it's us and spits in our food or something?"

"Let's assume he has too much pride in his cooking for that," she said.

Whatever his faults, Juan Aviles could seriously cook. I almost forgot about our investigation as we ate the appetizers and savory Peruvian lamb and spicy Brazilian seafood stew for dinner. When I felt like I couldn't eat another bite, Vince brought us the dessert menu. I actually groaned.

"Oh, we'd love to," Erica said. "But we're totally stuffed. The food was excellent. Is there any chance we could talk to the chef?"

He looked dubious, either because no one actually spoke to the chef except in movies, or because he was afraid to ask. But in a minute, Juan Aviles was walking toward our table with a wary look on his face. His expression turned even more confused when he recognized us.

"Hi, Mr. Aviles," Erica said far more graciously than I could have managed. "We just love your food and wanted to tell you that our meals were excellent."

"Okay," he said, allowing the customers at the next table to get by him and leave.

"We actually came here under a ruse," she said as if admitting to a naughty mistake. Was she seducing him or getting information?

"A ruse?"

"We are so concerned about the reputation of our shop and are hoping you can tell us anything that might help us figure out who may be involved in the robbery."

His face reddened. "Are you crazy? I'm not telling you nothing. I am very loyal to my friends and would never reveal anything about them."

"Reveal?" Erica said. "That's a very telling word. You must have something big that you're hiding."

"You need to leave." He turned around.

"I'm sorry to hear that," she said after him. "I'm sure the Rivers would be troubled to learn how you treat your staff."

He faced her again, his whole head turning red. I had an image of a cartoon thermometer about to blow its stack. "What are you talking about? These bozos are lucky to have jobs."

The host walked by close enough to overhear. She rolled her eyes.

"The Rivers are very supportive of workers' rights." Erica leaned closer to him and spoke lower as if telling him a secret. "And we saw you take that waiter's tip."

"How do you know what I was going to do with it?" He was all blustery. "I could've been saving it for him."

She shook her head. "It doesn't matter. We saw and we know. And if you don't want us to tell the Rivers that you cheat your hardworking staff out of their money, you will help us. I'm sure they'd be horribly embarrassed that they've been recommending your restaurant to all of their friends."

His eyes narrowed to deadly slits. "What do you want?"

"Anything you know about Dr. Moody."

He looked completely shocked. "Why do you care?"

"That doesn't matter," Erica said. "What do you know about him?"

"Nothing." He took a step back. I thought I saw a little bit of fear flash across his face. "Now pay your bill, leave and don't come back."

"But—" Erica tried.

He yelled at Vince, "Give them the check and make sure they get out."

"Yes, sir," Vince said with a hint of contempt that Aviles either missed or ignored.

Aviles stomped back to the kitchen as the other diners stared at us. I smiled to reassure them that we were no danger to them, but Erica went into thought mode.

Vince returned with the bill. "What'd you do?" he asked quietly.

"Asked him some questions about a murder he didn't want to answer," Erica said with her head angled away from Aviles. "Did you hear about Dr. Addison Moody?"

I took my time reading the bill and then pulled out cash.

"Oh yeah," he said. "It's all anyone's been talking about here." He looked over his shoulder. Aviles stood in the doorway to the kitchen, scowling.

Vince turned back. "Maybe if you come back after closing, you can see something that will help."

I jolted in my seat and had to start counting the money over.

Erica dug in her purse, pulling out a few ones. And a business card. "What time?" she asked.

"Midnight," Vince said. "He's gone by then."

"Awesome." She slipped her card into the small stack of money. "My cell number is on the card. Please call me to let us know when he leaves."

Aviles kept his laser beam eyes on us until we were out the door.

"Well, that was interesting," I said, feeling an oversized sense of relief at the cool night air. "Do you think Vince will really help us?"

"Oh yes," Erica said. "The enemy of my enemy and all that."

"So what do we do until midnight?"

"You know this is the witching hour," I said while we waited outside the restaurant. We kept the windows open to let the cool night air in. We'd spent hours at a smaller jazz club a few blocks away, and I was feeling the effects of the couple of beers I'd ordered. Erica had nursed one glass of wine and was sitting in the driver's seat while we waited for Vince the waiter to contact us.

The more crowded bar that Mark and Gretchen might still be in was open, with music and noise spilling out onto the street. For some reason, the crowd reassured me that nothing terrible would happen to us. At least not without a few witnesses.

"According to whom?" Erica asked.

To avoid a lecture on Wiccan practices through the ages, I changed the subject. "Want to wait in Mark's restaurant?"

She glanced over at me. "No."

"Are you sure you don't want me to beat her up?" I joked. "I could take her."

"No," she said. "It's not her fault Mark is a cheating jackass." She sighed and pulled out her phone. "Oh."

"What?" I asked.

"I just got an email from our African friend," she said. "And?"

"He agrees with me," she said, her voice flat. "The vase has an extra glyph. It's worth a million dollars."

I stared at her. "Wow. That's huge. We need to tell the police."

She nodded. "Soon."

"If this is about Bobby," I started.

"Of course it's not," she said. "Just give me time to figure it out."

Just then, Mark and Gretchen came out. He carried her guitar, and they were holding hands. Some of the customers on the street yelled out to her, "Good set!"

She waved back. "Thanks!"

We sat in silence for a minute. "She's seems too, I don't know, nice and peppy for him," I said.

"It's inexcusable," Erica said, bitterness creeping into her voice. "Colleen's at home doing homework and he gets to gallivant in music clubs with his young girlfriend."

Gallivant? I tried to figure out the right thing to say. "Colleen is doing fine. She's loving school right now. Do you remember that feeling?"

She nodded.

I tried to tread carefully. "Was she happy with him?"

"Not happy-happy," she admitted.

A group of intoxicated young women dressed in little black dresses stumbled by. "One of my customers told me something years ago that has stuck with me. I asked her if she was happy after her divorce, and she said that she wasn't really happy then, but that the divorce gave her the possibility for happiness in the future."

Erica nodded.

"Now Colleen has a chance at happiness. And that's an important, really valuable thing, isn't it?"

Her eyes softened. "That's true."

"Just like you have a chance at happiness with Bobby, once this whole thing is over and you get back together." As soon as the words came out of my mouth, I regretted them. The transition to talking about Bobby was not as smooth as it sounded in my head, and I sounded like a matchmaking idiot.

"Maybe." She didn't sound convinced at all as she glanced at her phone.

"He's going to be even more pissed at us if he finds out about this, you know."

"He sure is," she said, staring at the restaurant as if willing Vince to call.

"Especially if we find something," I said. "But it's not our fault he's always one step behind us. First the diary and then the college—"

Erica turned her head so fast her hair whipped around. "What. College?"

"Um," I said, fumbling around for a lie that might work, and then gave up. "Come on! You didn't really think I wouldn't talk to LibrarySophie?"

She narrowed her eyes. "And how did you find LibrarySophie?"

Uh-oh. No way was I throwing Zane under the bus. "Duh!" I said. "Even *I* could figure out that she must work at the college library. Anyway, she was on a plane back from some women's conference in Chicago. So she's totally cleared. And then Bobby saw me. He was driving in as I was driving off the campus."

She looked appalled. "I told you I didn't want you to bother her."

"Since when are you the boss?" I asked with fake outrage. "If I want to investigate somebody, I'm going to investigate them."

Erica's phone dinged with a text message. Saved by the bell.

"It's Vince," she said. "We can go in now."

We got out of the car. "But don't think this is over," she warned.

The front door was unlocked. Leaves rustled as a stray breeze blew down the street, pushing on the door as it closed behind me.

"Back here." Vince stuck his head through the serving window of the kitchen. All of the chairs were upside down on the tables, and the floor was damp with recently mopped cleaner.

We followed him through the kitchen to a back room that was filled with assorted restaurant essentials. A small desk was squeezed in between shelves and the wall. Vince brought up what looked like the inside view of the restaurant from a security camera. "Go at it," he said.

"Thank you so much for your—"

He waved a hand as if to brush her off. "You can thank me by getting his ass in trouble. You have half an hour while I finish cleaning."

Erica sat down in the chair and stared at the screen as I looked over her shoulder. "Is that . . . ?"

She right clicked on the mouse, checked the list of functions she could do and zoomed in on the dining table I'd pointed to.

"Oh my God," I said.

The professor was sitting at the table with Carlo Morales.

An hour later, I still couldn't get over it. Vince had helped us find six meetings at the restaurant between Dr. Moody and Carlo Morales in the last few months, and we'd printed out photos with the time and date stamp on them. Vince said that Aviles forwarded the previous recordings to some company to store, but he didn't know how to access those earlier files.

Vince also let us know that when Carlo was planning to eat at El Diablo, he made his reservation with Aviles directly and the chef whipped up a special dish that wasn't on the menu and took forever to cook—Feijoada, which was some kind of stew. I looked it up on the way home and it was actually a Brazilian dish that, cooked the traditional way, used parts of the animal not normally eaten by Americans. Well, that we knew of. In any case, Vince promised to text Erica the next time Aviles made it.

I felt a little punchy in the car, confused by the wild direction our investigation had just taken, the late hour, and probably the beer as well. Erica was quiet on the way home, most likely trying to figure out how this fit into the whole picture.

"So Moody had to be selling Maya art to Carlo, right?" I asked. "Why else would he meet with him so often?"

She shrugged. "We need to find out more about Carlo. Just because he's from Central America doesn't mean he's an art trafficker."

"He told me that he was an art dealer," I said. "I wonder if that includes stolen Maya antiquities."

"If the professor was selling art to Carlo, then why have the exhibit?" Erica asked. "Especially with a million-dollar vase. And where was he getting the art?"

"We should ask Lavender," I said.

"I'm not sure Lavender would admit to her employer doing something illegal," she said, but I could tell she was spinning all of this around in her head, trying to make sense of the latest puzzle piece. "You should ask Kona what she knows about Carlo, and I'll get Zane to dig deeper. And then we'll talk to Lavender."

She was still at it when I fell into bed, pacing back and forth above my head.

B y eleven the next morning, I was taking turns looking outside the store in case Deirdre turned up early and jumping at any sound coming from anywhere near the door. My mind was churning with what we'd seen at the El Diablo Restaurant. It didn't help my nerves that our dining area was packed way more than usual for a Saturday morning.

It also didn't help that I'd pissed off Kona. All I did was ask some innocent questions about Carlo.

"You think he's going out with me just to find out about your investigation?" she'd asked, her brown eyes flashing.

When I'd backpedaled, she hadn't given me a break.

"I know he's out of my league," she said.

"He is *not* out of your league," I'd responded, dismayed. "He's lucky to have you."

At her stunned expression, I'd tried, "Not *have* you–have you, but be dating you." Then I'd given up. "Never mind. I won't ask again."

She stayed out of my way as much as she could. I even caught her checking the clock several times, as if she couldn't wait to get out of there. I felt terrible, but had to focus on the big project of the day—finding out what the Rivers' house-keeper knew about the robbery and Dr. Moody's death.

I'd met Deirdre only once, when we were both reaching

for the same ear of corn at the grocery store. She'd been shy as we both insisted the other one take it, and we both moved on to another ear.

I remembered her as medium just about everything. Medium height, which was certainly taller than me. Medium weight, shoulder-length brown hair, and timid brown eyes.

Zane had uncovered some interesting facts about her. She was a total gamer, and had achieved a ninety level, whatever that meant, in World of Warcraft. What was more fascinating to me was that she and her mother shared a really big investment account that had been steadily growing for many years. I didn't want to know how Zane learned that. Maybe they got their financial advice from one of the Rivers.

"What's going on?" Kayla asked when she arrived right before noon. "Are you having some kind of Saturday sale I don't know about?" She yawned and finger-combed her blond curls so they fell even more adorably over half of her face.

Kona handed her a black coffee. "I have no idea, but get moving."

Kayla good-naturedly took a gulp, and then set it down to tie on her Chocolates and Chapters apron.

May peeked in and waved me over to the door. Today she was wearing a white shirt with large daisies on it. I felt the urge to buy a bunch of daisies, so the not-so-subliminal cues were working. "Sorry. I just snuck out for a second. Gary was insisting, so I moved the kittens a little early. They're in the back of my store. Coco only scratched me once. Come by and see them."

I felt a surge of need to see the kitties. May had let me name the boys Mocha, Truffle and Nibs, and she named the girls Lily, Poppy and Zinnia. The list for adopting them was so long, the Humane Society was sending May emails of all the kittens they had up for adoption.

Then May stage-whispered, "Is she here yet?"

"Who?" I asked, trying to ignore the sinking feeling in my stomach.

"Deirdre Cash," May said. "I heard through the grapevine that she's coming here to spill all the River family secrets."

"What?" I looked around at the customers eyeing the front door as if Ed McMahon was about to arrive. "How do you know about that?"

"Everyone knows," she said. "We can't wait to find out what she says." Someone stopped to look in her flower store and she held up a finger for them to wait a minute. "She refused to say anything to the police but you'll get her to talk. You're like Oprah!" The potential customer picked up a bouquet of yellow roses and May went to help her.

I found Erica in her office working on a publisher's online order form. "Everyone knows!" I hissed, looking over my shoulder.

"Knows what?" she asked.

"That Deirdre is coming in to talk to us," I said. "They'll scare her off."

"Did you tell anyone?"

"No!" I said, my voice rising. "How did they all find out about it?"

"Hmm," she said. "Could Deirdre have mentioned it to someone who unfortunately spread the word?"

"I don't know," I said. "But it's almost noon." I shook my head. "Our best lead is going to fall apart because someone opened their big mouth."

"Don't worry," she said. "We'll figure it out."

"I'm gonna call Jake," I said. If this many people knew about our little talk with Deirdre, he was sure to have heard something. I went back to my counter and pulled out my cell.

He answered after the first ring. "The Ear. Ready to listen."

"Hi, Jake," I said. "It's Michelle at Chocolates and Chapters."

"Hey," he said. "You getting ready?"

"For what?" My eyes were on the door.

"The big reveal," he said. "Deirdre Cash is coming over to tell ya all about the River family skeletons, right?"

"How does everyone know that?" I kept my voice down but still managed to sound shrill.

"No idea how it started, darlin', but it was all anyone was talking about last night. How she won't talk to the cops, but she's coming in to see you."

I swore. "Sorry," I added.

"Yeah," he said sarcastically, the clink of glasses in the background. "'Cause I never heard that before."

When I didn't say anything, he added, "You done?"

"Yeah, thanks," I said.

"Let's hope she makes it," he said. "Depending on what she's got, they might just knock her off before she gets there." He hung up.

Great. Something else to worry about.

Erica walked back to her cash register right at noon. I gave up any pretense of working and stood by the counter tapping my fingers and staring at the front of the store, willing our guest to arrive. At 12:01, Deirdre marched up to the store and opened the door, sending the bells jingling.

I drew in a breath.

She paused in the doorway, noting all the customers but

not reacting. With one long look over her shoulder, she straightened as if making a big decision and then stepped inside, turning around to gently close the door behind her.

Deirdre looked like she'd aged a lot since I'd seen her in the grocery store. She couldn't be more than a few years older than me, but had gray streaks in her hair. She hadn't bothered with makeup, which emphasized the fatigue on her face. I should let her go home and take a nap.

"Deirdre," I said, as if she was a long-lost friend. I made myself appear calm, hoping my face wasn't betraying how quivery I felt inside.

She walked through the gaping townspeople as if they weren't there.

"Have a seat." I gestured toward the counter stools as if I was Vanna White. "Would you like to try some Pumpkin Treats? Most people love the rush of allspice."

She barely glanced at the plate. "Can we talk somewhere private?"

"Sure." I suddenly felt even more uncertain. "We can use Erica's office in the back."

She nodded and followed me down the hallway.

"How are you holding up?" I asked, and then the front door slammed open with enough force to send the bells slapping against the frame.

"Ms. Cash!"

It was Adam River, looking frantic.

15

stole a look at Deirdre as he made his way across the store and saw satisfaction spread across her face.

He took her hand. "I'm terribly sorry." He turned to me. "Is there somewhere we can talk?"

Did he mean me? No, he meant Deirdre. "Sure," I said, not sounding sure.

"Not here." Deirdre dropped his hand.

"Of course." His voice oozed relief. "I'll take you back to the house."

She scowled. "Not yet."

Was she playing hard to get?

He blinked at her, realizing he wasn't out of the woods yet. "Okay."

Deirdre looked at me, her back ramrod straight. "Thank you for your offer. But now is not a good time." She turned to walk out and Adam silently followed her. He sent me a look as if trying to figure out what I was up to. At least he didn't threaten me like he had in the park with Jennie.

I had no idea what the hell was going on, but for some reason, I was rooting for Deirdre.

Our customers erupted with dramatic discussions and long looks at me. Erica joined me as I stood staring at the now-empty doorway.

"What just happened?" I was a bit bemused.

"We've been played," she said, her voice low.

"Really?" My voice squeaked my surprise and I cleared my throat.

"Deirdre must have been the one to spread the word that she was coming in to reveal the long-lost secrets of the River family. I imagine they waited to see if she'd really follow through and then made the call to hire her back."

I took a minute to think that through. "So she knows something. Something big enough for Adam to kinda humiliate himself publicly."

She nodded. "Maybe she wanted to get him back just a little, for firing her and kicking her out of the only home she's known."

"So, what are they hiding?" I asked. "And what does it have to do with stolen Maya art? And maybe murder?"

Erica kept her eyes on the now-empty doorway. "That's the big question, isn't it?"

Jake called me less than an hour after Deirdre left. "I hear you've been duped," he said. "Very Pink Panther."

"Didn't he always get his man in the end?" I reminded him.

He laughed and I was about to hang up on him when I realized he might be calling for a reason. "Have you heard anything else?"

"Just that she's safely back in her apartment on the River estate," he said. "You probably won't have another chance at her."

I was already mad, but that sent me over the top. I stomped over to talk to Erica. "We need to go all out," I said. "We're no further along than when we started."

"That's not true," she said. "Just think what we learned last night at El Diablo. And we've eliminated some possibilities."

I waved my hand around. We still didn't have any idea who actually killed the professor. "We can't do anything about Carlo until Vince calls us, but nothing's stopping us from going after Santiago Diaz."

Erica stared at me. "I wasn't sure I should tell you this, but Zane found some information on both of them that concerns me."

"What?"

"Except for an outdated website about Carlo's art business, nothing."

I waited for a moment. "So?"

"Do you know how hard it is to have nothing on the Internet?" she asked. "Neither one of them has any information online."

"That's impossible," I said. "Maybe they're not using their real names?"

"Possibly," she said. "But Zane is working on it with his comp sci professor."

"That's fine," I said. "But I have another way to find out more about our secretive Santiago."

. . . .

We decided not to wait until May and Nara met that night in the store for their weekly pre-manhunting, lucky-chocolate-eating visit, so I called Nara to let her know that she should come over early to test my new Caramel Apple Milks for her customers.

"Yum! I'll be over as soon as my newlyweds go back to bed." She chuckled. "Which should be in about five minutes, the way she's eating that whipped cream on her strawberry waffles."

Great. Now I wanted strawberry waffles. I popped a Raspberry Surprise to compensate.

I wondered if whipped cream would work on Bean. Who was I kidding? I wouldn't be able to pull that off without laughing.

It didn't take very long for Nara to arrive. "I was wrong. Three minutes." She was wearing a sari in a brilliant blue, which she hitched up to sit at the counter.

"You look gorgeous," I said. "Your parents here?"

"Oh yeah." She wore traditional Indian clothing only when her parents visited from New Delhi. "It's been just a *lovely* visit." It was no secret that her parents disapproved of her choice of occupation, her divorce, and especially her disregard of her heritage.

"That bad, huh?" I asked. "Maybe these will make you feel better." I pushed her plate closer, along with her favorite Masala tea.

She took a small bite of the Caramel Apple truffles, with their tiny chunks of tart dried green apples. "Hmm, this is heavenly."

Erica joined us and folded her long legs under the counter. "Hi, Nara," she said. "How are things at the inn?"

"Fine," she said. "Lots of reservations coming in for Columbus Day weekend."

"Great," Erica said. "Need any more coupons?"

"Not yet." Nara sipped her tea.

"How do your visitors like the Hemingway room?"

Nara had convinced the owners to give each of the rooms a literary theme, and Erica had helped her with the subtle finishing touches including the teapots decorating the Alice in Wonderland room, Georgian fabrics in the Jane Austen room, and colorful exotic plants in the Dr. Seuss room.

"They love it," she said. "Especially the quill and ink pot on the desk."

"Oh, good," Erica said. "I heard you have a very handsome man in there now."

Nara stopped midbite. "Wait. Are you guys trying to question me? You know I have a strict privacy policy with my guests."

Actually, that was so not true. She *said* she had a privacy policy but she still managed to sneak little gossipy tidbits into any conversation. I imagined she told May just about everything that happened at the inn when they went out on their manhunts.

"I know," Erica said in her *soothing yet tell me everything* tone. "But that's with upstanding, law-abiding guests. You may very well be housing a known felon."

Whoa. We didn't know that for sure. Erica was pulling out the big guns right away.

Nara's eyes opened wide. "What? I didn't . . . realize."

"Of course, you didn't," I said, taking the good cop role. "Who wouldn't trust such a charming man?"

"He seemed really nice," Nara said. "What did he do?"

Erica patted her hand. "Well, I don't want you to panic, but we think he may be involved in art smuggling."

Nara laughed in relief. "Oh, that's all."

"Mr. Diaz may have graduated to more violent crimes," Erica said, her voice getting lower.

Nara gasped. "The professor?"

Erica shrugged. "Could be."

"What should I do? Ask him to leave? He might get mad."

I took over. "No. Don't do that. We just want you to let me join your cleaning staff tomorrow morning and make sure he's not involved."

"You mean search his room?" She looked at me, worried. "But what if you get caught?"

"She won't," Erica reassured her.

She looked at her watch. "They're still working today."

Shoot. I wasn't sure I was ready for that yet. Then I thought about Deirdre's duplicity.

Erica met my eyes. "No time like the present."

At first, I thought that the worst thing about cleaning hotel rooms was the uniform. I considered telling Nara that this shade of mustard was simply ugly. And the polyester was itchy. What was she thinking?

But the absolute worst thing was that people are totally gross. Even though I joined the cleaning crew late, I couldn't arrive to "clean" only Santiago Diaz's room. I'd put on a baseball cap, hoping not to see anyone I knew, and kept it pulled down as low as I could.

I'd brought my heavy-duty up-to-the-elbow rubber gloves but wished I'd brought some farmers' up-to-my-shoulder, industrial-strength gauntlets for birthing cows. Or a hazmat suit. Or a full-body condom.

I imagined I'd be making beds and cleaning out trash, which was bad enough. But Nara's head housekeeper was not happy about my addition to her crew and she put me in charge of bathrooms. Which were disgusting.

Finally, we came to the end of the third floor, a spacious corner nook room with windows looking out over the side and back gardens. The Hemingway room was decorated in early Florida, with palm-covered wallpaper, wicker furniture and sea blue carpet. I closed the door behind me, a total no-no, but I was planning to claim forgetfulness. The housekeeper always knocked several times before entering, especially after we'd "surprised" the newlyweds who must have been so involved they didn't hear our knock. Too bad they didn't miss our mutual gasps when we opened the door and then slammed it shut again. Nara knew what her newlyweds were doing; she had to work on her communication with her staff.

As soon as I stepped into the room, I noticed the same men's cologne Mr. Diaz had worn at the reception. Very unique. I started at the tiny desk, which held a laptop. I quickly opened it but had no chance at guessing the password, so I gave up. Rifling through the papers on the desk, I realized I was at a distinct disadvantage not knowing Spanish. I pulled out my phone and started taking photos of what looked like business papers. Following what I'd seen on TV,

I pulled the desk drawers out and looked underneath and behind them. I repeated the process on the two small nightstands.

Nothing.

I scanned the room for possible hiding places. The armoire looked promising, but inside it held only a pole with a few dark suits and starched white shirts. Tiny shelves on the left held just a few other clothing items, stacked neatly.

Behind it though, I thought I saw something. I turned on the flashlight app on my phone and saw a small black pouch just beyond my reach. I strained to reach it, pressing my face against the side, sure I'd have a wood imprint on my face. I got it!

Just as I'd tucked it into one of the long pockets in my cargo pants, I heard a masculine voice say, *"Perdóname,"* out in the hall by the door.

I had just enough time to dive into the bathroom and turn on water in the sink before the door opened. I peeked out and saw Santiago Diaz look intently around the room. His eyes narrowed as he looked at his desk, and then they met mine.

I popped back into the bathroom like a gopher diving into its hole, hoping he hadn't recognized me in my baseball cap, and the head housekeeper spoke to Santiago from the hallway. The pouch felt heavy in my pocket.

He responded in Spanish, and she came into the bathroom. "Hurry up," she ordered in English. "He's going downstairs for twenty minutes and wants you to be done by then."

When they both left, I breathed a deep sigh of relief that he hadn't recognized me. I finished cleaning the bathroom and when I came out into the room, I saw Santiago had left a folder on the desk.

With one look toward the door, I opened the folder. It

contained pages of a spreadsheet, the words in Spanish. I
used my cell to take photos of every page, closed it the way
I found it, and got the heck out of there.

Somehow I made it all the way back to the store before
opening the pouch. Shoot! It didn't seem like it was
something that belonged to Santiago. At least, I didn't think
so. It was an expensive tortoiseshell-colored manicure set,
most likely left behind by another guest who was female.

My only hope was the photos on my phone.

Of course Erica knew enough Spanish to start interpret-
ing the documents right away. She was most interested in
the spreadsheets with dates and amounts in what might be
dollars or euros. Each entry had jumbled-up letters that we
had no idea how to decipher.

Then May popped her head into Erica's office. "You girls
need to see the kittens. I swear they're getting cuter by the
minute." She glanced at the spreadsheet on top. "What's
that?" she asked and then answered, "Oh. Art sales."

Erica and I stared at her. "How do you know?" I asked.
It may have sounded a little unbelieving.

May shrugged. "I don't know for sure, but I used to do
bookkeeping for an art gallery and the owner used codes
like that."

Erica jerked her head in a *get her out of here* way.

"Thanks so much, May," I said, taking her arm. "I'd love
to see the kitties now."

We entered the flower shop through the back hallway we
shared. The kittens were all asleep after their big move. May
had provided a lovely box filled with soft towels, food and

water, and a litter box. Coco raised her head once when the chime announcing the front door opening sounded, took note that I was there and promptly went back to sleep.

The kittens were turning into pudgy balls of fur. Cutest things ever. I sat on an overturned flower bucket and watched them sleep until May finished with a customer who wanted a purple arrangement.

"I told Reese she wasn't allowed to put that camera in here," May said. Today she was wearing peach to match her sale on pale carnations. "And to get her flowers online from now on." She snorted. "She must be feeling very guilty about that horrible blog post, 'cause she didn't even argue."

"Leo has his friends protesting on and off all day, and they went around town and returned all of her papers to her storefront," I said. "At least she hasn't posted anything crazy lately."

I used one finger to pet a few kittens while Coco purred in her sleep. Kittens sure were a stress relief.

Our house phone rang again very early in the morning. I didn't know why we still had the thing, except every time I considered getting rid of it, Leo talked me into keeping it for emergencies.

Confused by the noise, I picked up my cell phone, which said it was 4:32 a.m. Who was calling at this ungodly hour on a Sunday morning? By the time I'd stumbled my way into the kitchen, I could hear Erica on her way downstairs, talking into the cordless phone. "Reese, please. Take a deep breath and start over. I have no idea what you're talking about."

I may have been slightly delirious but I thought I heard Reese yelling something about blood.

Erica walked right by me and opened the front door. "Oh my," she said.

I joined her in the doorway.

Pointy little tubes were scattered on our front porch in a puddle of blood.

"Are those . . . ?" I asked her, willing my brain to start working.

"Stingray spines," she said. "Used for Maya bloodletting rituals."

I stared at her. "And for killing Professor Moody."

16

I f I thought Bobby was mad about the diary, he was posi-
tively livid when he arrived at our house. When Erica told
Reese we had the same display on our porch, she'd hung up
on her and called 911. Chief Noonan must've pulled the
short straw and went to Reese's house, and Bobby and Detective Lockett were standing on our porch, taking photos.

We hadn't touched anything, which I thought was very
nice of us, and let them do their policemen thing.

It reminded me that Bobby was probably still mad about
the whole LibrarySophie thing, and I should be extra careful
with him.

Erica immediately brought her laptop downstairs to the
kitchen table, and was trying to find where someone could
buy stingray spines. Unfortunately, a lot of marine biological
supply companies sold them to anyone who wanted them.

And these spines were cheap, not like the murder weapon used on Professor Moody. That had been a special blood-letting tool. A hundred-thousand-dollar genuine antiquity made of jadeite.

I knew the Internet had everything, but selling stingray spines was going too far. And since when did so many marine biological supply companies exist? How many customers wanted puffer fish that looked like they were holding their breath?

Soon the crime scene techs arrived and took fingerprints of everything on the porch. The blood was thankfully red paint, but the intent had surely been to scare the crap out of us.

Detective Lockett knocked on the back door.

I led the way to the kitchen.

"You ladies at it again?" He was dressed in jeans and a black button-down shirt, all slightly rumpled, like he'd jumped out of bed and picked up the closest thing he could find to wear. Of course, I was wearing sweatpants with holes in the knees from sliding into home too often at softball practice.

"At what?" I asked in my most innocent voice.

He shook his head. "What are we going to do with you?"

"Do you have a specific question, Detective?" Erica asked.

He scratched his head and shuffled his feet as if trying to think of something.

"Really?" I said. "Do you think you're Columbo or something?"

He smiled, but there was something determined behind it. "You do remember that you were almost killed a few months ago."

"Of course," I said.

"Here's the thing I've learned about people who kill," he said conversationally. "If they've done it once, they're much more likely to do it again. Just like what almost happened in May."

I couldn't help the shiver that ran up my spine.

"You two should take that warning out there to heart," he said.

"Not 'yinz guys'?" I said, borrowing some Pittsburgh-ese.

He looked at me, not distracted at all.

Erica broke in. "It seems like we must be getting pretty close to something important if we're making somebody, not necessarily the murderer, nervous. I'm not sure a splash of red paint and a few stingray spines equals much more than vandalism."

"Vandalism?" Lockett repeated. "You think some bratty kid did that?"

"No," Erica said in her *I'm trying to be reasonable in the face of your hysteria* tone. "It's obviously a warning, but not necessarily by Dr. Moody's killer."

"So you're saying you don't have to worry?" Lockett asked.

She didn't answer him, looking uncertain.

"Right." He pulled out a kitchen chair and sat down at the table. "Let's just get to the nitty-gritty. Why don't you tell me what ya learned that might've got you two in trouble?"

Erica looked at me and I nodded. She told him what we knew so far, except for the million dollar vase. Or my little field trip to Santiago's room and the spreadsheets. Because then we wouldn't have to worry about someone else killing us—Lockett would do it for us.

Lockett wasn't happy. He even stopped taking notes after

a while and rubbed his eyes with both hands. "Nothing stops you two."

Erica lifted her chin. "If you were smart, you'd use us."

"Yeah right," he scoffed.

"For example, I could offer my expertise on Bertrand River's diary," she suggested.

He stood up. "Even if I thought that was a good idea, your boyfriend would stop it in a second."

"He's not my boyfriend," she said. "Not that it has anything to do with my expertise."

He started to say something about that and realized it might get him into trouble. "This is getting messy. Really, stay out of it." He went outside to talk to the crime scene techs.

Bobby came in demanding that we promise not to do anything that anyone might consider to be "investigating." If he could've, he would have put us under house arrest.

I leaned over to Erica and said in a stage whisper, "Is he going to break up with you again?"

Bobby stomped out as if he couldn't trust himself to be around us. It didn't help that the same scene of stingray spines and red paint was found outside Reese's storefront, our store, Lavender's hotel, and even Gary's coffee shop. It seemed like whoever had done this was also trying to warn off anyone who was known to have talked to us.

By some miracle, we still opened at our normal Sunday time of eleven. I was arranging my Orange Hot Cocoa boxes on a display table when Gary called my cell. "I hate to bother you with everything that's happened, but the cats are back, and May didn't answer her phone."

"I'm so sorry," I said. "I'll be right there."

I grabbed a box and drove over, wishing I had the

baby-blanket-lined basket that May had used to move them. Different crime techs were finishing up in front of the Big Drip, and I went in through the back, heading up to the front to let Gary know I was there.

Gary gave me an exasperated look from behind the counter. "Same place."

One of his skater buddies was asleep on the couch. I ignored him and went to the storage room. "Come on, Coco," I said quietly. She let me grab the little mewing kittens and put them into the box, and then she jumped in with them, complaining loudly.

Gary came back to watch, sticking out a finger to pet one of the kittens. "Don't tell anyone, but I kinda miss them."

I smiled. "I can imagine. They're irresistible." I pointed to Reese's webcam and computer still in the closet. "Is Reese taking those out?"

He rolled his eyes. "I've asked her to a bunch of times, but she's busy. She said they're turned off."

I put the box down. "I'll just clean up in there and go out the back."

"What'd you do to my brother?" he asked. "He told me not to talk to you."

Hmm. Did he mean talking to Jennie or trying to get Deirdre to spill the River family secrets? "I'm sorry to cause you to disobey his order," I said. "You can tell him this time it was Coco's fault."

He frowned. "I don't take orders. From anybody."

Oh good. He fell for it. "He'll calm down," I said. "As soon as they catch whoever did this." I pointed to the guy on the couch. "Did he see anything?"

"No," he said, disgusted. "Too messed up." He snorted.

"Don't do drugs, kids," he said and then seemed to relent. "I let them crash here when they can't see straight enough to drive, but it's getting to be too much." He went back to the counter.

I quickly cleaned up Coco's mess. She'd once again shredded a bunch of poor Gary's napkins, and the industrial-sized box was pretty empty. I put the last few packages on a shelf and took the box out of the closet to recycle. When I came back in, I noticed a small door with a padlock, probably leading to plumbing that hadn't been used since the whole building had been repiped decades before. The cement had crumbled around it, leaving a hole barely large enough for Coco to squeeze through.

I was going to tell Gary and suggest that he try to close up the hole on both ends of wherever the panel led, but he was trying to handle a few upset skater boys.

"Dude!" one of them yelled to the passed-out kid. He kicked the couch leg and woke him up. The poor guy looked like he could use a lot more sleep, and a lot of coffee. "You gotta put the key back in the hiding place, you moron. You passed out and we couldn't get in."

"Leave him alone," Gary said. "You did the same thing last week."

The first irate skater dude saw me holding the box and abruptly stopped talking. I waved to Gary and went out the back door.

May was in her shop when I got back, and I handed her the box of kittens. "Oh, thank goodness," she said, her hand on her heart. "I got back from church and I was so worried!" Coco circled, meowing her head off, until they were all settled back in their spot.

Kona asked to talk when I got back to the store. She

started to say something and then stopped, looking miserable.

"What?" I asked.

"It's just, I couldn't get your question out of my mind and I realized that Carlo had asked me questions about you and Erica last week."

"Oh," I said. "I'm sorry."

"So he *was* using me to find out what you guys were up to." She sounded sad and mad at the same time.

"That's not true," I insisted. "He liked you the minute he met you, before the . . . whole mess started."

She shook her head.

"When did he start asking questions?" I asked.

"I'm not sure," she said, sounding troubled. "He was pretty subtle about it. Like asking how the shop worked and then about the festival and murder investigation stuff around Memorial Day. I totally told him you were *not* getting involved in this Dr. Moody case." She paused and then admitted with a sideways look. "But I did kinda brag that if you were, you'd figure out who the bad guys were way, way before the police did."

Great. Maybe Carlo was the one trying to scare us with stingray spines. I tried to keep the worry off my face.

"Can you stay away from him for a few days?" I asked. "We actually are looking into a few things."

She nodded, no longer resentful of my concern. And not surprised at all that we were investigating. "Yeah. He texted me this morning, but I'm not going to answer."

I went back into Erica's office and Zane was there. "We need to find out more about Carlo. Like now."

"Why the urgency?" Erica asked.

My voice started to shake with outrage. "He asked Kona

about us and if we're investigating the professor's murder. He was using our Kona."

Zane cleared his throat. "Kona told me that last night and I did some digging with my comp sci professor." He typed on his computer and turned the screen to us. "She's done some consulting with a few government organizations and reached out to someone. He told her that Carlo has been suspected of international art trafficking for years, but it's never been proven."

I sat down hard in a chair. "Oh my God."

Erica looked upset for a moment and then took a few deep breaths.

"Why didn't Lockett or Bobby tell us?" I asked. "They have to know that."

"This might be why Bobby was so adamant about us staying out of the investigation," she said.

"Let's back up. If Carlo was responsible for the robbery and the professor's death, then why is he still here? Wouldn't he be out of the country by now?"

Erica's cell phone dinged with a text. "Speak of the devil," she said. "Vince the waiter said Aviles has been making Feijoada since early this morning. He thinks Carlo is coming for lunch this time." She told Zane what we'd learned about the professor meeting with Carlo at the El Diablo Restaurant. "Let's go see who he's meeting with."

"It's already eleven thirty," I said. "We have to get over there right away."

The idea of staking out a suspect sounded exciting but in reality, it was totally boring. Zane had insisted on joining us. He'd quickly borrowed a van from a friend and loaded it up with cameras that were now trained on the street outside the restaurant. We all sat in the back of the van, which got stuffy even though we'd parked in the shade and cracked the front windows a couple of inches.

At first, anytime someone walked even close to the restaurant door, we all stared intently at the laptop to see if the person was our target. Vince had texted to let us know that Carlo hadn't arrived yet, and his special dish was still stewing.

By the time two o'clock rolled around, we were wondering if the whole thing was a bust. And then Zane pointed out a man in a baseball cap on the screen. "This is his second time walking down the street."

Erica and I leaned forward to look at him closer. "How do you know?"

He zoomed the camera in and brought up footage that had been captured fifteen minutes before. Same man.

"What is that he's wearing around his neck?" Erica asked.

Zane zoomed in even further. The man wore a large light green necklace that wouldn't be so obvious except he'd opened his shirt a few buttons past *Miami Vice*–style.

"That's K'inich Ajaw, the classic Maya sun god," Erica said.

"Maya?" I said. "That can't be a coincidence."

"It's most likely a copy that is pretty common—sold to tourists even," she admitted. "Unless that's real jadeite."

"Jadeite?" I asked. "Isn't that what the murder weapon was made of?"

"Yes. I'd have to see it closer to be sure." She stared intently at the screen.

Amulet Man walked past us and soon our camera was looking at his back. Which was how we captured the look on Carlo's face as he came around the corner and recognized him. Carlo was furious. They had a short argument in Spanish and the Amulet Man slunk away, throwing a resentful look over his shoulder.

Carlo's eyes darted around as if searching the area. I actually ducked when he stared at the van for a moment, even though there was no way for him to see us. Then he made a quick phone call and turned around to go back the way he'd come.

"We have to follow him!" I said as he disappeared around the corner.

I ignored Erica's protest and slid open the van door.

Santiago Diaz stood on the other side, a gun in his hand.

17

My mouth formed the word "What?" but no sound came out. He gestured again with the gun and I moved backward into the van. He coolly climbed in and shut the door. He seemed like a more lean version of Carlo, all hard angles in his face, and hard muscles under that dark suit.

What was wrong with me? Why hadn't I yelled and run? Or better yet, slammed the door in his face?

"Hands where I can see them, Mr. West," Santiago said. "I'm afraid I'll have to take that laptop."

Erica didn't look frightened at all. "Why would you want our surveillance of Carlo Morales?"

"Such an official word, Ms. Russell," he said, "for your, how do you say, hijinks. Let's just agree that this is bigger than the unfortunate death of your professor."

He held out his hand for the laptop with the gun in the

other. Erica nodded to Zane, who unplugged the computer and handed it to Santiago. Erica stared at me and I could tell she was willing me not to do anything stupid.

"All of you should pay very careful attention to what I'm about to say." He pointed the gun directly at Zane. "Stop your investigation into Carlo Morales immediately. All of your lives may depend on it."

Zane stared back at him, as impassive as Erica.

We watched Santiago tuck the laptop under his arm and pull the door open, slipping his gun into a shoulder holster. Then he smiled and slid the door shut.

I went to open the door and follow him, but Erica said, "Michelle!" in such an authoritative voice that I stopped.

Zane immediately typed into his cell phone, and then yelled, "Shit!"

I had never heard him raise his voice, let alone swear. "What?"

"He jammed my transmission," Zane said. "He has the only recording of the meeting on that laptop. Hold on."

Erica sat still, trying to make sense of what just happened.

"Did you get it?" Zane asked someone on the other end, and then made a fist and yelled. "Yes!"

"What?" I demanded.

"I sent a photo of that guy with the necklace to my professor as soon as I captured it," he said. "At least we have that."

Everything looked the same back at the store, but I felt like some kind of monumental shift had happened. Why did Santiago want our recording of Carlo's meeting with

Amulet Man so much he'd risk an armed robbery on a busy street? Why was Carlo arguing with Amulet Man? And how was I serving Rum Raisin Milks to a table of grandmother church volunteers without shaking?

We'd decided to wait and see what Zane's computer science professor came up with before saying anything to the police, especially after Bobby's hissy fit following the stingray spine incident.

By late afternoon, it all seemed like a weird dream. Zane was working with another of his laptops, although he was pretty angry at losing his favorite. He was muttering about not being able to access the dark web, which sounded like some video game.

Erica got ready to leave for her flash mob work party at the high school. I didn't know how she could think about that now. Of course, I was selling truffles.

"Let me know if Jennie River makes it," I told her as she went out the door.

Kona and I were discussing the chocolates we'd make on our Magic Monday, when Zane came out from the hallway and gestured for me to join him.

"I'll be right back," I told Kona.

Zane rushed back to the office he shared with Erica, and an enlarged photo of Amulet Man we'd seen outside the El Diablo Restaurant was up on his screen. I was just about to tell him to be more discreet when he excitedly said, "You won't believe this, but I think we took the only photo, like ever, of a famous forger."

"Are you kidding?"

"No," he said. "My professor's government contact is super psyched. She wasn't supposed to tell me anything, not even which agency her contact works for—I suspect Homeland Security—but they only had a description of the guy—no photographs. He goes under the name Sincero and he provides forged documentation to show that antiquities have been purchased legitimately, when they're not. He wears a baseball cap and an amulet, just like that guy. ICE, the FBI, Interpol—they've all been looking for this guy for years."

"ICE?" My brain was moving too slowly to keep up with Zane.

"Immigration and Customs Enforcement," he said. "They're responsible for finding art that has been sold illegally and sending it back where it belongs."

I was feeling more confused by the minute. "A forger? So he might be connected to the robbery and by default, to Dr. Moody's death?" I asked. "Shouldn't we just give that info to Detective Lockett and let him pass it on to the right people?"

"Um," Zane said. "I'm pretty sure that just happened through my professor's government guy."

"Okay," I said. "I need to talk to Erica. Can you, I don't know, keep digging?"

"Sure." He seemed energized by his big win.

I let Kona know I was running over to the high school for a little bit. The first serious flash mob rehearsal was taking place in the gym and I was dying to see it, in addition to filling Erica in on this Sincero guy.

"It's the candy lady," one of the kids painting long strips of paper in the hallway yelled as I entered the front door. "You got some M&M's?"

"Sorry!" I called out. "You gotta upgrade those taste buds." The strips of paper seemed to form a huge background of a jungle with a stone edifice rising out of it.

"Nah," he said. "I love all the chocolate."

Jennie was painting a bunch of intricate parrots in a tree. I was delighted to see her there. She used her finger to make an artful smudge and then wiped it on her shirt that had hearts all over it. When she saw me, she gave a timid smile and then got back to adding detail to a wing.

"Where's Erica?" I asked.

"In the gym, I think," one of the students told me.

I never failed to feel nostalgic in the gymnasium, where I'd spent so much of my high school years at basketball practice and games. It smelled the same, that mixture of old popcorn, sweet spilled drinks, and teen sweat.

The high windows that never let in enough light were the same, but the beat-up floor and bleachers had been replaced after years of fundraising by the hardworking PTA.

Jolene Roxbury was looking down at a printout of the mural and hollering out orders. "Jim, to the right one step. Hold your weapon higher."

That caused a cascade of giggles that Jolene ignored. "Winnie, to the left, half a step." I watched as each student followed her directions until it was set up exactly how she wanted it. A long line of Maya warriors and royalty dressed in vibrant colors of red and orange, and warm, earthen browns. If you didn't look too closely at the papier-mâché helmets and fake weapons, it was almost believable.

"Mark it!" she yelled at last, and four students with different colors of tape started placing tape strips on the floor with a reasoning only drama people would understand.

I walked up to Jolene. "How's it going?"

She grinned. "Amazing. These kids are amazing. And the whole thing is going to be amazing." She handled a few questions by students working with maps of Main Street. It seemed like they were figuring out what streets to block off to keep possible bystanders out of the way during the filming.

She sent them on their way to do her bidding and I snuck a question in before she started her next job. "How's Jennie River doing?"

She looked over her shoulder to make sure no one was around. "Good, I think. Very shy even though she's a little older than these kids. But she paints beautifully. I'm glad you suggested I reach out to her. One of the art girls has taken her under her wing."

I was having such a good time watching the innocent fun of the teens that I'd forgotten about Zane's discovery. "Where's Erica?" I asked.

"Workroom," she said, waving in the general direction of the theater. "Behind the stage. It's confusing back there, so just ask a kid when you get close."

I found my way, after opening the costume room and a rehearsal room first, and found Erica repairing a few papier-mâché helmets and a spear. She looked up, surprised to see me.

"Hey," I said. "I have some news from Zane."

I could tell that she changed mental gears reluctantly. I felt the same way. Flash mob mode was way more fun than murder investigation mode.

"That guy we photographed goes by the name Sincero. He's actually a big-time forger," I said. "Customs has been looking for him for years because he provides documentation that art traffickers need to prove their pieces were bought legitimately. You know, when they're not."

She frowned. "And Carlo knows him. He probably uses him."

"Why do you think Carlo was so angry?"

She paused to think. "Maybe being seen with him in public? Maybe something about their business?"

We stared at each other, both troubled. "Zane said his professor will inform the right government people, but maybe we should let Lockett know," I said.

"You're right," she said.

I breathed a sigh of relief, feeling like a big weight dropped off my shoulders. It shouldn't be up to two shop owners in small town Maryland to bring down an international art trafficker. "I doubt that anyone really believes you're a suspect anymore," I said. "Our job is kinda done."

"Do you want to do the honors or should I?" Erica asked.

"You do it," I said. "I'm heading back to close down the store."

"I'll probably be here late," she said.

"No problem," I said. "Although, can you make sure you walk out with someone?"

"Sure," she said.

Before she could dial, Jennie came into the room. "Mrs. Roxbury said I should help you paint the helmets."

Uh-oh. Had she overheard any of our conversation?

"How's it going?" I asked.

"Good," she said. "This is fun."

I looked at Erica and she shook her head slightly. I dove in anyway. "How's Deirdre?"

Jennie gave me a funny look. "Fine," she said and went to pick up a few art brushes. "That was all a big misunderstanding. She didn't steal anything."

"That's good," I said. "It would be hard to have a criminal, like, living with you."

She picked up a helmet. "You want me to paint this to match that?" She pointed to a photo of a Maya nobleman on the wall.

"That'd be great," Erica said. "You get started, and I'll be back in a minute." She waved her cell at me to let me know she'd make the call.

I drove through town to the store. West Riverdale was already quieting down for Sunday dinner, and our early Sunday closing time was fast approaching. Some of the maple trees were just beginning to change for autumn, slight touches of red and yellow at the edges of their leaves.

I arrived at the store to find an ominous black Lincoln Town Car parked in front. Instead of driving around and parking in the back as usual, I pulled into an open spot in front. Before I dashed inside, I called Bobby.

He answered with a rude, "What?"

I was just grateful that he took my call. "I'm not sure what's happening but I need you at the shop. No sirens. Just casually stop in." I hung up before he answered, confident that he'd be there.

Kona was standing behind the counter looking upset as Carlo leaned over it. The store was empty of customers, although I knew Colleen had to be cleaning up somewhere.

"How's it going?" I asked. "Those kids at the high school are awesome." I pretended to just realize who was standing there as he eased back, looking stony. "Hi . . . Carlo. Everything okay?"

"Yes," Kona said, her chin up. "He was just leaving." She was angry, not afraid.

"Carlo," I said, trying to draw him away from Kona. "As you may have heard, we're trying to help the police with their investigation." I took a step back, hoping he'd follow me.

He turned his head, still angry, but curious.

"We found these spreadsheets in Spanish that appear to be for art sales."

Now I really had his attention.

"Would you be willing to look at them for me and provide your expert opinion?"

I gave him my best wide-eyed look, just as Bobby walked in.

"Hey, Bobby," I kept my voice casual. "Chocolate run or caffeine run?"

He nodded to Carlo and played along. "Coffee, please," he said to Kona, and took a seat at the counter.

"I'll be right back." I practically ran to the office and back again with one of the spreadsheets. "Want to sit here?" I gestured toward a chair where Carlo could see Bobby but Bobby couldn't hear what I was about to say. He would so not approve.

Carlo crossed to the table, moving with an elegant grace that still seemed threatening. His face was wary.

I took the seat across from him. "This was provided to us, anonymously, and the only thing we can tell about it is that it seems to be a handwritten recording of sales. But why wouldn't it be on a computer?"

His eyes went to the paper as soon as I said "handwritten." "Anonymously, you say?"

"Yes." I improvised. "Dropped through our mail slot. It seems like someone is trying to help us, but we're too stupid to figure it out."

He froze as soon as he saw the spreadsheet, and then his eyes zeroed in on my face. He leaned toward me. "Where did you get this?"

I gave up the pretense as well and tried to look tough. "Why? Is it yours?"

His eyes flicked toward Bobby. "What do you want?"

"It's simple," I said. "Stay the hell away from Kona."

He didn't reply, his face becoming stony.

"You'll miss her," I said, as if it was a done deal. "But don't come back."

Carlo stood up until he was looming over me. "Who's going to ensure it?"

My hands started shaking at the menace in his voice and I clenched them into fists. I stood as well, drawing myself up as tall as someone as tiny as me could and took a step into him the way Leo had taught me to push back against bullies. "You should know," I said in a low tone, "that I'm very, very protective of Kona."

Bobby spoke from the counter. "Back up, Mr. Morales." I didn't have to look at him to know that his hand was on his gun.

Carlo didn't take his eyes from mine. "There's no cause for concern, Detective Simkin." His voice was silky smooth. "I was just leaving."

We all watched him turn around and go out the door. I knew it wasn't rational, but I ran over and locked the front door.

"What was that about?" Bobby demanded as Kona dashed angry tears away. "Did he threaten you?"

I shook my head slightly at Bobby and asked Kona in a gentle voice, "What did he want?"

"He wanted to know why I didn't return any of his texts or calls," she said. "Like he owns me or something."

"What did you tell him?"

"That I knew he was going out with me just to get information on your investigation," she said.

Bobby stared at me, and then shook his head. "Look what your damn investigation got you now."

Bobby seemed pacified as soon as I told him that Erica had called Detective Lockett about the photo of Sincero; that Carlo had seemed to recognize the art sales, but why Santiago had it was a mystery; and that we weren't investigating anything. The "anymore" was implied, but he didn't call me on that. Bobby called Lockett, who told him that someone in ICE was deciding the next move, since Carlo running into a known forger on the street wasn't exactly a crime.

I was ready to ask about the definite crime of Santiago pulling an armed robbery, when Bobby spoke into the phone. "What blog?" He looked at me. "Can you bring up Reese's website?"

I groaned. "What did she do now?"

A few clicks of my computer and her blog was on my screen. "A Million Reasons for Murder?" screamed the headline, with a photo of a vase. *The* vase. The one Erica said was worth one million dollars.

18

"Sonofa—" Bobby said. "You amateurs are killing me."
While I couldn't argue with him, I had nothing to
do with Reese's big mouth. "Hey! We didn't blab that on the
Internet."

He stared at me. "But Erica knew, didn't she?"

I opened my mouth and then shut it.

He spoke into his phone. "How long has this been up?"
He listened to Lockett for a few minutes and then hung up.
"I have to track down Reese," he said. "Can you stay out of
trouble for a few minutes at least?"

I nodded obediently, unsure how to handle this obviously
worried Bobby. "What's going on?"

"I'll stop by and fill you guys in later," he said and left.

I read the blog and then called Erica. She groaned out loud.

Kona and I finished cleaning up and shutting down for the night. "Where's Colleen?" I asked.

"She left a little early," Kona said. "It was a pretty dead night."

"So you were alone when Carlo was here?" A shiver went up my spine. What would've happened if I'd come back later? "Do you and your roommate want to stay with us tonight? I don't want you to be alone. I feel like . . . I don't know. Something bad might happen."

"Are you serious?" she asked.

I nodded. "Just for a night or two."

"Fine," she said, with no trace of her usual good humor. "My roomie's at her parents' house for some kind of family thing tonight. I'll crash at Kayla's."

I had totally assumed that Reese would keep a low profile after Leo's protest of her office, at least until after the next town council meeting when Leo's friends were going to propose some kind of sanctions against her. But apparently not.

Once I got home, I reread the blog. Again, Reese went after Erica, implying that anyone who knew anything about Maya art would have known the true value of the antiquities on display.

Jolene had forced Erica to leave the high school when everyone else did, and we were sitting at the kitchen table, contemplating our next move, or if we had any moves left. Bobby had let her know that Santiago had moved out of Nara's bed-and-breakfast, and Carlo had checked out of his hotel in Frederick.

Too much had happened and we were both exhausted. Just when I was thinking of going to bed, I got a text from another blocked number. *You should see what's happening at the West Riverdale Examiner headquarters.*

"That's weird." I turned the phone around for Erica to read. "I don't know who this is."

"Let's go," she said, "but I'm calling Bobby."

It took only a few minutes to get over there. Erica's electric car was almost silent as we stopped halfway down the block. Reese's place was totally dark, and I felt foolish for calling the police station. "It was probably Reese messing with us."

Bobby pulled up beside us in his police car, and Erica put the window down. "Stay in there," he said in his tough-guy voice. He didn't wait for our response, just swerved to park his car at an angle in front of us, either to protect us, block our view or keep us from moving forward.

He and Junior got out with their guns pulled, and suddenly I felt like we were in a cop movie right before something terrible happened.

Before they had taken two steps, the movie special effects took place. A flash of light seared my eyes quickly followed by a loud boom, and the front windows of the newspaper office blew out all over the road.

An hour later, Erica and I were standing by her car which was blocked in by a fire truck. Leo had called to make sure we were okay and to say the protest group was backing off.

I had to clear my throat to ask my question. "But none of them . . . did this, right?"

"Of course not," he said, but I couldn't help but worry that his group were actually reasonable suspects.

Bobby and Junior were unhurt, and the blast seemed to have done the most damage to the front windows of the building. Erica had recovered faster than I had and was out the door and running to Bobby seconds after the blast. He and Junior were on the ground and he seemed a bit groggy when he sat up.

He'd grabbed her tight and then started bellowing at her to get back in the car. But I'd seen the panicked look in his eyes before he realized she was fine.

Then he'd checked on Junior, and started yelling all kinds of codes into his radio, and soon the place was filled with backup of every kind—police and firefighters, with the ATF not long behind them.

Chief Noonan had questioned us, but we really, really had no idea what this was all about.

When Reese arrived, she ran out of her car and left the door open, taking photos as she moved. Bobby had to tell her to put the camera down several times while he attempted to ask her questions.

May heard the news and joined the growing crowd around us, all watching the officers work. May tsk-tsked several times before saying to Reese, "Oh, for heaven's sake, Reese Everhard. Put that thing away. You coulda been in there!"

Reese turned to look at her and then at the damage and suddenly broke into tears, her bony shoulders heaving.

May said again, more kindly, "Oh for heaven's sake," and went over to give Reese a hug.

It didn't take long for Reese to recover and get back to taking photos of anything she could. More than one bystander glared at her while she covered the crowd. Then the van from a Baltimore news station pulled up and she was immediately on her computer in her car, uploading her photos and writing her story before they could.

Erica and I got into the car, which seemed so quiet compared to the chaos outside. I leaned back with my eyes closed, while Erica stared at the scene. I knew she wasn't really seeing it. "I don't think it was someone from Leo's group," she said. "The timing's not right. This was most likely a warning to Reese. And us."

I reluctantly agreed with her. "That's why whoever it was texted us."

She nodded. "That article must've really angered someone."

"I can imagine. The buyer had the most to lose, right? Reese's blog was like free advertising for all of his competition," I said. "Hey, all of you buyers of illegally obtained art, come and get it!"

"There must be something holding up the sale," she said. "And maybe the seller didn't want all that publicity and even more attention than this robbery has gotten."

"Then he shouldn't have killed the professor," I said.

"That's certainly where he, or she, went wrong."

Then Bean texted me. *You guys okay?*

I got a warm, fuzzy feeling and responded that we were both fine and that no one was injured.

He texted back. *Heard serious intel that EGB is headed for West Riverdale. He wants that vase.*

El Gato Blanco? Great. Another ruthless man after Maya artifacts. Just what we all needed.

Let me know if he gets here, I texted back. I felt a little sad and added, *Can't wait for "this" to be over.*

I waited for him to respond, wondering if I'd revealed too much. And then came his text. *Me too.*

Detective Lockett came out of nowhere, opened the back door and slid in. "When are you guys gonna learn?"

"I don't know what you're talking about," I said as we both turned in our seats to look at him. "You may not have noticed, but it's Reese who set him off and Reese's office that was blown up. We were innocent bystanders."

"Not from where I'm sitting," he said. "He texted you, not her. What do you know about this vase?"

Erica explained. "My friend says that if it was authenticated, it could be worth almost a million dollars."

"Who's got the photos?" he asked.

"Reese for sure," Erica said. "She gave us the copies. And they're on my computer."

Lockett then repeated all the same questions Chief Noonan had asked, and we answered. "I need your phone," he said and I handed it over without a protest. He got out with a warning. "Seriously," he said. "You're out now."

Bobby walked to the car, and I could feel Erica stiffen up. He'd avoided talking to us, or even looking in our general direction, ever since their mutual grab-a-thon after the bomb went off.

He stuck his head in my side. "You guys can go home," he said. "Junior and I will take shifts in front of your house."

"Shifts?" I asked. "Are you kidding? For how long?"

"Until we find this guy." He sounded exasperated. "It

would be helpful if you two stayed together as much as possible. We won't be able to watch you all the time."

Erica began to protest and I broke in. "Can you give us any information about what happened?"

His mouth tightened, but he answered. "Seems to have been a pipe bomb attached to a timer. Amateur stuff."

That shouldn't have made me feel better, but at least it wasn't an international art thief cartel targeting us with state-of-the-art bombs. Wait. "So it would've gone off even if we weren't here?"

"But he made sure you were here, didn't he?" He straightened up.

I looked up at him. "When do I get my phone back?"

"That's up to ATF." He knocked on the roof of the car to say *get going* and told the fire truck blocking us in to move out of our way.

There was something reassuring about having a police car tailing us home and then parking in front of the house. So much had happened that the house smelled different to me. Something familiar, but I couldn't figure out what.

I was so exhausted I was worried about falling asleep over the grinder, but made coffee and added cream and sugar the way Bobby liked it.

"You should take this out to him," I said, after seeing Erica's eyes go to the window several times. I opened the door to the cooler I kept at home, and piled chocolates on a plate. "And give him these."

"Since when did you become a matchmaker?" she asked, the joke falling flat with her voice sounding so tired.

"He deserves some coffee and a treat, and maybe a real conversation with you."

....

The next morning, I skipped my run and invited an exhausted Bobby in for breakfast. He refused, saying he was just waiting for Junior to show up and then he'd head home to sleep. His tired face made my chest hurt with guilt. Our little investigation was affecting a lot more people than just us.

Erica was downstairs when I went back in.

"How'd it go with Bobby last night?" I asked.

"As well as it could have," she said. "I think we're friends again."

I wanted to ask if they were "friends" or "*friends*," but restrained myself. We were both pretty subdued as we got ready for work, especially with Junior following us in. He took off as soon as we were safely inside.

My Magic Monday didn't feel so magic. I decided to repeat last week's chocolate-making plan, which allowed me to keep thinking about what had happened. In my head, I started comparing all the different parts of the mystery to ingredients. And Dr. Moody was the main ingredient. He was the chocolate base and everyone else was less important. He wasn't around to answer questions but the next best thing was. Lavender.

I took off my gloves, reached for my cell phone in my spine pocket, and remembered that the ATF still had it.

I found Erica, who was chatting with Kayla about a stack of boxes full of colorful journals in the back hallway.

"We need to talk to Lavender today," I said.

Kayla covered her ears. "I hear nothing. I know nothing."

"Sure," Erica said. "But I just texted May that we're stopping over for a kitten break."

I took off my chocolate-spattered apron and walked down the back hallway to May's shop. All six kittens were latched onto Coco, eating.

"Look at Coco's pretty collar," May said in a voice normally reserved for talking to babies.

"Very spiffy," I said.

"It has a GPS tracker," she said. "So I'll know if she's trying to go back to Gary's coffee shop."

"Cool," Erica said. "High-tech kitty."

"What a terrible thing to happen to Reese," May said. "She's a pain in the ass, but no one should have to go through that."

"I know," I said. "Leo's even calling off his protest."

Kayla texted Erica that my phone had been delivered, but I had to be the one to get it.

I sighed and stood up, not wanting to face the rest of the day just yet.

After showing ID to the uniformed deliveryman, I took my phone out of the sealed plastic bag and left it for Zane to check out. I was probably being paranoid, but I wanted to make sure the ATF or whoever else checked it out hadn't put anything weird on it.

When Colleen arrived, we slipped away. Junior was nowhere to be seen, which was good because none of our police friends would be happy with us. We found Lavender enjoying the last offerings of the free continental breakfast her hotel offered. She had chosen a table by a beautiful bay window and the sun was shining through lace curtains.

When she saw us, she closed her eyes for a moment as if expecting, and dreading, our visit.

"Good morning," Erica said. "Sorry to disturb your meal."

As an answer, Lavender pulled a large manila envelope from her bag. "Here. Take it and go."

Erica took the envelope and much to Lavender's dismay, we slipped into chairs at her table. The dining room was almost empty and two women in white aprons were setting the tables for lunch.

"I'm really sorry to bother you with a few more questions," I said. "We saw something on security footage at the El Diablo Restaurant—"

The way she stiffened let us know that she knew exactly what we were talking about.

"Did you know Dr. Moody was meeting with Carlo Morales?" I asked.

She lifted her chin as if to refuse to answer and then her whole body seemed to deflate. "Yes," she said.

Erica took over. "Do you know why?"

Lavender nodded.

"Was he selling Maya antiquities to him?"

Lavender nodded again, looking down.

"Illegally?"

Lavender bit her lip.

Erica seemed stunned for just a moment that our suspicions were correct. "That wasn't like him. Can you tell us how it started?"

Lavender played with the lace around the place mat for a minute. "A year ago, when Addison was having . . . all the trouble at the university, he got a phone call that he got very excited about," she said. "He left the office right away saying it could be a way out of our problems."

"Do you know who called?" Erica asked.

"No," she said. "He started having these secret meetings every couple of weeks."

"If they were secret, how did you know they were happening?" Erica asked.

"He'd have me reserve the time and put 'Frederick' in the calendar," she said. "But he wouldn't tell me anything else about them."

"He wanted to protect you," Erica said. "How did he appear before and after these meetings?"

When Lavender looked unsure, Erica added, "Was he nervous? Excited? Was he more generous afterward?"

Lavender thought for a minute. "All of those."

Erica tilted her head. "You were curious, so you followed him," she said, sounding sure.

Lavender started to shake her head and then stopped. "Yes," she admitted. "I followed him once."

"Of course," Erica reassured her. "It was your job to take care of him even when he might not take care of himself."

She was really piling it on.

"And you saw him meeting with Carlo?" Erica asked, keeping a close eye on Lavender's face.

She nodded. "I didn't know who he was at first. But Addison started to have more money and I asked him once where it came from."

She stopped, staring out the window as if thinking back.

"And?" I couldn't help but prompt her.

"He said I didn't want to know," she said.

"Did you recognize Carlo at the party?" I asked.

She nodded.

"Dr. Moody told the police that he didn't know Carlo," I said in an accusing tone.

Erica shot me a look that screamed *shut up.*

"He didn't discuss it, but I can imagine he couldn't afford for anyone to make the connection," Lavender said. "I was in charge of invitations and I don't know how Mr. Morales got one."

"So Dr. Moody was selling Maya antiquities to him before the reception." Erica's voice was gentle. "Do you know where he got the art to sell?"

"No." Lavender seemed relieved not to know something about her boss's criminal activities.

"Did you try to find out?" Erica asked.

"A little," she answered. "But not too hard. I didn't really want to know more at that point." Her face shone with a mixture of shame and grief.

"Do you have any ideas?" I pushed.

She looked at me. "He knows a lot of people who own this kinda stuff."

Then I thought of something important. "Do you have any proof of any of this? Documents, receipts, anything?"

She shook her head, as if she was scared. "I did." Her voice was practically a whisper.

"What do you mean?" Erica asked.

"A few months ago, Addison left me a letter to open only in the event of his death."

"Oh my," Erica said. "Did he say what he was worried about?"

Lavender's face crumbled like she was about to cry. "No. He said it was just insurance."

"Did you give it to the police?" I couldn't help but feel terrible asking when she was distraught.

She shook her head. "It's missing."

Erica and I exchanged a glance. "How?" Erica asked.

"Someone searched my room the morning after he . . . died." Her breath seemed to catch in her throat. "I came out of the shower and my bag was dumped. It was gone. At first, I didn't think anyone would believe me."

"And then?"

She didn't say anything.

"You read the letter, right? A long time ago?" I didn't know how Erica could stay so calm. "And you didn't want anyone to know what was in it."

Lavender's eyes leaked tears. "He admitted everything," she said. "That he was selling art on the black market, and that Carlo Morales was the one making it happen. And that if anything happened to him, to tell the police."

"Did the letter say where the art originated?" Erica asked.

"No." Lavender sniffled.

Erica reached across the table to take her hand. "You have to tell Detective Lockett."

Lavender pulled back quickly, her feet knocking against the table leg. "No! They can't know. His reputation . . ."

I held my breath until Erica said, "I think it's more important to find out who killed him, don't you think? And make sure he doesn't kill again."

Lavender looked down, defeated, and then nodded. "Do you know I can't even go to his funeral?"

"I'm really sorry," Erica said gently. "That must be very painful for you."

"His parents are holding one in Chicago," she said. "And I'm not allowed to leave the state."

"I really need a diagram of all this," I said, while Erica drove back to the store. "There are just too many moving parts for me."

"Let's start at the beginning," she said. "Moody started selling Maya antiquities to Carlo a year ago but we still don't know where he got them."

"Jennie took a class from him six months before that," I said. "Maybe she has a houseful of them we don't know about." Then I remembered something. "Wait. Wasn't he meeting with a former student the day he was murdered?"

Our eyes met, and then I said, "It's impossible. She's just a lost kid."

Erica added, "If she was selling art, it would be unlikely she'd support making such a significant donation to the museum."

"Okay," I said, feeling a little relieved that neither one of us could imagine Jennie as a killer. "But only some of the donations were stolen. Maybe Jennie didn't agree with the sale and took them back. Maybe because of Dr. Moody's class, she knew how valuable that million-dollar vase was."

Erica shook her head. "An entry-level class most likely wouldn't cover something like that."

"You know, Adam is some kind of brilliant businessman," I pointed out. "Wouldn't he do the research to figure out what the pieces were worth, independent of Dr. Moody's evaluation?"

Erica nodded. "You're right," she said. "Too bad we can't get to him."

"But we can ask Gary," I said.

Kona called when we were approaching West Riverdale. "We're having a run on the Flag Furls," she said. "Mayor Abby wants them for a staff meeting this afternoon. You have some at home, right? Can you swing by and bring them in?"

"Sure," I said. The red, white and blue spray-painted white chocolate in flag shapes had been one of my popular items all summer, and I had a few trays of them in one of the coolers in my kitchen.

I directed Erica to detour by the house. "I'll be out in a minute," I said and ran into the kitchen.

Bean was sitting in a chair at the kitchen table with his eyes closed, holding a bloody towel to his arm.

19

"Oh my God! What happened?" I asked.

He swayed in the chair. It was then that I noticed the amount of blood on the floor. I ran to put more pressure on his wound. "We need to get you to a doctor."

"No," he said, almost mumbling. "Gunshot wound."

Panic set in, making my hands shake. "Okay, then we need to get you to the doctor, like, *now*."

"No," he said, more insistent. "They'll be forced to call the police. No police."

"Not even Bobby?" I asked and he shook his head.

I heard the front door open. Erica must've realized I was taking too long. "Erica!" I yelled.

She rushed in, her worried face turning to alarm at the sight of her brother bleeding.

"He said no police," I told her, my voice cracking. "What do we do?"

"Call Tonya," Erica grabbed a clean towel and took over applying pressure to the wound. "Tell her we have an emergency but she has to keep it a secret. She trusts you."

Tonya was on my softball team and worked as a nurse at West Riverdale Urgent Care. She'd spent many hours studying in our shop, where I gave her endless refills of coffee.

She didn't ask any questions when I called to say we needed her for an emergency at our house but she couldn't tell anyone. "I'll be right there."

We moved Bean to my bed, and he groaned loudly, making me wonder if we were doing the right thing. Especially when he passed out.

Luckily, Tonya arrived before I passed out as well from worry. She was in serious nurse mode, carrying a medical bag just like on TV. Usually, her face was as expressive as a mime on steroids, but now she was totally professional.

"What happened?" She gestured for Erica to move aside and looked under the towel at the wound. Blood burst through and she put the towel back. "Gunshot?"

"We're not sure," Erica hedged. "But he's working undercover on a big story and said he can't have the police notified."

Tonya shook her head. "Hold on." She expertly applied a tourniquet. "He needs to be hospitalized."

I could see Erica wavering. "What about Leo's friend Oakes?" I suggested. "He was a medic in Iraq."

"Oh yeah," Tonya said. "He's a rock star. He could definitely take care of this."

I left the room to call Leo and told him an abbreviated version of what was happening, my voice quavering.

Leo wasted no time. "We'll be right over."

Tonya evaluated Bean further. "He might need a transfusion. I can give him some antibiotics, but if he spikes a fever, you won't have any choice but to take him in."

"Okay," Erica said. "But we're going to do everything we can to stay right here."

I looked down and saw drops of blood making a path from the back door and realized that Bean had taken all the same precautions to protect us, parking far away and walking across the field, even so badly injured.

There were way too many guns in my life.

I cleaned as much of the kitchen as I could before Leo and Oakes arrived, the Harley roaring up over the sidewalk to the front porch where I was waiting. Oakes jumped off the back before Leo had even stopped, and ran up the stairs.

"Where's the patient?" he asked. He was dressed in a camouflage T-shirt and beige shorts that had seen better days, and radiated both confidence and competence. I rushed him back to the bedroom, and he handed his medical bag to Tonya. "What ya got?" he asked her.

He took a look at the wound and I gasped. Without looking at me, Oakes said, "Out." Then he spoke to Tonya. "I'll need novocaine and a suture kit."

Leo grabbed my arm and we went to the living room. While we waited, he paced, stopping every once in a while to reassure me. "Oakes is the best. Don't worry. He'll be good as new soon enough."

Perhaps I should've worried about Leo's reaction to all of this, but my mind was filled with the image of Bean's blood dripping down his arm.

I had no idea how much time passed before Erica came in, looking relieved. "He's going to be okay," she said. "Calling Oakes was a genius move." She gave me an intense look and held out her hand. "Come and see."

Bean's arm was bandaged up and he seemed to be sleeping normally, but was so pale and drawn that I had to fight back tears. What if he'd been too far gone and I'd pushed Erica to keep him here?

Leo stuck his head in. "Lookin' good," he said. "Nice job, Oakes."

Oakes was packing his bag. "Back on his feet in no time."

He tried to get Leo to loan him his Harley, but Leo just laughed.

Leo looked Erica in the eye before he left. "You call me when you need me to take a shift, okay? You both need to rest too."

Tonya had weaseled a promise out of Erica to have their family doctor visit the next day, and Oakes had seconded the motion. The doctor was pushing ninety, but still practiced one day a week. A self-proclaimed crotchety old man, he just might be happy to break a few rules for them.

After I changed my bloody clothes, I dialed Kona, who had called my cell several times. She took my head off until I promised to explain in person. I told her I'd deliver the chocolates myself to the mayor's office. Erica wasn't going anywhere and Bean didn't need both of us to keep an eye on him, much as I wanted to stay.

Erica watched over Bean from a chair in the corner, and I showed her the chocolates from the doorway so she'd know what I was up to. He looked so different from the last time I'd seen him. He'd shaved the sides of his head and let his beard grow out, which probably gave him a much tougher look, at least when he wasn't pale as a ghost. Tonya had cut off his dirty T-shirt and he had a dark tan in the shape of a tank top. The bandage practically glowed on his arm.

That was so not the way I wanted him to end up in my bed.

I delivered the chocolates to Mayor Abby, who was delighted to have them for her meeting, if a bit late.

Back at the store, I told Kona an abbreviated version of the story, and then let Colleen know the whole deal. She wanted to rush over to see her brother, but her ex-husband was about to deliver her kids. I reassured her that Erica was taking great care of Bean and she should visit later, alone.

I couldn't concentrate, even though Erica and Leo had reassured me that Bean would be fine. I flitted to my kitchen, then my storage room, then to Erica's office, like an agitated butterfly. Rifling through her papers, I found a copy of the spreadsheet I'd borrowed from Santiago.

Art sales? Wasn't high-end art usually sold through auction houses? On a hunch, I retrieved my computer from behind the counter and returned to the office, bringing up the website of the only auction house I knew by name, Sotheby's.

It listed completed auction information. I clicked on a date from May that matched the spreadsheet.

Oh. My. God. The lot was entitled *Maya Blackware Carved Cylinder Vessel Late Classic, CA A.D. 850-950.*

I checked the spreadsheet codes. *BW CY VE AD850.* That couldn't be a coincidence.

The dollar amounts—$9,300—matched exactly.

Zane walked into the office and I said loudly, "Look at this!"

He raised his eyebrows but looked at the computer screen. I jabbed my finger at the description on the website and then the spreadsheet, and he understood immediately.

"Can I check the next one?" he asked.

I was already getting out of my chair to let him work his computer magic. He quickly searched a few older dates. Not all of the sales on the spreadsheet were on the website.

"This is interesting." He pointed to the column titled *SC*. "For each one of these sales that were handled by Sotheby's, ten percent is deducted. Maybe this column is what was paid to Sincero."

"And maybe the other ones are private sales," I added. "He gets paid five percent, because the forgery doesn't have to hold up as well."

Ten, or even five, percent of all of these sales was a lot of money. "Is there any way to find out who the seller is?" Could it be Santiago who was behind everything? This was his spreadsheet. But the tape at El Diablo Restaurant and Lavender's confession pointed directly to Carlo.

"Yes," he said. "But it means some serious hacking."

Whoa. No way could I bother Erica with this decision tonight. "Erica's . . . not feeling well," I told Zane. "Don't do anything yet. Can you, I don't know, back all of this up somewhere and we'll ask her what to do in the morning?" Suddenly I was exhausted and the whole investigation, and Bean's injury, was just too much.

He squinted at me, but didn't ask any questions. "Sure."

"We have to make sure that you're not messing up your future because of something like this." I was getting emotional and his eyes widened. It seemed like every step we took had consequences for a lot of people, not just us. "Nothing we do is going to bring back Dr. Moody, so don't jeopardize what's going to be an incredible career for this, this, whatever it is. Okay?"

"Okay." He stared at me in horror as I blinked back tears.

I choked out a wet little laugh. "It's okay," I said. "I'm not going to cry."

When I got myself together and left the office, I was pretty sure I heard him give a big sigh of relief.

I was not my normally friendly self to my customers, but no one except Kona seemed to notice. "Your face is going to freeze that way," she said, and pressed a finger between my eyebrows, where I was already developing wrinkles from worrying too much.

I tried to smile. "Sorry. Lots on my mind."

"Well, stop thinking and go cook or something," she said. "I'll take care of the customers."

An overwhelming need to escape hit me and I closed myself off in my kitchen. Breathing in the chocolate-filled air was usually all I needed to feel back to normal, but the Mint Juleps cooling on the racks weren't enough to quell the anxiety rushing through me.

My cell phone buzzed with a text from Erica. *Bean's sleeping peacefully. Reading you know what. It ends with a bombshell that changes everything.*

I texted Erica to call me when she could. I couldn't leave Kona alone yet again to man the store. She'd worked way too many hours lately with me disappearing all the time to investigate.

A few minutes later, Erica called and spoke in a low but urgent voice. "You won't believe this, but I think Bertrand's diary was the target the whole time."

"What? Not the million-dollar vase?" *Or my bowl?*

"Bertrand River fell in love in the British Honduras," she said. "He got married and had a child."

Oh. My. God.

My head actually started to spin. "Hold on," I told her and dropped the phone on the metal utility table with a clang. I sat down on a stool, put my face into my hands and took a few deep breaths. I could faintly hear her calling my name.

I picked up the phone. "Tell me again."

"The analysis of the last few pages that were damaged came back," she explained slowly as if to a child. "The diary is authentic. It belonged to Bertrand and is in remarkable condition given its age. And get this. Bertrand wrote about falling in love, getting married and having a child. In what was then the British Honduras. It's now Belize."

"So the River family has another branch?" I asked, imagining a map of an actual river. "Do you think they know?"

"I'm not sure," she said. "But if one of the Rivers knew what was in that diary, getting rid of it would keep a lot of money in the family."

I remembered Rose Hudson yelling about curses at the reception, the event that had caused this whole mess. "I think this is what we call a motive," I said.

We were both silent for a minute, thinking about all the ramifications.

"Rose Hudson is the only one old enough to remember what happened," Erica said.

"Wait. Should we be doing this now?" I asked.

"Let's just talk to Rose," she said. "And then we're done."

I decided not to keep the latest news from Erica. "And talk about a bombshell, you won't believe what Zane and I figured out."

I told the long-suffering Kona that I owed her big-time— maybe all-expenses-paid-vacation-in-Hawaii big-time—to hold down the store while we visited Rose. Monday afternoons were unpredictable in the store, but she'd be able to handle whatever happened.

Erica had called Leo, who was happy to watch over the still-sleeping Bean. She'd convinced herself that he'd want her to pursue any lead she could.

The grounds for the Village Retirement Community reminded me of a well-kept golf course, the grass trimmed to perfection and the trees and flowers placed with symmetrical precision.

We parked in the visitor parking lot and walked in the front door, narrowly avoiding what seemed to be a hundred-year-old man in a fast-moving golf cart. A huge flower arrangement with orange birds-of-paradise and striped tiger lilies sat on an ornate antique side table in the lobby. And I thought the mixed bouquet I'd picked up for Rose from May's shop was big.

"Can I help you?" The uniformed customer service rep sat behind an information desk twice the size of my store counter.

"We're here to see Rose Hudson," Erica said.

"How nice." The rep brought up Rose's information on her computer and typed in our names. "Rose is in the Vintage Garden outside the west wing." She handed us visitor badges to clip on, and another uniformed woman came to show us the way.

Rose sat on a wicker chair looking at the beautiful view of rolling hills that met the mountains in the distance. A gardener used small pruners to clip purple flowers from a bush. Other patients sat in groups or alone, all across the lawn and gardens.

"Rose." Our guide bent down to meet her eyes. "These two young ladies are here to see you."

Erica took the seat beside Rose as I handed her the flowers. "Hi, Mrs. Hudson. This is Michelle and I'm Erica from Chocolates and Chapters."

She looked up, her wrinkled face wrinkling even more as she tried to place us. She focused on the flowers. "What beautiful lilies. Adam, can you put those in a vase for me?"

"It's Steve, ma'am," the attendant corrected kindly.

"Oh, I'm sorry," Rose said. "Steve. Of course." She shook her head at herself and then grabbed Erica's hand. "How are you girls doing? Isn't it a beautiful day?"

Erica went right along with her. "It is. And we're good. How are you feeling?"

"Oh, I'm just fine," she said. "Viv is picking me up soon."

"That's nice," I said with a sideways look at Erica. We had to move the conversation along fast before Vivian arrived.

Erica took my cue. "We're so sorry that the display in our store upset you."

Rose tilted her head. "Upset me? Oh, you mean the curse." Then she smiled. "It's okay. Adam told me there was nothing to worry about anymore."

"Of course there's not," Erica reassured her. "What could you possibly be worried about?"

"That Bertrand," she shook her head indulgently. "He could always stir the pot."

"That's actually why we're here," Erica said. "To find out more about him."

Her face became sad. "He's dead, you know. He was too sad for this world." She looked intently at Erica's face. "Everyone said it was a heart attack, but it was really a broken heart. He was in a dark place. The Rivers got that problem all over the place. That's the real curse."

"Bertrand?" Erica asked.

Rose laughed out loud, a twinkly laugh that drew a smile from the gardener. "Oh yes, you ladies love my Bertie. But he's taken, dear." She looked at her watch. "Viv should be here. We're going to Sanders for ice cream."

Startled, I looked at Erica. The Sanders ice cream parlor in the next town had closed ten years ago.

"That will be fun," Erica said, her voice careful. "What's your favorite flavor?"

Rose got a confused look on her face, and then she said, "Vanilla." She nodded once as if confirming the answer to herself.

Suddenly, Steve was at my side. "I'm sorry, but Mrs. Hudson has an appointment right now. You'll have to leave."

"Oh, that's too bad." Erica stood. "It was lovely to see you."

Rose grabbed her hand again. "Thank you for your visit. Please come again."

Steve seemed anxious as he escorted us out, and even the lady at the front desk gave us a strained smile.

"What was that about?" I asked after we'd walked slowly to the car.

"I'd say that someone doesn't want us talking to Rose Hudson," she said.

20

Erica wanted to check on Bean so she dropped me off at the store.

I walked in to find Detective Lockett waiting for me. Great. I didn't even bother to say hi, just led the way back to Erica's office.

"Any idea who just called me and demanded that you and your buddy stop harassing their family members?"

"Joe Jonas?" I asked. "I'm president of his fan club so I'm allowed to contact him whenever I want. It's in my contract."

He ignored my joke. "Adam River. Imagine my surprise to hear that you and your buddy were pestering an old lady."

"Pestering?" I asked. "Who uses that word? You sound like an old lady yourself."

He assumed his normal long-suffering expression when dealing with me. "First, I keep Bobby off your back about the librarian suspect. Then you say you're done investigating. Instead you *pester* old ladies."

"We weren't pestering anyone," I said. "Visiting is not pestering."

"What were you *not pestering* her about?" he asked.

I debated telling him about the diary, but too much had happened. "We saw the analysis of the damaged pages in Bertrand River's diary."

He straightened in the doorway. "How the hell?" He changed gears. "What did it say?"

"That Bertrand fell in love during his travels," I said. "And got married and had a family."

His jaw tightened. "You two . . ." His voice trailed off and then he made a decision. "You're coming with me to the station." Grabbing my arm, he tugged me through the whole store to the front door.

I sent a wide-eyed look over my shoulder to Kona. "I'll be back," I yelled.

"No, she won't," Lockett yelled as he dragged me outside.

Lucky for me, Detective Lockett was driving a normal sedan and not his state police car. I got in the passenger side, put my seat belt on and crossed my arms while he stood outside and made a call on his police radio.

"What do you hope to gain by acting this way?" I demanded as soon as he got in.

"Just be happy I didn't cuff you." He backed out of his parking spot and headed over to the police station. "Did you imagine that the analysis of the diary just might be a motive for murder?"

I huffed. "Of course. That's why . . ."

"That's why you ran off to interrogate someone who might be able to provide the police with valuable information. And now you've warned the family so they can prevent access to that individual."

"We never mentioned the diary," I insisted, feeling guilty.

He glanced over at me and it was like he read my mind. "Only because you didn't get a chance, right?"

"Sorry." My voice was a little grudging. "We should've told you."

"No shit," he said. We pulled up to the white building that served as a police station. Lockett said, "Go back to the lunch room," before stopping in Chief Noonan's office to tattle on us.

It didn't take long for Erica to arrive with her big bag in tow. She pulled out her laptop, looking totally fine about the whole thing. That must've been what Lockett's police radio call was about.

I talked quietly in case someone was listening. "Leo still hanging out?"

She nodded. "Everything's fine."

Detective Lockett, Bobby and the chief all came into the room and sat down. The chief spoke. "Okay, ladies. What ya got?"

E rica told them everything we'd learned about the murder, Carlo, Santiago and Sincero, even Zane's breakthrough on the spreadsheet. Bobby still wanted to lock us up until they had someone in custody, but the chief let us go with a last-chance warning to keep our noses out of police business.

It was totally selfish of me, but I stopped at home before going back to the store. Leo was holding a beer, with his head in the refrigerator.

"You're not giving that to Bean, are you?"

He smiled over the fridge door. "Nope. It's all mine."

"How's the patient?" I asked.

"Last time I checked, sleeping. Your turn to baby him?" he asked.

"Sorry," I said, itching to peek in. "I have to get to the store."

"'K," he said. He pulled a few bags of cold cuts out, and then folded a few slices of salami over a slice of cheese. "The doc was here and said he wasn't going to win any beauty contests with the scar he's gonna have, but there's no nerve damage or anything." He took a large bite of his make-shift sandwich.

"Has Bean told you anything?"

"About getting shot?" He took a sip of beer. "Nope. Before he left, he was asking about some paramilitary groups farther out in Maryland, but that's all I know." He gestured with his beer bottle to the back door. "I cleaned up his trail out there. All the way to his car."

"Thanks." Scrubbing the blood from the kitchen and bedroom had been hard enough. "You doing okay?" I asked. "Not bringing back any, I don't know, bad memories?"

He smiled. "I'm good. It's a happy ending, right?"

I couldn't resist giving him a big hug. "Stay good, okay?"

Bean opened his eyes when I stepped into the room, and gave me a sloppy smile. "He-ey."

"Are you okay?" I asked. "Your voice sounds slurry. Should I call Oakes?"

He shook his head. "Nah. Leo gave me some really . . . nice painkillers." That explained the glassy eyes.

"They seem to be working." I should probably talk to Leo about modifying the dose.

"Oh yeah." He patted the bed. "Sit down. Take a load off." He grabbed my hand and started rubbing my palm with his thumb. "Sorry for the mess."

"No problem," I said, not sure how to handle this injured, drugged-up Bean.

He turned his head and blinked as if he had trouble focusing on me. "This isn't how I imagined being in your bed."

I gasped. I'd thought the same thing! I felt a deep blush move up my face. "How did you imagine it?"

He looked around as if seriously considering my question. "Sexier. Wa-ay sexier." His smile was a little loopy. "And I thought both of our 'this's' would be over."

Leo stuck his head in the doorway. "He lives!" he said in a friendly tone. He must not have heard Bean talking about my bed.

I stood up. "Sorry. Gotta get back to the store."

Bean's eyes closed and then opened as if he was fighting fatigue and the effects of the drugs. "Bring me some of those flag ones."

I was happy to forget all about murders and burglaries and just work, even taking over making caramel when Kayla took over for Kona.

Kayla had insisted on taking a turn stirring the industrial

sized pot when the flash mob practice ended up near our store. "You have to see it. It's so cool!"

Students were rushing down the street acting out various scenes—from short battles to elaborate rituals—while "soldiers" with spears stood at attention to keep innocent bystanders out of the way. Luckily, Main Street of West Riverdale didn't have a lot of bystanders on a Monday evening.

Wink was working with a woman who seemed to be the director, and a camera man who kept holding his hands up to make little squares as if evaluating camera angles while they walked up and down Main Street. Every once in a while, they'd ask the students to run through a scene. They were all having a blast.

May closed up and stood watching with me. "Don't worry if you see Coco outside. I had to open her cat door," she said. "She insists on going out, but she always comes back to her babies."

Rehearsals continued past closing time, and I left Erica talking flash mob business with Wink.

Leo and Star were eating Zelini's pizza in the kitchen when I made it home. It had been a long day, but seeing the students having so much fun working on something so worthwhile made me feel close to normal.

"We saved you some," Star said, grabbing another plate and setting it on the table.

"Great," I said. "I'm starving."

I pointed to her arm, where her biceps rippled. "You been working out?"

Star was a personal trainer to serious athletes only. She flexed, showing a deep ridge. "I picked up a few new clients and they are kicking my butt."

"I thought it was supposed to be the other way around," I said.

She nodded, a little of her hair falling across her face. "Gotta make sure they know I can do what I make them do."

Leo pushed the hair back behind her ears, in a show of tenderness that made me smile. "We're going to take off," he said, getting to his feet and piling the dishes in the sink. "I just gave Bean a pill, so he'll sleep for a while."

"Thanks," I said, and took another huge bite. "I'll walk you out. Bean's chocolates are still in the car."

I finished my slice on the way, said good night and brought in a box of the flag chocolates Bean had requested as they drove away. They were the first chocolates of mine he'd ever tasted. Maybe he was being romantic in asking for them.

I debated leaving the door unlocked. Erica would be home soon, but I decided to err on the side of caution and locked it.

I turned around and Carlo was standing at the other end of the hallway, holding a gun aimed right at my heart.

21

let out a tiny scream.

Carlo made a slow and deliberate *shush* gesture with his finger that was ominous even without the gun pointing into the living room. Did he know Bean was sleeping right on the other side of the wall?

I slid by him into the room, turning the light on. It didn't make me feel any better.

"Have a seat," he said.

When I didn't immediately sit down, he added, "I must insist."

I sat. "How did you get in here?"

He gave me an "oh please" look. Locks on hundred-year-old doors must be no match for an international art trafficker.

"What are you doing here?" I tried.

"Please put your phone on the floor." He sat between me and the door. "And don't try anything. I'm an excellent shot." He said it almost as an apology.

"Why are you doing this?" I asked. "Because I told Kona to stay away from you?"

"Of course not," he said. "Kona is, was, a beautiful diversion, but nothing gets in the way of my business."

"Which business?" I asked. "The legit one or the illegal trafficking in antiquities one?"

His eyes narrowed and I regretted my outburst.

His voice grew hard, with none of his usual charm. "You will end up like the professor if you do not answer my questions. Who are you working with?"

"No one," I said, ashamed of the slight wail in my voice. "You killed the professor?"

"His death didn't matter," Carlo said. "He'd become useless."

My face must have shown my shock.

He looked at me as if evaluating the best way to proceed. "How did two country mice like you uncover the identity of Sincero? You must have had help."

"What are you talking about?" My voice shook.

"Come now." He settled more comfortably into the chair. "You don't last long in this business without many connections."

"Connections?" I asked.

"Did you think I wouldn't hear of your now-famous photo?" he asked. "I have people everywhere." He let that sink in. "You're remarkably foolish. I would have paid a great deal to keep that photo secret."

"Why are you here?" I asked.

"To find out who you are working with." He moved the gun in a circle. "One way or another."

"Look," I said. "We didn't work with anyone. We just stumbled around and got lucky. It's how we do things."

"Solve mysteries and mete out justice from your little shop?" he asked, not believing me.

"No meting out anything," I said. "Whatever we find, we give to the police. So it's too late. We gave them everything we know."

He cocked his head. "If that's true then you can tell me about your Santiago."

"He's not *my* Santiago, and isn't he one of you? You know, the bad guys?"

"I wouldn't be so sure," he said. "Did he ever tell you about El Gato Blanco?"

"Really?" I bluffed. "The white kitten? Is that name supposed to be intimidating?"

He smiled as if enjoying my joke at Santiago's expense. "I would love to attach a face to the El Gato Blanco myth. A dead face."

And then I heard a creak in the hallway and Carlo whirled around. Santiago stood there, dressed all in black, a gun in his hand.

It was obvious from the way they glared at each other that these guys were not on the same side.

"Oh for heaven's sake," I said. "You two need to take your little feud somewhere else." Inside, I was quivering.

"Why don't we?" Santiago said backing up a step.

Carlo didn't move.

"The testosterone in this room is getting overwhelming." I took a step toward the door. "Can I go?"

"No," Carlo said at the same time Santiago said, "Yes." They moved in unison into the hall, not quite mirror images. Two handsome bad boys that no one should mess with.

Then I heard sirens in the distance, and I almost wept in relief.

Carlo shook his head. "*Cobarde*," he said, his voice filled with disgust.

"Looks like I'm getting that vase," Santiago taunted.

Carlo scowled. "Perhaps. But I'll get it in the future." He slipped out the back door and Santiago let him go.

"I called the police," Santiago admitted. "Knowing he'd scurry away like the rat that he is."

"So you're really El Gato Blanco?" I asked. "You couldn't come up with a more original nickname?"

He smiled as at least two cars screeched to a halt in front of my house. "That's my cue. Remind them that I'm with ICE, loosely, if they try to shoot me."

The next morning, Junior was relieved of guard duty in front of our house when word got back to the West Riverdale police that Carlo Morales had crossed the Mexican border and that Santiago was not only El Gato Blanco, but surprisingly, was also the consultant to ICE he'd claimed to be. He was something of a Robin Hood, responsible for repatriating thousands of antiquities back to their country of origin, sometimes in cooperation with ICE, but usually not.

"You're sure he's really El Gato Blanco?" I'd asked Bobby.

"Don't romanticize the guy," Bobby said. "A long time ago, he was a low-level drug dealer in Panama until his children were wiped out by a rival gang. I guess it's good that he's at least trying to make things right."

The chief seemed to believe that Carlo's conversation with me was a confession for the professor's murder, but Erica and I weren't buying it. It just didn't add up.

Bean was healing fast, sitting at the kitchen table eating the eggs and toast that Erica had made with one hand. He felt terrible for sleeping through the evening's adventure with Carlo and Santiago, and was determined not to be a burden anymore.

Overnight, Erica had researched state-of-the-art security systems and one was being installed in our house in a few days. She'd also read quite a lot of Bertrand's diary and couldn't stop talking about it. "It sounds like their wedding was beautiful," she said. "By the twentieth century, most Maya were Catholic, but they still retained a few traditions. The groom had to work for four months in the field of the bride's father before the wedding. Bertrand's bride, Maria, wove and embroidered her own *huipil*, and Bertrand bought one from a ritual *compadre*. Bertrand seemed to revel in the Maya customs. He thought it was romantic that they wouldn't wear their bridal outfits again until their funerals."

From the sound of Erica's voice, she found it romantic as well. "You're adorkable," I said.

Bean's surprised laugh burst out of him, and then he cringed as if it hurt. "Adorkable?"

"You okay?" When he took a deep breath and nodded, I defended my word. "You know, the adorable nerd. I've heard the kids say it, and I've been waiting for the right time to use it."

"She *is* pretty adorkable," Bean said with affection.

Erica rolled her eyes. "If you two aren't interested in Bertrand's captivating stories, then I have things to do." She picked up her papers and went upstairs.

A sudden tension filled the room when we were alone. Oh please let it be sexual tension.

"You okay?" he asked. "I know all of this is difficult to say the least."

"Your 'this' or my 'this'?"

He smiled. "Either. Both. All of the above."

"It's kind of a toss-up between you getting shot and international art thieves threatening a shoot-out in my living room." I tried to sound carefree but my voice shook a little halfway through. I cleared my throat. "So are you going back?"

He shook his head. "No." He paused. "I'm not sure if it's because I have enough for the story or," he looked down at his arm, "because of this rather major wake-up call."

"And don't forget bleeding all over my kitchen," I reminded him.

"Yeah. That too." He stared at me. "So."

"So?"

"Wanna go out?" he asked, as if he already knew the answer.

"Like on a date?" I acted surprised.

His smile dimmed. "Yes. Like on a date."

"I'd love to," I said.

He grinned and grabbed my hand.

Erica came back in through the door, carrying her cell phone.

Could she have worse timing?

"The Village called," Erica said. "Rose Hudson is demanding to see us."

....

"Are you sure we should do this?" I asked as we drove out to the retirement facility. "Adam made it clear we weren't allowed to talk to her." And I didn't want to even think about Lockett's reaction.

"Rose's attendant said they have strict rules, and if they feel that their client is clear minded, they follow her directions," Erica said.

Rose sat in the same chair, facing a beautiful view of mountains. "Michelle and Erica," she said, looking totally clear minded to me. "Thanks for coming back. I'm sorry if I wasn't all there during your last visit."

We sat down.

"Adam tells me that you found Bertrand's diary and the secret is out. I wanted to explain, as well as I could, the bit that I know."

"Of course," Erica said. "He was a fascinating man."

She smiled. "Oh, he was. Especially in person. Why, he'd just light up a room."

"So what happened? After the end of the diary?" Erica asked.

Rose's smile disappeared. "You have to understand that it was a different time back then. Our father had grand plans that Bertrand was not interested in at all." She looked out over the field. "Bertrand came home and told our parents what he'd done. That he'd gotten married."

She shook her head. "My father refused to give him any money to go back to Central America. Bertrand fell into a terrible depression after that. Our side of the family, well, let's just say we have a history of that."

She took a deep breath. "And soon after that, Bertrand up and died. I was very young, but I knew why. He'd called Maria the love of his life. I'm convinced he died of a broken heart."

Her voice faded, sadness in every syllable. "I tried to help him. He told me to hide his treasures so that he could sell them when our father wasn't paying attention, and get the money to go back."

"And did you hide them?" I asked.

Her face became mischievous, looking decades younger. "Oh yes. I hid many of them, but not all, along with his diaries. And they're still there!" She paused, looking confused. "At least I think so. I don't know how his diary got . . . out."

Erica moved forward a little closer to Rose. "Where did you hide them?"

"You'll never guess," she said. "It's a secret hiding place."

"Who else knows about it?"

She looked shocked. "No one!" Then she paused, as if remembering something. "Except for Bertrand. He visited me." Then she shook off the thought. "No, that's impossible."

"But I can tell you." She leaned close to Erica's ear and whispered so low I couldn't hear her.

She sat back, and then her face became melancholy. "He changed at the end, you know. He met some archaeologists, and started feeling bad, taking all those pots and things away from their homes. He wanted to make things right."

"What did she say?" I asked as we left the retirement home grounds.

"She told me where she believes the hiding place is,"

Erica said. "Behind one of the furnaces in the basement. But there's no way the Rivers will let us in there."

"Can Lockett get a warrant?" I asked. Look at me, trying to walk the straight and narrow.

"I doubt it," she said. "Their lawyer would say it's the ramblings of an elderly woman with dementia."

Something made me check out the rearview mirror. "We have trouble," I said too late, as a black BMW passed us moving fast and then cut us off.

22

Erica screeched to a halt as Santiago got out of his car. He held his hands up to show he wasn't holding a weapon, and then he pointed to the window.

"Back up," I told Erica.

"He'll follow us," she said. "And maybe do something more dangerous. I think he just wants to talk."

She pushed the button to lower her window two inches.

"It seems I underestimated you," he called out and moved closer. "When I fed you that spreadsheet, I didn't expect you to get this far. My friends at ICE have arrested the infamous Sincero and now they are no longer one step behind me."

Erica seemed to evaluate what he'd said. "You fed us the spreadsheet?"

He nodded.

"But why?" I asked. "You work for ICE."

He laughed. "Oh no. Let's say I'm a consultant." He paused. "When it's mutually beneficial."

"Why are you telling us?" I asked.

He took another step. "I'm making an official request that you cease and desist from your amateur investigation. You're not only embarrassing the big boys, but you've put the bad guys on notice."

"And?" I asked.

"And?" he repeated. "I like to have my bad guys stupid and unknowing."

Erica narrowed her eyes. "What exactly is your role?"

"Everyone said you were the smart one." His tone was admiring. "And your Michelle is the tenacious one. But perhaps you're learning from each other." He paused. "I heard a rumor. That dear pillaging Bertrand's diary contains an amazing Hollywood ending."

"What do you mean?" I said, a little too quickly.

He smiled, delighted. "So it's true. He got married and started a family in Belize. I can't tell you how exciting this news is." Then he grew serious. "But I must reiterate. Stay far, far away from Carlo."

"I'll need something more . . . official if you want us to leave it alone," Erica said.

In a split second he was at her window. "Listen. I will control the result of Sincero's arrest, but I need Carlo in place. I know how he works. He must continue doing what he does so I can continue doing what I do."

"And what *do* you do?" Erica said.

He took a step back. "That's not your concern. But if you lop off his head, someone new will take his place. And I'm getting too old to learn a new dance."

He walked back to his car and we watched as he drove away slowly at first. Then he gunned the engine and disappeared over the rise.

"Whoa," I said. "He really is El Gato Blanco."

"What is going on?" Erica pulled out her phone. "Zane? You need to find out everything you can about Santiago and El Gato Blanco. Go deep."

"I guess there's no reason to remind you that we're really done with this investigation."

Back at the shop, it was hard to stop thinking about Santiago's request. He had to know that an official investigation into Carlo was far outside of our control. And why was he so interested in Bertrand's family?

"I forgot to tell you," Kona said, as we cleared the remains of the Realtors' meeting on the back table. "That mom you said was pregnant because she didn't finish her Mocha Supreme?"

"Samantha?" I asked.

"Yes. That's her name. She *is* pregnant," Kona said. "Diagnosis by truffle really works."

I was feeling pretty proud of myself when Vivian River came through the door.

"Oh my God," I said to Kona. Maybe she'd heard of our visit with her mother. "She's never been in here except for the reception."

Vivian looked around the dining room and chose a small table in the corner.

I gave Kona a gentle push. "You go see what she wants."

Kona went over with a smile and returned with a frown. "She wants a decaf cappuccino, one caramel, and you."

I felt my shoulders droop a little. I so didn't want more drama with the Rivers. I took a deep breath and crossed to her corner. "Vivian," I said. "How nice to see you."

She didn't smile. "Please sit down and join me for a few minutes," she said.

I did as she asked, feeling like way too many people were telling me what to do lately. "What can I help you with?"

She paused as if considering. "Since turning back time and deciding not to open Pandora's box is out of the question, I would ask that you and Erica please keep the news of Bertrand's"—she sniffed—"family to yourself until we have sorted it all out."

"Sure," I said. "I don't think anyone knows except, you know, the police." I looked over my shoulder to make sure Kona was working on that cappuccino.

"Yes." Her disappointment in our not being able to keep our mouths shut was clear. "Apparently, they feel that it presents some kind of 'motive' in the death of the professor."

"That's too bad," I said, in a tone as if that idea was news to me. "So, I should get back to work . . ."

She looked like she wanted to say something else, and then changed her mind. "Of course. Thank you for your time. And your discretion."

The weather couldn't have been more perfect for the filming of the flash mob, in spite of the storm warnings from local news stations. I was amazed at how many Main Street shops were open early, getting ready for the big moment. Many of the store owners and workers had bit parts, whether it was to look surprised at the folks running through town in centuries-old garments, to surreptiously hand out props or to gather at various scenes that needed an active audience. All of West Riverdale was behind the project.

Erica was heading to the high school, doing what she did best: ordering people around in the nicest possible way.

Kona and I delivered free coffee and caramels to the professional film crew that was setting up, with huge lights, screens and some kind of serious dolly that would allow them to track the student actors' movements down the whole street. They even had a cameraman on a crane by the community center, where the final scene would be shot. I didn't want to know who was paying for all of that equipment.

Wink and Jolene were in drama-nerd heaven, rushing around to consult with the film director, cameraman and Erica, in between herding actors and gathering costumes and props. I recognized members of Erica's comic book club—the Super Hero Geek Team—taking some of the leadership roles in the project.

It wasn't until Bobby and Junior closed Main Street to traffic that I realized how big this venture had become. Mayor Abby stood at her station, blocking off access from White Stone Alley, and members of the town council were all at their assigned spots. Word had spread and the sidewalks were packed with people from neighboring towns.

Then whistles blew up and down the street, the signal for everyone to be silent.

Spanish guitar music floated out from hidden speakers. The entire arrangement had been written and recorded by the school band. Then the Latin beat picked up and the first scenes unfolded. A royal child was held up and subjects rejoiced. At the same time, across the street, slaves worked with food, a woman wove cloth, scribes wrote on huge books, and a god wearing an elaborate headdress, as tall as his body, demanded obedience.

The cameras captured multiple angles, especially the delighted, surprised and sometimes confused reactions from spectators, always my favorite parts of flash mob videos. Many brought out their own cameras to capture the moment.

The camera moved on to ballplayers throwing and catching a small black ball, wearing their sumo-style costumes, and dancers performing in elaborate feathered back racks as large as a Vegas showgirl's. A king in animal prints moved between fawning women, and three men of royal birth challenged each other through dance with large plumes of fabric pressing out from their hips.

And then the music changed and the battle began.

Trumpets blasted and banners flew. Combat ensued with spears clashing, soldiers falling, and fake blood flowing.

A captive was on his knees, pleading for his life, the press of a spear to his heart and then his lifeless body on the ground. A new king ascended to power.

I ran as fast as I could to see the finale, and got there just in time to see all of the actors meet their marks. They assumed their positions, looking royal with chins held high, in front of the community center, which held the huge mural they'd painted at the school. It looked just like the photos of Bonampak in the book, an ancient stone edifice rising from the jungle.

A banner unfurled from the top of the building announcing the exhibit information and dates.

The sheer pageantry of the ancient Maya could not have been brought to life any better.

The director yelled, "Cut!" into his megaphone and the students erupted with cheers.

Hours later, Jolene was trying to herd the last of the celebrating students out the door of Chocolates and Chapters, telling them once again that no, they could not take their costumes or spears or headdresses home. They had discussed their favorite moments over and over with squeals of laughter and smiles of pride.

The director finally packed up his equipment. He'd kept cameras running all night, hoping that the film of the flash mob would be so popular that people would also click on his "behind the scenes" video.

Erica and I were finally able to close up. The heavy rain clouds that had been promised by the local weatherman suddenly delivered, and the rain was starting to fall.

The lone streetlight bordering the parking lot was struggling to keep back the dark, but nothing could deflate my good mood. As I pulled out onto Main Street, Erica waved me down from in front of her car.

"Coco just came out of her cat door with a kitten," she said, holding the hood of her raincoat over her head.

"Shoot!" I said. "She's taking it back to the Big Drip."

Erica got in my minivan. "Let's try to cut her off."

I sped the few blocks to Gary's coffee shop. "What if she already put one, or more, inside?" I asked. "They can't be left alone overnight."

"Maybe we should let her be until Gary opens tomorrow," Erica suggested.

I thought about the storm warnings. "Gary leaves a key

for his skater buddies to crash there," I said. "Maybe someone will let us in." Although if they were anything like the one who was there before, he'd be too far gone to answer the door.

"Okay." Erica sounded dubious.

I parked the minivan in front of the coffee shop with the headlights shining on the front corner, illuminating the front door and part of the side wall.

I grabbed an empty box I'd used to deliver candy bars and handed it to Erica as she hopped out to huddle under the little bit of roof hanging over the building.

The wind whipped my hood off as soon as I got out of the car. Great. Water was already dripping down my neck. I pulled it back over my head and knocked on the front door.

Nothing.

"I'm going to check the back," I told Erica as her phone rang. "Don't answer that—you have to grab Coco."

She looked at the screen and hit a button. "It's Zane," She had to yell a little bit over the sound of the rain. "I'll call him back."

The streetlight was out on the other side of the coffee shop, and the dark was a little overwhelming. I was grateful for the feeble porch light over the back door. I knocked again and then tried to see where Gary might hide a key for his buddies. It was pretty easy to spot. A small sign in the shape of a skateboard read *Deliveries only*, and a key on a chain was wrapped around the hook holding it to the wall.

Should I?

It was definitely breaking and entering, but for a good reason. I was picking up kittens, not stealing cash from the register. After a short debate with myself, made shorter by the rain dripping down my face, I pulled the key off its hook and unlocked the door. Erica would vouch for me if I set off the security alarm and the police came.

I stepped inside, sliding my hand along the wall until I found the switch. The sudden light was blinding, but I blinked a few times and made my way to the storage closet. I opened the door to see that Coco had created yet another nest of torn-up napkins and had already deposited four of her six kittens there.

I heard a noise and stuck my head out of the storage room to see a dripping Erica coming down the hall. "What are you doing?" she said in a stage whisper. "We have to get out of here, now."

"Just a minute," I said. "Four of the kittens are here. Give me the box."

She handed it to me. "I can't believe you broke in," she said. "Zane called back. He thinks Gary was supplying Maya antiquities to the professor. We have to get out of here. Fast."

"Gary?"

She joined me in grabbing the squirming kittens. "Zane doesn't give up. He figured out how to hack into the Big Drip accounting system. He saw that Gary put in a bunch of cash right after a bunch of the sales on that spreadsheet."

Now I understood her alarm. Coco stuck her head through the hole in the plaster, a kitten still in her mouth, and then backed up out of our reach.

"Damn it," I said.

"Let's go," she said.

"Here, Coco," I cooed, but she could probably sense the worry in my voice and stayed in her hole.

An enterprising kitten, the one I'd named Truffle, stepped

on his sister to catapult himself out of the box and escaped out the door. Erica went after him just as Coco stuck her head out again. I moved faster this time, grabbing her by the scruff of her neck, but let go when I heard something terrible in the hallway, a loud *thunk* followed by the sound of something falling.

"Erica!" I rushed out of the storage room.

Erica was slumped on the floor.

Gary stood over her holding a crowbar. "I knew those cats would ruin everything."

23

"Erica?" I rushed toward her.

"Stay back," Gary warned, lifting the crowbar with both hands as if to hit her again.

Erica moaned and moved her legs.

She was alive. The white-hot panic that paralyzed me lifted just a little.

I took a deep breath and decided to act dumb. "What is wrong with you?" I said. "Call 911. You know we're not here to rob you. Just to get the kittens. You didn't need to hit her."

He made a scoffing sound and shook his head. "Right. The police. That's just what I need." He stared at me intently as if trying to figure out what to do next.

I tried again. "Gary. You can fix this. Just get Erica an ambulance."

"Give it up," he said. "I heard what you guys said in there. You know about the pottery, so you know about the professor."

"What are you talking about?" I was grasping at straws.

"I *can* fix this," he said. "I just have to get you two out of the way for a little bit." He pointed toward the dining area with his chin. "Go sit in one of the chairs."

When I didn't immediately follow his order, he tapped the crowbar in his hand. "Do you want to see what happens to her special brain after another hit?"

I walked sideways to the dining area, sneaking a peek at the box full of kittens in the storage room. Coco was attempting to settle them and paid no attention to me.

My heart lurched when Gary grabbed Erica by one arm to drag her along the linoleum with him. "Sit," he ordered.

He stayed a safe distance, giving me a wide berth until he reached the counter. With his eyes on me, he dropped Erica's arm. The only light came from the hall, shadowing half of his face.

He looked down behind the counter for one second and reached for something. I stood up, ready to lift the chair and throw it at him, but before I could even get it in the air, he brought out a gun.

Another freakin' gun.

I sat back down, and he smiled.

"I still don't understand," I said. "Why did you need to steal the display if you were already working with the professor to sell all that art?"

He scowled. "Your precious professor screwed me over. He went around me to my brother to get that donation. Adam didn't even notice that stuff in the house until Moody told him some crap about how important it was. Like Moody cared about that. He just wanted money and prestige."

Erica's phone rang and Gary's eyes widened. "Shit." He reached into her pocket, pulled out her phone and turned it off. "Give me yours."

"It's in the van," I said.

"Right," he said. "Empty your pockets."

I realized that even with the gun, he didn't want to get close to me. I stood up and reached into my pockets, pulling out notes for a recipe I'd forgotten to give Kona, a few dollars and change, and my keys. Then I turned around to show him that my back pockets were empty, hoping my secret spine pocket still hid my phone.

He looked like he didn't trust me. What was he planning to do with us?

Maybe I could get him talking and someone would come and find us. "How did the professor steal from you? You know, he wasn't my favorite person in the world either."

"He shortchanged me, but I got him back, didn't I?" He rustled around in another shelf and pulled out black straps that might be used to tie surfboards down on a car roof.

"What are you doing?"

He walked toward me. "Put your hands through the back of the chair."

"No," I said.

"Do what I tell you, and you'll both get out of here. I just need to get my stash to my car and eventually, someone will find you."

If my hands were behind my back, maybe I could get to

my cell phone. I did what he said, feigning reluctance. "Why did you leave stingray spines on your own doorstep?"

"They wouldn't suspect me then, right?" He wrapped a strap around my wrists, yanking them tighter than I expected.

"Ow!" I felt totally helpless. "Is that vase really worth all this?"

"You have no idea."

Out of the corner of my eye, I saw him go back to the storage room, shoving Coco's box out of the way.

I maneuvered my fingers into my pocket and felt the outline of my phone. I pushed the button to turn it on and tried to aim toward where I knew the phone icon was located on the screen.

Gary appeared in the hall, carrying a small bottle. He went to the counter and dropped a pill into a cup of water, mixing it with a spoon. Then he walked over to grab my chin, and I could see the sheen of perspiration on his face.

"What are you doing?" I yelled, wrenching my face away.

I ended up tipping over the chair and falling heavily on my side.

"Have it your way," Gary said, and sat down on the floor. This time he held on to my chin tight as he poured something medicinal from the cup into my mouth.

Erica groaned and shifted, and he looked at her.

I silently spit out as much as I could but could tell I'd swallowed some from the medicinal aftertaste in my throat. Was he trying to poison me or drug me?

I obviously hadn't spit out enough, because soon I felt like I was on a roller coaster ride of spinning colors.

Gary moved toward Erica, and I watched helplessly as

he repeated the process with her. Then he walked back to the storage room and brought out a wide bowl, a padlock hooked onto the belt loop of his jeans.

I recognized that bowl. It had been in the display case at the reception. Gary hid them in his storage room?

Then time became a kaleidoscope of scenes that flashed into my brain and slipped away before I could make sense of them. Sensations of panic and fear crested like waves and then receded, replaced by a tidal wave of sleep.

I woke up in the dark. I heard a car engine, and realized I was in the trunk of a car, with a red light in my face taunting me. I moved and the back of my head bumped into something. Something that moaned. The brake lights flashed and I saw Erica's face. A bunch of small boxes were lined up behind her. I thought about pulling the wires out from the light. Someone might notice.

I willed my hands to move and realized they weren't tied. I reached out and yanked. And my eyes closed.

Voices woke me up. My spine tingled as the phone vibrated in my secret pocket. I struggled to pull it out and hit it against the top of the trunk, knocking it from my grasp. I fumbled around in the darkness to find it, feeling like I was moving through Jell-O.

The voices moved closer. I tried to yell but only a croak came out. So I kicked as hard as I could. The sound echoed in my head.

Nothing.

I kicked again.

Tears came to my eyes. It was hopeless. I closed my eyes, unable to fight the drugs.

Lightning flashed and rain fell on my face. Gary stood outside the trunk, the rear red lights illuminating one side of his face. A policeman stood beside him, looking stunned. His face hardened and he spun Gary around and out of my sight.

And then I saw more red. A lot of it. I heard endless deafening sirens.

Bobby and Leo's worried faces appeared in front of me, and I gave in to the drugs.

24

The next time I woke up, I was in a clean, dry and way-too-bright hospital room. I turned my head and saw Erica in the next bed.

Bean dozed in the chair against the wall, his arm in a sling. He must have heard me stir, because his eyes popped open immediately. "You okay?" he whispered and grabbed my hand.

I nodded and then regretted it. A wave of nausea came over me.

Bobby stood from where he'd been waiting on the other side of Erica's bed, in full uniform.

"Is Erica okay?" I whispered.

"She will be," Bobby said. "She has a mild concussion."

"What happened?" My throat felt as dry as a desert.

"Gary hit Erica on the head and drugged you both." Bean's voice was angry.

A memory of being trapped in the car flashed through my mind. I winced and the machine I was attached to started beeping faster.

Bean said, "It's okay. You're safe now."

I tried to breathe deeply, and the machine beeps slowed.

"That's my girl," he said. He pushed the nurse call button and said, "She's awake," when the nurse answered.

"I'll be right there," she said.

"Coco and the kittens?" I asked.

"They're all fine," he said. "Back with May."

Then Leo appeared in the doorway with two cups of coffee at the same time as the nurse.

"One of those mine?" I asked him, my voice hoarse.

He smiled, losing the worried squint between his eyes. "It is now."

The nurse played along. "Oh no, it's not." She moved Bean aside to take my blood pressure and temperature. "You girls are sure popular." She took the thermometer out of my mouth and patted me on the arm. "The doctor will be in soon."

"Can I sit up?" I asked.

"Sure, dear." She raised the bed and plumped my pillows, while both Bean and Leo looked a little helpless. The movement made me feel light-headed and I closed my eyes.

"Worst day?" Leo asked, with more urgency than usual.

It was all I could do to shake my head once before I was out.

I woke again, feeling more like myself, in time to hear Bobby talking to Erica. "I'm so, so sorry."

From the glassy look in her eyes, she was still under the

influence of something. Even in my state, I could tell that he should save whatever he was trying to tell her until she could understand him.

"It's okay." She sounded hoarse like me.

"No," he insisted. "It's not. I get it now. You're smarter than me. I'm okay with that."

She blinked. "What?"

"I'll apologize. I'll do anything." He was beginning to sound desperate. "Anything you want." Finally he focused on her and seemed to realize she wasn't taking in what he was saying.

Then Bean walked in. Our eyes met and I felt light-headed in a whole new way. *Anything you want*, my heart whispered.

"Hey," he said. He dropped his backpack, took my hand and kissed my forehead. "You look like hell." He looked at me as if I was unbelievably precious. Maybe I should get drugged by a killer more often. Wait. Maybe not.

I noted his drawn face. "You've looked better yourself."

I was pretty sure the smile on my face was as goofy as his.

The nurse bustled in. "Everyone out but my beautiful patients," she said. I couldn't believe how great it felt when she put ice chips in my mouth.

"Do you remember anything?" Erica asked when the nurse had gone.

I shrugged. "Not much."

"I don't either," she said. "Retrograde amnesia, just like Farley." She scrunched up her face as if she could force herself to remember.

"That asshole drugged us," I said.

When Bobby, Bean and Leo came back, we demanded to know what had happened while we were unconscious.

Bobby seemed the most reluctant to talk, but Leo filled us in. "From what I can piece together, you were breaking into the Big Drip to pick up the kittens, not your best move, I might add, and Erica got a call from Zane that made her think puny little Gary was the big ol' bad guy."

"Oh right," Erica said as if she finally remembered something important. "Zane kept digging. Somehow, he was able to . . ." She paused and looked up at Bobby. "See something about the Big Drip bookkeeping. He figured out that the coffee shop's income increased right after some of Carlo's sales."

Leo was enjoying himself too much to let Erica take over the storytelling. "So instead of being as smart as she supposedly is and calling the cops, she followed you into the bad guy's store to make you leave." He settled himself into a chair. "Lucky for you, Zane *is* smart. When he couldn't get either of you to answer your cells, he called Bean. And then Bean used some kind of creepy phone app that allowed him to track you. Which you both owe me an explanation for, by the way."

Bean cut in. "I called Bobby to tell him you might be in trouble at Gary's, but you were gone when he got there. On the app, I saw that you were moving, so we tracked you."

"Bean was too candy-ass weak to be useful." Leo smirked as Bean looked up at the ceiling in exasperation. "So he called me. And because police cars are slower than a snail in peanut butter, I almost beat him to you."

"You rode your motorcycle in that storm?" I asked.

Leo waved away my concern. "It was a good thing I did, because Lieutenant Bobby was pounding the crap out of ol' Gary."

Erica's eyes shone with a little bit of hero worship.

"Wait," I said. "I remember another policeman."

"Yep," Leo said. "A rookie traffic cop. He pulled Gary over for his brake light being out and heard you kicking inside. Then Bobby arrived and lit into Gary. If I hadn't pulled him off, he'd have killed that scum for sure."

Leo sounded a little regretful he hadn't let Bobby finish the job.

"Where was Gary heading?" I asked. "What was he planning to do with us?"

Bobby's eyes narrowed. "Bluebird Park," he said. "Where he killed Dr. Moody."

That sobered us all up.

"And then the whole freakin' cavalry arrived," Leo added cheerfully. "Chief Noonan, state police, ICE, FBI. It was an acronym free-for-all." He patted my hand. "All to save your sorry asses."

It didn't take long for the nurse to hustle everyone out so that we could sleep. I was suddenly so tired that I didn't even complain. I woke up in the hospital in late afternoon and Erica wasn't in her bed.

But Adam was in the room, staring out the window. He turned around, his brilliant blue eyes on me. I noticed how much like Gary's they were, and I couldn't help the flare of alarm I felt. I fumbled for the nurse call button.

"It's okay," he said and kept his distance. "Erica just went for a walk up and down the hall."

The room now had a bunch of flowers and balloons. I

must've been asleep for hours for all these deliveries to happen. Erica walked in holding on to Bobby's arm. She looked like she was feeling a lot better.

"You okay?" she asked, meaning, *okay enough to deal with our visitor.*

Bobby added, "You don't have to hear about this yet if you don't want to."

I shook my head and this time it felt normal. "I'm good."

Adam cleared his throat, obviously uncomfortable. "First, I want to apologize on behalf of my entire family for what Gary did to you. Last night and, before."

I nodded.

"It seems that Rose had mistaken him for Bertrand at some point and told him about the many boxes of Bertrand's antiquities hidden in a secret room in the basement of our home. And, to get back at me for trying to control his trust fund, he began selling them on the black market." He took a deep breath. "Gary has had . . . issues with honesty in the past, but we all thought, or hoped, he was outgrowing them. But apparently, he has not."

Adam continued. "We were especially pleased that Gary was making a success of the coffee shop, but even that wasn't true. He was simply using it to launder the money from the art sales." There was so much pain in Adam's voice that I had to stop him.

I raised my hand. "It's okay," I repeated. "It's not your fault."

He nodded. "Just one more thing. Gary does seem to regret how far it all went. Once he realized how ruthless that . . . man was, he got scared." He stopped, probably aware of how feeble the excuse sounded.

. . . .

With all the nurse and doctor comings and goings, it took forever to get the whole story. The abundance of attention probably had something to do with the Rivers paying for some kind of VIP healthcare for us. But we just wanted to go home.

We talked the doctor into discharging us, promising to rest in bed all day.

Bean volunteered to be our nursemaid so that Leo would go home and rest. He let in Detective Lockett and Bobby.

Erica and I shared the couch, and I hoped the pillows and blankets made us look enough like invalids for them to go easy on us. We *had* told them we were done investigating after all, but perhaps they never believed us.

"Gary is cooperating in exchange for leniency," Lockett said, sitting back in his chair, seeming a lot less intense now that the killer was found. "Rose told Gary where the pottery was hidden at the same time Jennie was taking a class from Professor Moody. Gary approached him about being the go-between and Moody was desperate enough to set up a meeting with Carlo."

"How did the professor know about Carlo?" Erica asked.

Bean answered. "Carlo's well known in the museum world as the go-to guy for anyone who wanted to enhance their Central American art collection and wasn't too picky about where the stuff came from."

Bobby took a turn. "But the professor got too greedy. He took a much larger cut than he'd agreed to. Which was working fine until he went around Gary to convince Adam to make the big donation. Moody was attempting to help his reputation, but with all the attention the pieces were getting, Gary did some research and figured out he'd been shafted for months. So he followed Dr. Moody to his meeting with Carlo. He wanted to eliminate the cheating middle man."

"So who stole the stuff in our display?" I asked. "Gary or Carlo?" And where was my bowl?

"That was all Gary," Lockett said. "He had access to the drugs through Jennie's friends, and he knew the security guard's schedule. The professor figured it out and threatened to tell everyone, so Gary killed him. He's claiming it was an accident, but Gary's the one who set up the meet and he knew what happened to that creek when it rained, like it was supposed to that night."

And like it did the night he drugged us.

"Why did Gary keep everything at the coffee shop?" Erica asked. "It's so public."

"The only business close to that park was the storage facility," Bobby said. "Gary's buddy had been letting him use an empty unit and pay under the table, but with the police investigating that area, Gary had to move his stash somewhere."

I'd finally realized that the padlock on the metal panel inside the storage room was hiding a lot more than old plumbing. "No wonder he was so frustrated about the kittens," I said. "Especially when Coco kept bringing them back."

"Exactly," Lockett said. "Those kittens and that webcam were blocking his access to the pottery, and Carlo was not the patient type. He wanted that vase and put a lot of pressure on Gary to produce it."

"But Carlo had already left town," Erica pointed out. "Why was Gary at the coffee shop that night?"

"He was heading to Mexico. He'd told his family he was going to New York for a meeting, but his computer showed a map from West Riverdale to the border," Bobby said. "He was meeting up with one of Carlo's guys. And he wasn't coming back. He just needed to make sure no one raised an alarm for twenty-four hours."

I shuddered. "Did he admit to planning to . . . ?"

"No," Lockett said. "He said he was going to hide you in the storage facility so he could get out of town."

"Do you believe him?" Erica asked.

He met her eyes but didn't answer.

"Why was Carlo so pissed off at Sincero?" I asked. "And why did Santiago steal Zane's laptop if he's working for ICE?"

"We're speculating, but we believe Sincero was growing impatient with the delay as well," Lockett said. "He never stayed for long in one place to help avoid detection. Carlo did not want to be seen with him, for good reason, it turns out. Because of you, we now have Sincero."

"And Santiago?" Erica asked. "What is his story?"

Lockett frowned. "He's . . . something of a consultant, who doesn't always do what he's told."

"But he's done a lot of good," Bean insisted. "Just not always the way ICE would like."

"What happens next?" I asked.

Lockett stood up. "You two rest. And try to stay away from homicide investigations in the future."

Once again, Coco was a hero. She'd delayed the bad guy from selling off national treasures. Of course, if Coco hadn't left May's store, we wouldn't have been in danger in the first place. But then Gary might have got away with those precious antiquites. And the professor's murder.

May had belatedly figured out that Coco didn't like the smell of the flowers, so she had moved the whole family to her home, with a high-tech cat door that only worked with the GPS on Coco's collar to let her in and out. This time, she seemed to be staying put. Maybe she'd even set down roots in May's house, instead of wandering the shops of Main Street.

25

Santiago dropped in during the half hour I'd been allowed to be alone in days, popping his head into the living room where Bean had put me with my laptop and a Netflix subscription. "You are one popular woman." He took a seat across from me, his hair hanging freely around his face, looking more gorgeous and relaxed than he had any right to be.

"How did you get in here?" I demanded. "I'm going to fire that security company."

He shook his head. "Don't bother. I get through them all."

"What do you want?" There was no heat in my voice now that I knew he was one of the good guys. In his own way. And was he even more tanned than before? How did he find the time?

"Thought you might want to know that the right thing will be done with Bertrand's treasures," he said.

I gave him a pretend scowl. "What did you do?"

He laughed. "So suspicious. I just made sure that the right people connected to the Rivers pointed out that Bertrand's diary is rather like a will, and he wished that he'd never taken the Maya people's property. Once I suggested that it all be returned, the Rivers readily agreed."

"All of it is going back?" I asked, not sure I totally trusted him.

"Almost," he admitted. "And I must confess a more personal agenda I had concerning Bertrand's diary."

"Personal?" I asked.

"What would you think if I told you that my middle name was Rio?"

My mouth dropped open. "Even I know that's Spanish for 'River.' Are you a descendant of Bertrand's?"

"Yes," he said. "And I have a lot of cousins, all with the same middle name."

I was stunned. The infamous Santiago, El Gato Blanco, was a River?

"Are you guys, like, all moving here?" Could they all be as complicated as Santiago?

"Of course not," he scoffed. "We have our lives in Belize. But some of the River estate would go a long way to improving our little town."

"What did Vivian say?" I couldn't resist asking. "Are you a cozy member of the family now?"

He smiled. "That may take a little longer, but I'm sure we'll come to some agreement." He made an elaborate hand flourish and suddenly a bowl, *my* bowl, was sitting in the palm of his hand. "This is for you."

I gasped.

"A present," he said. "A thank-you. For your contribution to the Maya."

"I . . . couldn't," I choked out.

"Michelle," he said. "You must know by now, that I won't leave you a choice." He placed the bowl on the coffee table and stood, ignoring my thanks and disappearing as silently as he'd arrived.

A couple of nights later, we were all heading over to the high school auditorium to see the showing of the flash mob video. It was the first time I'd left the house since coming home from the hospital, and Bean insisted on keeping his arm around my waist. I didn't complain.

We drove into the high school parking lot. At least twenty students came up to us to share their excitement.

"Who'd believe you used to hate kids," Erica said.

The anticipation in the crowd reached tsunami levels as the first scene appeared on the huge screen in the auditorium. Everyone cheered each time they recognized themselves and their friends on the screen, especially at the bloody battle scenes.

The short movie was wonderful. The film company had done an amazing job, somehow making it seem professional while still retaining a charming amateur quality.

The crowd erupted in applause at the climactic scene in front of the community center, as the music came to a crescendo and the museum's banner unfolded.

Jolene took to the stage and raised her cell phone over her head. "You've all just received the link. Now post it to

Facebook, email it to your grandmas, tweet it, Instagram the sucker. Get the message out."

The students' thumbs went crazy, sending their video out into the world with exclamations of "Mine was RT'd." "Mine was favorited." "Mine was shared." The noise grew crazy loud. A tech person brought up the YouTube page and kept refreshing it until the number of views reached one hundred. Two hundred.

Then the director from the film company came on stage and cheerfully yelled, "Quiet down! We have something else to share. We hope you like it."

He gestured toward the tech gal in the back, and the behind-the-scenes video began. I was happy to see lots of shots at Chocolates and Chapters. And then the students started talking to the camera, gushing about Erica and Wink's vision, and Jolene, Steve and Janice's hard work pulling it all together. All of the adults, and quite a few students, had tears in their eyes when it was done.

That time, the applause was deafening.

Bean and I ducked out the back to avoid the news crew from a DC television station, attracted by the connection to the murder of Professor Moody and arrest of Gary River. That would surely help the video to go viral.

Detective Lockett was leaning against Bean's car. He straightened and they shook hands. "Came to give you an update," he said. "Gary's info paid off. We got Carlo and he's cooperating. We're going to bring down a lot of traffickers."

Already, Vivian was spreading the word that Gary had been under the control of Carlo and was just a young kid searching for meaning in his life.

But I was there and saw his eyes.

Gary was desperate, yes, but some part of him was enjoying it. Who knows what would have happened if we'd arrived at Bluebird Park?

Something of what I was thinking must have shown on my face because Lockett cleared his throat and nodded. He understood. He shook Bean's hand and when he tried to shake mine, I reached up and gave him a hug.

"Ms. Serrano," he said. "I hope I never see you again."

We watched him drive away, and focused on the first of the teens to leave the school, flush with victory.

Bean was smiling at me. "You know what?"

I smiled back. "What?"

"Both of our 'this's' are finally over." He grabbed my hand. "So, how about that date?"

RECIPES

• BY ISABELLA KNACK •

❋ Bourbon & Apple Wood Smoked Salt Truffles
(YIELDS ABOUT 15 PIECES)

4 ounces heavy whipping cream
7 ounces dark chocolate, chopped
½ ounce butter, softened
1 ounce bourbon whiskey
Pinch of salt
Cocoa powder for dusting

Bring the cream to a boil. Pour one-third of the cream over the chopped chocolate. With a spatula, mix rapidly to obtain a smooth and glossy texture. Gradually add the remaining cream, making sure to keep the emulsion smooth and glossy. Mix until the dark chocolate is completely emulsfied.

Stir in softened butter and mix thoroughly. Then add the bourbon and stir. Add salt and mix into ganache. Place ganache in refrigerator to chill until set, about 12 hours. With a melon baller, scoop ganache into individual balls and dust with cocoa powder.

✺ Mocha Truffles
(YIELDS ABOUT 60 PIECES)

2 ¼ pounds bittersweet chocolate, finely chopped
4 ounces milk chocolate, finely chopped
1 ¼ cups heavy whipping cream
1 ½ tablespoons instant espresso powder
2 tablespoons Kahlúa or other coffee-flavored
*   liqueur*
60 candy coffee beans or mocha beans, for
*   decoration*

Place 12 ounces of the bittersweet chocolate and the milk chocolate in a 2-quart mixing bowl.

In a 1-quart saucepan over medium heat, bring the cream to a boil.

Remove the pan from the heat, dissolve the espresso powder in 3 tablespoons of the cream, then blend this mixture back into the rest of the cream.

Pour the espresso cream into the bowl with the chocolate and let the mixture stand for 1 minute.

Stir together with a rubber spatula until thoroughly blended.

Stir in the Kahlúa and blend well.

Cover the truffle cream, let cool to room temperature and chill in the refrigerator overnight.

Chill the covered truffle cream for another 2 hours in the freezer.

Remove the truffle cream from the freezer and bring to cool-room temperature so that the outer coating won't crack when they are dipped. Melt and temper the remaining 1 ½ pounds of bittersweet chocolate.

With a melon baller, scoop ganache in individual balls.

Place a truffle center into the tempered chocolate, coating it completely. With a dipper or fork, remove the center from the chocolate, carefully shake off the excess chocolate, and place the truffle on the wax paper.

After dipping 4 truffles, center a candy coffee bean on top of each truffle before the chocolate sets.

❉ Bananas Foster
(YIELDS ABOUT 40 PIECES)

4 tablespoons butter
¼ cup brown sugar
1 tablespoon rum (optional, can substitute vanilla
*   extract or rum flavoring)*
½ teaspoon cinnamon
Dash nutmeg
1 ripe banana, sliced

¾ cup heavy cream
8 ounce semisweet chocolate, chopped
½ cup cocoa powder, for dusting

Place the chopped chocolate in a medium bowl and set aside for now. Melt 2 tablespoons of the butter in a 7-inch skillet over medium heat. Once melted, add the brown sugar and stir it until the brown sugar melts as well.

Add the rum, cinnamon and nutmeg, and stir until the mixture is bubbling and fragrant.

Place the banana slices in the middle of the sugar, and cook them for one minute on each side—no longer, or they will overcook and become mushy.

Once cooked on both sides, remove the banana slices from the saucepan. Add the heavy cream to the saucepan—the cream will first cause the sugar to seize and you might have bits of hardened sugar floating in your cream.

Whisk the cream and sugar together over the heat until the sugar dissolves, the mixture is smooth and the cream is almost boiling.

Pour the hot cream over the chopped chocolate in the bowl and let it sit and soften the chocolate for 1 minute. Once softened, whisk the cream and chocolate together until it is smooth and no bits of chocolate remain.

Add the remaining 2 tablespoons of butter and whisk it into the chocolate.

Chop the cooked banana slices into small pieces and stir them into the melted chocolate as well.

Let firm up overnight.

Place the cocoa powder in a bowl and dust your palms

with cocoa. Use a candy scoop or a small teaspoon to form 1-inch balls of ganache. Roll them between your hands to get them round. If they start sticking, dust the balls with a little cocoa powder. Repeat until all of the truffles have been formed.